Godmother:
The Secret Cinderella Story

By Carolyn Turgeon

Rain Village
Godmother: The Secret Cinderella Story

Godmother:
The Secret Cinderella Story

Carolyn Turgeon

headline
review

First published in 2009 by
Three Rivers Press
An imprint of the Crown Publishing Group
A division of Random House, Inc.,
New York.

First published in Great Britain in 2009
by HEADLINE REVIEW
An imprint of HEADLINE PUBLISHING GROUP

1

Hardback ISBN 978 0 7553 5115 2
Trade paperback ISBN 978 0 7553 5116 9

Typeset in GoudyHundred by Avon DataSet Ltd,
Bidford on Avon, Warwickshire

Printed and bound in Great Britain by
Clays Ltd, St Ives plc

Headline's policy is to use papers that are natural, renewable and recyclable
products and made from wood grown in sustainable forests. The logging
and manufacturing processes are expected to conform to the environmental
regulations of the country of origin.

HEADLINE PUBLISHING GROUP
An Hachette UK Company
338 Euston Road
London NW1 3BH

www.headline.co.uk
www.hachette.co.uk

To my mother, father, and sister

CHAPTER ONE

I loved arriving at the bookstore first thing in the morning, when the streets were still quiet, the sun half risen, and the whole place felt like a secret meeting room. I liked walking through the still-dark city, as if I were wading through air – the buildings like shadows looming on either side of me, the streets rushing forward in black rivers. There was something about the empty store, too, the books piled all around, that made you want to whisper and walk as slowly as you could. The city was always on top of you, pressing in, but the moment you stepped inside Daedalus Books, it felt like you'd closed your eyes and gone to sleep.

That day it was so hot the place was stifling when I walked in. August had made the whole city seem to melt and turned the air to water. It sat on my skin, sank into it. I switched on the giant fan in the corner and stood in front of it, breathing in. Outside, I could see the glimmer of light from the bakery across the street. The steam of coffee, the baskets of bread being put out.

I had a ritual. Before I began sorting through the piles of

books, organizing and cataloging and shelving them, before I began attacking the dust that had accumulated the night before, I stooped down in front of the shelf of rare books behind the register. The books glittered like jewels behind the glass, with their ornate covers and bright gold edges. I unlocked the case, slid it open, and then paused, listening for any sign of life upstairs.

The smell of the old books was sharp as it hit my face. I loved the earthy scent of them, straight from another time. I could almost imagine I was being hurled back. I was always seeking out things and moments and places that were filled with the past, that made history seem like something you could touch.

I reached in and pulled out my favorite – the book at the end of the bottom shelf, tucked away, the pages like onion skins. I moved my palm over the raised cover.

I drew a deep breath, taking in its rich bark scent, then pulled back the front cover, carefully, as if I were juggling glass, and peered in. George had many old collections of tales, but this was my favorite. It had the most delicately rendered drawings, separated with translucent gold-speckled sheets that crackled when I turned them.

I felt something catch in my throat the way it always did, and I turned the pages, barely touching them, pressing them lightly with my palms so they wouldn't crumble.

The text seemed to have been stamped on the pages, among images of a girl sweeping the chimney and the floors. Scenes of a dance, a hall filled with men and women twirling like tops. The girl was drawn in pen and ink, her hair a mass of black lines. Leaves fluttered down the sides of the pages.

George had found the book, he said, at an estate sale, buried in someone's attic, with a stack of other books. *Peter Pans, Alice in Wonderlands*, wonderful old books as heavy as stones, filled with drawings and crinkled paper. He had bought the whole lot for barely anything at all, he said, and refused to sell them. I didn't question George. The store had been his father's, and his father's before him.

I sat down, pulled the book close to me, against my chest. I loved that each book had its own history. I kept a box under the counter filled with the ephemera I'd found in them, the notes and receipts and lists and bookmarks and bits of feather or plastic that people stuck between pages and forgot to pull out again. Once I'd opened a copy of *Middlemarch* and found a dried sprig of lavender and one pink rose. Another time a love letter had fallen out as I flipped through the pages of *Thérèse Raquin*. '*I can't see anything but your eyes*,' the lover had begun, and I would wonder who it was, if the lovers even remembered the fever that had passed over them once.

I loved the scribbles in the margins, the notes in the front of the books that told their stories, the ways they passed from one person to another. '*To Jennifer, Christmas 1921. May these words stay with you.*' The stray phrases and numbers jotted on the side of a page – '*Indian Taj, 74th Street*' emerging from the margins of *Utopia*, '*BUY PUMPKINS*' blaring up at me from the back cover of *To the Lighthouse*. As I sat behind the register, carefully erasing the penciled marks, I felt as if each book had a secret to tell, only to me.

In this one, my favorite one, someone had scribbled on the inside of the back cover, in French: '*Tous mes anciens amours vont me revenir.*'

All my old loves will be returned to me.

I had often imagined who had written it, the faded pencil, the strange scrawl. Sometimes I imagined a young girl, day-dreaming. Sometimes an old woman like me, left with nothing but memories. I wondered what had happened to the woman, if she'd ended up having a life rich with love or if she'd lived how I had lived, starving and alone. It could have been anything, an artist's note or a quote to tell a friend, but I felt I could see this woman, her face lit with hope, the pencil poised in her hand like a swooping bird.

I set the book down. What would someone say if they saw me? Silly old lady crying over a book for children. I put it away carefully. Locked the case. I used a mixture of white vinegar and clove oil to wipe it down, erase my fingerprints, and then I stood up slowly, facing the window.

The sun was starting to rise, and the light moved over the shelves, streaming in and onto the counter. Outside, the city breathed, groaned. Its hot breath steamed up the windows, and my own face stared back at me from the glass. The wrinkled, hanging skin, the dull hair that spiraled out like wires, the sunken dark eyes. I hated catching myself this way, by surprise. *This is not who I am*, I thought. Sometimes I ached so badly for my former beauty that I wanted to pull off my skin like an old robe.

I grabbed the broom and began tackling the floors. As I cleaned, I ticked off my day, what I had to do. Inventory, pricing and shelving, bills. There were boxes of books in back that George had dropped off the day before, and a few bags that customers had brought by to sell. This day I would be alone all afternoon while George headed upstate to track down some rare book. He was always off chasing treasures, and there was always someone in his array of contacts who would pay the price he asked for them. I thought of the bills I needed to pay and felt a twinge. The bookstore had limitless funds, thanks to George's family's other ventures – their horses and restaurants – and his own rare-book trade on the side. I was always struggling.

When I finished sweeping, I rubbed the shelves and counters with a damp cloth, then watered the plants I'd stuck in the windows. I straightened the books that had slumped over during the night, all the shelves the customers had wrecked the day before. It was mindless work, but satisfying: The dull floors began to gleam, and the dust-covered shelves came to life. During the day there was never enough time to fix what the customers unfixed, but here, now, in the early-morning hours, the place was perfect. A completeness and fullness that came as close as I could remember to life in the other world.

At ten A.M., I turned the Closed sign to Open and wheeled out shelves of one-dollar books onto the sidewalk. A man passed me, walking his dog and carrying a newspaper under his arm.

I stood on the sidewalk. Stared out at the world, the comfort and hush of the store behind me. A few groups of people sat in the bakery now, sipping coffee, eating pastries. A woman stared intently into a laptop, tracing the screen with her fingers. Cars twisted down the street, nearly silent.

I went back inside. There were always mountains of new books to contend with, and the shelves were constantly shifting, transforming. Customers started trickling in, shuffling through the aisles, paging through books, slipping science tomes into the poetry section, picture books in American history, Gabriel García Márquez next to Evelyn Waugh next to Casanova. I picked up a box of dusty children's books and got to work.

Around noon the back door opened and George walked in. He lived upstairs, in an apartment I'd never seen.

He had a book in one hand, a cup of coffee in the other.

'Good morning,' I said as he approached.

'Hey, Lil.'

'How was your date?'

'Oh,' he said, yawning and setting the book on the counter. A well-worn copy of *Revolutionary Road*, I saw. 'It was a disaster.'

'It was?'

I stared at his long-fingered hands, his famished eyes, the dark streak of his hair.

'Yeah,' he said. 'I just . . . Oh, I don't know. I guess I'm not much of a ladies' man, Lil, despite all appearances to the contrary.'

I laughed. I wished I could say something. I never knew what to say. He stood there for a moment, watching me, and then he walked away, disappearing into the back office.

I stared after him. I didn't know why I cared the way I did, but I wanted so much for him to be happy. I wanted it more than my own happiness. A remnant from my former life, this feeling. It was always rearing its head.

I put a pot of coffee on the table by the register, and I could see George turning on the computer. It glowed on his face and he sat hunched over it, oblivious to anything else. I moved through the narrow aisles, straightening books, and watched him out of the corner of my eye. There was this look that came over his face when he was concentrating, on a book or on something he was writing. He was writing now, his long fingers scrambling across the keyboard. I wished the women he met could see him like this, the way I saw him, all loose and flushed and taken over.

The bell tinkled, and a customer came in. I moved away.

A young man, a college student obviously, came up and asked for Shakespeare and Chaucer. 'Cadbury Tales,' he pronounced it. I found the books for him and rang him up. Another group of customers swept in – more college students, looking for records and graphic novels – followed by a dreamy young woman who went straight to the poetry section, browsed the Baudelaire and the Lorca.

Once the store cleared out, I poured a fresh cup of coffee for George, adding in one teaspoon of milk, one packet of sugar, and went to the room in back. He had left. The computer was dimmed, but when I tapped the keyboard, it sprang to life again. I was tempted to sit down, retrace his steps, but I could hear the door opening and shutting out front, the bell tinkling, books falling from the shelves and to the floor, the dust multiplying. The hours stretching out before me.

By seven P.M. I was exhausted. I took care of the till, shut off every light, and locked the door.

The sky was still bright, as if it were the middle of the day, as if it were right on top of you.

I stepped into the street. The West Village, right here, was the part of the city that was most like the old world: the cobblestone streets with trees hanging over them, the balconies and wrought iron, the rustling leaves. Brownstones with bright flower boxes and glittering windows, ivy lacing up the shutters. Stone steps leading to arched wooden doorways that opened into secret, unknown worlds. You could see the odd framed picture or chandelier through open curtains, an occasional cat curled and sleeping in the sunlight. A man stood cooking at a stove, oblivious to the people walking by.

I turned and trudged up Hudson, past all the strolling couples, the outdoor cafés packed with people talking and laughing. Thin women with bare shoulders and dangling earrings, men who looked like they could be in cologne ads, baring their teeth. Hudson turned to Eighth, and I walked until I couldn't feel my legs anymore – through Chelsea, past Madison Square Garden and Penn Station, past the fabric stores and office buildings, the pizza shops and hardware stores, up to Thirty-eighth Street. My favorite diner was in the middle of the block, an unassuming place I'd been coming to for as long as I could remember. I sat down at the counter, at my usual seat by the swinging kitchen doors, where I couldn't see myself in the mirror behind the counter. The fan blasted on me, mercifully, almost making me shiver. There was only one other person at the counter. A teenage boy sipping coffee across from me and looking around nervously. His glance met mine and then he looked through me, as if I weren't there.

'Hey, Lil,' Mike said, walking up to me in his white apron. 'You want the usual?'

I nodded. 'And just water, please.'

A second later he set a glass beside me. I picked it up and took a long swallow. The clink of spoons against mugs, forks against plates, made me feel safe and warm.

I devoured my burger when it arrived, letting the thick grease and meat collect in my mouth, then ate the french fries one by one, drowning them in ketchup. I paid and headed home, walking back to Eighth Avenue. The streetlamps lit the sidewalks. If you squinted, you would never think you were in this massive, breathing city. The buildings like mountains, the water towers on top of them like island huts. I liked to play this game, to make the city into something else, to seek out the places that didn't fit. I walked past the corner bodega, turned onto Thirty-sixth Street. Past 'Non Stop Fashion,' through the door, and up the flight of stairs. I locked the front door after me and one by one clicked the dead bolts shut, then leaned into them, letting relief pour through me. I was safe.

I shrugged out of my clothes, unwrapped the bandages from around my chest, and drew a bath, pouring in the mixture of herbs I kept on the shelf in a jar – eucalyptus oil and winter-green oil, rosemary and thyme and dried mustard. A film of sweat stuck to my skin. The fragrance wafted up to me, sent a tingling through me. I let the potion spread out and cloud over, then leaned down and dunked my hands in, making circles in the water. Steam filled the bathroom. I stared and stared into the water, as if it were fire. With the potion suffusing it, the water was the color of a river, a deep yellowish green. I breathed in. The scent curled around me.

I stepped into the tub, lowered myself in. Instantly I felt better.

All my old loves will be returned to me, I thought.

I relaxed and lifted my arms out of the water, one at a time, to watch it drip down my skin. I moved my palms across the surface and over my stomach, up my breastbone and to my neck. Everything seemed to slow down. The water pressed into me, filled every pore.

I was alone, finally, completely free. I leaned forward and unclenched my back. A pure feeling of bliss moved through me.

My wings unfurled. White feather by white feather, curving out and up toward the ceiling, spreading to their full span, like two halves to one heart, until they tapped the walls.

CHAPTER TWO

he water was bright blue and tasted of berries. Far above us, I could see rays of light cutting through the lowest of the tangled branches dipping through the lake's surface. We were half in shadow. I stretched out my arms. Maybeth, my sister, slept next to me, wrapped in a yellow water lily and her own wings. I reached over and shook her awake. Her eyes flung open – bright blue eyes, water eyes. She unwrapped herself from the thick petals and kicked herself up toward the surface. I spread out my wings and drifted up behind her. On the lake floor our friends were still sleeping, tiny lights like stars nestled among the roots and flora and waving grass.

We floated up past the elders in their thrones, the gnarled branches swaying back and forth in the water. Quiet, we made our way through the vines that stretched out on every side of us, until we broke through the surface into air.

I opened my eyes. The trunk of the great tree stretched in front of us, bathed in sunlight. From a distance I could see the storm that was hovering over the kingdom of humans. 'Look.'

'What?'

'Rain. The sky's gone dark.'

'Oh,' Maybeth said, flipping herself into the air. 'I guess you'll just have to stay with me, then.'

I clutched the wooden pier and pulled myself onto it. 'I have work to do,' I said. 'Plus what's a little rain?'

'Do it later!'

'I can't do it later!' I laughed at her, flicking my hand and spraying her with water. A scented breeze whispered through the trees that lined the lake, rippling through the leaves. The water shone in the light, and the rocks and pebbles gleamed like gems. On the bank, two human men lay sleeping, enchanted. A few fairies stood around them, poking at their armor.

She flicked a few droplets back at me. 'But I hate it there,' she said. 'Hate it hate it hate it.'

'You don't have to come.'

'Oh, fine,' she said. 'Just leave me all alone.'

'Leave who all alone?'

I turned and our friend Gladys was hovering behind us, her wings shimmering out behind her, fluttering like a humming-bird's.

'Lil's going into the human kingdom today,' Maybeth said, folding her arms.

'Oh, really? How fun! Let's go turn a lady into a frog!'

'Gladys,' I said, 'this is important.'

'How important can it be?' Maybeth said. 'Kings, queens, they all get old and die, anyway.'

'We need to make this girl a queen before she can die as one,' I said. 'I told you what the elders said.'

'I think it sounds marvelous,' Gladys said. She caught sight of herself in the surface of the water and peered in, moving her face back and forth. 'I hear she cries all day long every day. Poor girl.'

'They say she is the most beautiful girl in the land,' I said. 'With hair like starlight.'

Maybeth made a great show of stretching up her arms and yawning as wide as she could.

'I'm sure she is simply dazzling,' Gladys said. 'But can she do this?' She flipped her body over and balanced herself on the water with one finger. Her wings pulled her up into the air behind her. 'And won't she turn old in seconds, practically?'

'Get old and die, you mean,' Maybeth said.

'I think you're just jealous,' I said.

'Of a human?'

'No,' I said. 'Of me.'

Right then Lucibell emerged from the water and threw her arms around Maybeth, knocking her over and into the lake. They were both laughing so loudly I covered my ears.

'What are you thinking about?' Gladys asked in her soft voice, almost a whisper. Suddenly she was right next to me, leaning into me.

'The work I have to do,' I said.

'I did like Cinderella's mother.'

'Me too.'

'I was sorry when she died. I saw it written in the leaves and I wished I could change it.'

'Don't say that,' I whispered.

'It was just a thought, that's all.'

I looked back at the other world, their world. The dark sky in the distance, curling in on itself, the light shooting down through it. It was our job to make sure that everything happened as it was supposed to happen, the way it was written in the branches and vines of the great tree, the way the elders interpreted. When necessary, the young fairies, like me, who still left the water, helped humans meet the fates the elders decreed. We were inextricably bound to humans, no matter what we thought of them.

'Lil thinks I'm jealous of Cinderella,' Maybeth said.

'Well, I am,' Lucibell said. 'I'm going to change my hair into pearls. Then the prince will marry me instead of her! What will you do then, Lil?'

'Ha,' Maybeth said. 'You won't be able to compete with my golden breasts!'

'Lucibell! May!' I said.

'You should not even kid about that,' Gladys said, gasping exaggeratedly.

'Thank you,' I said.

Gladys left my side and spread her crazy butterfly wings with the bright blue markings on the sides. 'Because we all know that no human can resist these lustrous wings coupled with my violet eyes. What do I need with gold or pearls?'

I sighed as they burst into laughter, but it was true: Gladys was the most beautiful of us, and took great joy in appearing in rivers and in sunlight to human men, who would write reams of poetry and sometimes even go mad altogether as a result. Still, it was not a proper topic for conversation. Cinderella was not an ordinary human. She was destined to become queen, and it was my task to ensure it.

Just then the sky lit up in the distance. Lightning.

'I need to go,' I said, standing up on the pier. 'Much as I am enjoying this stimulating conversation.'

'I'm coming, too,' Gladys said. 'I can help.'

'Oh, a great help you'll be,' I said.

'We're coming, too,' Maybeth said, dragging Lucibell behind her.

'Don't you have work to do?'

'We can work later,' she said, waving her hand. 'For now, we might as well see our *competition*.'

They all laughed, but I stayed silent. They were starting to annoy me. The elders had chosen me for this task, not them. I was the one who was to get Cinderella to the ball now that human vanity had conspired against it.

It had been a dark, wintry night when the elders summoned me to the court. Ice dripped from the trees and every creature in the forest was in hiding. Snow and ice had coated the lake's surface, icicles breaking off and falling into the grass at the bottom of the lake as we slept. I had thought I was in trouble when the message came, as if the elders could sense my desire to be out in the world, to run through the snow, but then I found myself in front of the council. Prince Theodore, they told me, was going to throw a ball and pick a wife. It was important, they said, that Cinderella attend, and yet her stepsisters and stepmother were going to prevent it. It was a great honor for me to have been chosen. For my sensitivity, the feather wings that marked me.

Now I spread my wings and flew up into the wind and beyond the fairy lake, which was in the center of the dark forest. The others flew close behind, and the air against my face was like mist. My whole body relaxed into it. We passed over the ancient trees, the secret hovels of elves and witches and gnomes, and a group of men searching for their two lost companions, whom they would never find – I could feel the fear coursing through them – and headed toward the palace in the distance, rising up into the storm clouds. Slowly my annoyance disappeared. There was nothing like the feeling of flight, of navigating whole worlds with one's heart and body.

I pushed myself into it, faster and faster, and soon the rain lashed against my skin, the temperature dropping to a heavy coldness. I gave myself over to it, all of it. I laughed with the others, screaming against the rain and thunder.

We landed in the field of a large estate on the outskirts of the kingdom. Gladys dropped into an upturned leaf that was filling with rain. 'I'm drowning!' she cried, as Maybeth flopped into the mud and covered her skin with it.

'I believe I have turned to chocolate!' Maybeth called out.

I laughed, then looked up at the huge black horse in front of us, quivering as thunder shattered the air behind it. He stamped at the ground.

'Lovely creature,' I breathed, and he looked at me then, his enormous eyes meeting mine. I flew up, against the rain, to him. He had long black lashes and I could see the scars on his side where he'd been lashed.

Maybeth was by my side in an instant. 'He's a pretty thing,' she said.

'He sees us.'

She neared the horse and gripped his mane. She leaned in close to his ear and whispered. Through the whooshing sounds of the storm I could hear her words, soothing him.

'We should go,' I said.

The horse calmed as she spoke to him. I flew down and pressed myself against his soft coat, as black as ink. The horse's eyes focused in on me and he blinked.

'A creature like this shouldn't have to stay here, not this way,' Maybeth said.

'I know.' For a moment I could see the rain and the fields and the black trees through the horse's eyes, feel the fear slowly leaving him as his wounds closed and disappeared.

'Good boy,' she whispered, stroking his coat. Her face soft, open. We had both inherited it, this love for beasts.

'Where are the others?' I asked.

Lucíbell and Gladys were no longer in the grass, I saw then, but hovering up ahead, next to a carriage that was stuck in the mud. As Maybeth and I approached we saw a man wrenching himself out of the carriage and screaming at the horseman, his clothes getting soaked with rain. The horseman was pulling on the reins frantically, but the horses were refusing to budge.

Obviously, the two of them were up to no good. 'What are you doing to that man?' I said. 'Quit making mischief!'

'Oh, Lil, we're just having fun,' Gladys said, pouting. She glowed against the night like a firefly.

'I am quite sure he deserves it,' Lucíbell said.

Thunder clapped above us. I spread my wings. We left the horse and the carriage and the field behind, and moved through the dense, wet air. The kingdom spread out below us, all human life as we knew it. We passed noble manors, with their massive gardens and the lines of huts the peasants lived in, the fields full of crops and grapevines and livestock, the little chapels. We passed villages, with their rows of shops, their butchers and blacksmiths and seamstresses, their elaborate churches and stone taverns with the horses hitched up outside. We passed small forests without enchantments, filled with pheasant and other prey, and roads being traveled by knights and bandits and kings and beggars, until we came to the silver palace, which glittered under us, which reached up to us with its massive heart and all the desire that collected in it. And then, finally, after crossing the river that flowed like mercury, we came upon a dark manor on the other side of the kingdom that looked, from above, as sad as any tear. Its garden was overgrown, its crops untended. The stones in the façade were beginning to crumble. I had seen the place behind my eyes, from the lake, but here, now, it seemed enormous. Lightning cracked open the world. I could feel her in the house, and her presence came over me with such force I almost cried out loud.

We were silent as we came upon the long windows, pressing our foreheads against the glass.

'Up here!' Maybeth cried, and we all fluttered to the second floor, where, in a gaping stone room, three women stood huddled over a bed covered in dresses and fabric.

'Which one is she?' Lucibell breathed. 'None of them looks very beautiful to me.'

'Well, they're not going to be, not to us,' Gladys said. 'She's human after all.'

'This isn't her room,' I said, trying to interject. 'She's not here.'

'Oh, but her mother was gorgeous,' Lucibell said to Gladys. 'Remember? I loved her. I loved watching her.'

Gladys shrugged. 'She was half fairy. Wasn't she?'

'Yes,' I said. 'A fairy fell in love with her mother, Cinderella's grandmother.'

'That's disgusting,' Maybeth said.

'She was supposed to have been astonishing,' I said. 'He came upon her bathing in a stream and it happened then. Her husband never knew.'

Lucibell shuddered. 'I can't even imagine.'

'He was banished, right, the fairy?' Maybeth asked. 'For that, he must have been.'

'Of course,' I said. 'Anyway, those are the stepsisters and their mother. Cinderella's in the kitchen. I can feel her.'

The sisters were pulling up dress after dress from the bed and throwing them onto the floor. Rich fabrics of velvet and tulle and silk, every color woven into them.

Before I knew what was happening, Gladys pushed her way into the room, dissolving into the glass and reconfiguring herself on the other side, and Lucibell followed. I watched for a minute as they flung themselves onto the pile of fabric and began pulling the dresses away every time the sisters reached for them. The sisters, already in a state of anxiety and despair, started stamping their feet with frustration.

I grabbed Maybeth's hand. 'Let's go,' I said. We moved along the stone, passing room after room full of heavy tapestries and furniture, servants moving through them like ghosts, until we were outside of the great kitchen at the back of the house, just off the dining room with its table set for one hundred, though only the mother and her two daughters ate there every night. The door to the kitchen stood open as a maid lugged in a bucket of water from the well out back, next to the stables. We made our way inside, where servants bent over piles of meats and vegetables, large black pots and skillets. Dried herbs hung from the ceiling, batches of thyme in front of every window.

'To attract fairies,' Maybeth said, clapping with delight.

'She put those there,' I said. 'I feel her on them. She must have grown up hearing stories about us. I bet she knows all the songs, all the prayers.'

'I bet she leaves out bowls of milk next to her bed.'

'They probably don't let her,' I said. 'Look at her.' I pointed, then pushed my way to the back of the room, to where she was on her hands and knees on the floor.

'That's her?' Maybeth asked, shocked.

Her hair was bound in a dirty scarf, her body covered in rags. Her skin was smudged with dirt and ash. I felt her despair so strongly I had to stop and lean against the counter to recover. Rotting vegetables were piled on the counter, the smell moving into me like a hand down my throat.

'This is the girl who is to be queen?'

'Yes,' I said, clutching my stomach.

Maybeth appeared at my side, squatting down on the counter and pressing her lips to my ear. 'Are you sure about this, Lil?' she asked, and her voice, then, was less sure, more afraid.

'What do you mean?' I asked. I turned to her sharply.

She looked down at the ground, and then back up again. 'I just mean, it is a lot to do. She does not look right.'

'I will be fine, sister,' I said. 'I am prepared for this. That is why they chose me. Remember that: I was chosen.'

The girl paused in her work. She wiped a small hand against her forehead, which glistened with sweat, and left a line of dirt across it. She raised her eyes and for a moment they seemed to rest right on mine, and then they flicked to something behind me, to something that only she could see.

'She's so sad,' Maybeth whispered. 'What happened to her?'

We heard peals of laughter then, and looked up. Gladys and Lucibell, their faces red, hurtled toward us.

Cinderella looked up again quickly, squinting her eyes. *She senses us*, I thought.

'Back to work,' a low human voice said. I started, and looked around to see where the voice had come from. An older man sat deep in a chair beside the fire. Cinderella's whole body stiffened. I could feel it, that stiffening, through mine. I had never felt so sensitive before, to a human, the way I was to her. Usually I could feel them, sense them, hear their thoughts and dreams in a way that was uncanny – I was the best at this, of all the fairies – but not like this.

'Are you all right?' Maybeth whispered.

I nodded as Gladys and Lucíbell swarmed around Cinderella's head. Two tiny lights sparkling and glowing, dipping down and then back up again. But I was not okay. The man rose from the chair and walked behind Cinderella, stood there with his arms folded, watching as she scrubbed the stone. I could feel his hands on her, where they had been.

'Cinderella!' a voice screeched, from a distance. We all covered our ears. 'Cinderellllla!'

A bead of sweat passed down her face and dropped in the dust on the floor. Her hands on the stone, scratched and hardened. The brush under them, sweeping back and forth. Slowly and wearily, she lifted her head to the sound of her name, and then stood, every bit of her body aching. I felt it moving through me. All of it.

'Yes,' she said. 'I'm here.'

One of the sisters stormed into the room, dressed in a long purple gown and holding a pink and yellow one so heavy with jewels I was surprised she could carry it without tipping over.

'There is an emerald missing from this gown!' the sister said, looking down at it in disgust. 'Fix it!'

'Yes, ma'am,' Cinderella said, taking the gown carefully.

Gladys opened her mouth wide and looked at me. 'How can they treat her like that?'

Lucibell fluttered to the sister's neck, leaned in, and bit it. The girl started and flinched, slapping at bare skin. Gladys landed on her wrist and kicked it with all her might.

'You're a witch!' the sister said to Cinderella, clutching her wrist in her hand. 'You and your herbs and spells! A witch!'

'I am sorry,' Cinderella said softly, flinching. 'I will fix this for you.'

Gladys gave the sister's wrist another kick.

'Stop it, you two!' I said. 'She will have her time. You can be sure of that. We should go back.'

Lucibell gave the girl's neck one last nip as Cinderella carried the dress through a vast doorway and toward a flight of dusty stone steps.

'We need to go now,' I repeated, and lifted myself into the air. *I need to go now*, I should have said, *before my heart breaks.*

One by one we spread our wings and flew back into the cold, storm-filled human night, under a sky with not one star in it. We made our way back to the forest, to the fairy world that was all light, that was always light, and the lake that was the bluest blue you can imagine. I forgot everything and moved straight into it. Down into the depths of it, to the flowers and grass that swept out from the great tree that held all human fate. It was not in our control. The world grew quiet and calm. Everything was exactly as it should be. Me and my friends. My sister. I looked back at her – her ecstatic face, her sharp chin and wild hair, her huge glittering eyes.

*

I started awake, gasping for air. My mouth was dry and bitter. I blinked against the dark room, wondered where I was. For a moment I felt my heart burst open, a fluttering enter my throat. Instinctively I looked for her, my sister. I thought I saw the flicker of a wing, the glint of hair. My wings tensed up against my back. Anything seemed possible.

As my eyes adjusted to the dark, the room slowly came into relief. My room. The same dull flaking wallpaper, the dresser with the small television propped on top, the poster of Rita Hayworth on the wall.

The pain came at me like a fist. I became conscious of my body, the way my legs ached, the rawness where the sheets had rubbed my cheek and arms. Waking was always a huge shock. Even in dreams, the other world felt far more real than this room, this wallpaper, this dresser, this aching body.

I closed my eyes and tried to go back, concentrating as hard as I could on the image of Maybeth's face, her wings spread behind her. Outside, I could hear workmen shouting, the hum of the trucks, and, farther away, a wailing siren. The fan was useless in the city heat. I shifted and heard my bones crackle. Pulling a pillow to my chest, I burrowed my face into it, pushed my shoulders down. Sometimes I could do it, slide back into the other world for a little while longer, stave off the crushing loss. This morning there was a dream there, the tail end of one, like a ghost at the edge of the room.

After another few moments I sat up, throwing the covers off me. I looked at the clock. It was five A.M. I lay back on the bed, tossed and turned and sat up. I was exhausted but knew I would not get back to sleep again.

I heaved myself from the bed. I clenched in my wings, as hard as I could, and then slipped on a shirt and long skirt, the gypsy kind I always liked to wear, and a pair of comfortable sandals.

I was empty, starving. I thought about going to the diner for breakfast, but I was low on money, bills were due, rent was already late, so I shuffled to the refrigerator to see what was there. The shelves were empty except for some milk, a few eggs, a jar of pickles, and a bottle of ketchup. I would go shopping later, I decided, at the Gristedes between here and work – buy a whole chicken and boil it with celery and carrots and a few bay leaves, cook it up in a large pot and have soup for the week.

I pulled out three eggs and cracked them into a frying pan, then cut off a hunk from the loaf of French bread I'd bought a few days before. I pushed the eggs around, watched the whites fill out, the oil pop and fizzle. Cooking was a necessity with my income, as much as I loved having dinners a few nights a week at the diner or ordering large extra-cheese pizzas from the shop on the corner. I was always hungry, it seemed.

I ate standing by the front window, shoving the food into my mouth, soaking the bread with the split-open yolk. The street was just starting to fill with workers. I stared out: the brown brick buildings like rotten teeth, the old-timey slogans and advertisements painted on the sides, the round water towers perched on the rooftops. Smoke puffed from the buildings. It didn't feel like it was real, like any of it had anything to do with me at all.

I closed my eyes, thought of my sister hovering over me, beckoning me to come play.

What I would give, I thought, to go back.

I couldn't wait to get to the bookstore. On a morning like this, the apartment was unbearable. I had been raised with my sister and my friends all around me. Every day, all of us, down by the lake. Now it was just me. I turned on the television to hear the sound of voices, and they soothed me as I folded in my wings, clenched them against my back until they hurt. I pulled off my shirt. Then I lifted an Ace bandage from my dresser and slowly wrapped it around my body, from the front to the back, over my wings and my breasts. I stood in front of the mirror, facing to the side, to check. My back looked flat and normal. Human. Wrinkled. Old.

I shook the image away, rinsed my plate, the pan. I watched the water stream over the grease and the dish soap cut through it. I stacked the clean dishes in the rack by the side of the sink, then wiped the counter and stove. For the millionth time, I wondered what it would be like to live this life with someone, to have someone to cook for and clean up after. In the shop, people asked all the time if I had children or grandchildren, and usually I said yes, smiling warmly, because I knew that I looked as if I should. People saw me and imagined their grandmothers pulling steaming casseroles or piping-hot pies out of the oven, old ladies clucking away as they deposited fragrant dishes onto hot pads decorated with roosters and ducks. I made them feel safe. When I told them about a book they would love, or quoted them a price on a book they were selling, people felt they could trust me.

Nobody knew that I wasn't really old like this. That it was all a mistake.

George, of course, knew that I was an old lady who had never married, never had anyone. But that was something he liked about me, he said. George believed he was meant to be alone, too.

I could hear laughter from the television and went back into the bedroom. The sheets were strewn through with feathers. On the screen a morning talk-show host was laughing with a guest. Behind them the city seemed slick, ferocious. Like a different place. I sat down, lay on my back.

I stared up at the ceiling, the cracks shooting out in every direction, like my legs with the spider veins bursting over them. My apartment was caving in on itself, dark, falling apart. The old velvet-lined wallpaper – probably lovely at one point, carefully selected by some romantic soul – crumpled up at the edges of each wall and peeled down in strips across them. I turned my head, felt a feather brush against my face. I leaned into it, let the long strands graze my cheeks.

I could feel it come over me then, a terrible grief. Like a wave that rises from nowhere and pulls you into itself. On the television the women talked about their children, the way that one woman's five-year-old begged for Peking duck for his birthday and then refused to eat it. Everyone laughed. I had no idea why they were laughing.

I stood up quickly, clicked off the television, and brusquely made the bed, swiping the feathers onto the floor. I swept them up into a dustpan and dropped them in the trash. Smoothed the covers, the old-fashioned quilt that lay over them. I needed to get to work, to get out into the world before I was sucked under completely. At night my apartment became a haven and a sanctuary; in the morning it was the bleakest, emptiest place in the world. Grabbing my keys and wallet, I headed to the door.

I had just finished locking up – my two regular locks and two dead bolts – when I heard my name.

'Ms. Lillian?'

I focused in on the gray, badly lit hallway, the man stepping up to me. It was Leo, my landlord's grandson.

'Hello, Leo,' I said, breathing out and attempting to sound normal. 'How are you? I almost didn't recognize you.'

'I've been trying to reach you,' he said. 'My grandfather passed away a few months ago. Did you get my messages?'

'Oh,' I said. 'I didn't. But I heard about your grandfather. I'm so sorry.' Instinctively, I clenched my wings, ground my teeth. 'What can I do for you?'

'Well, we have some things to talk over. You know, I own the building now, all my granddad's buildings. How long have you lived here? God, you were here when I was a boy.'

'A long time,' I said slowly.

'Ahh,' he said. 'My mother said you used to tell her her fortune once a month or so. That you predicted I'd be a boy.'

'Did I?' I said.

'Well, that's what I hear.' He smiled. He couldn't have been more than twenty-five. It had to have been several years since I'd seen him last. 'I was trying to find your original lease, but my grandfather's papers are a bit messy. When did you sign one?'

I hesitated. 'I don't quite remember,' I said.

'It's amazing – it must have been some time in the seventies? You don't even seem as old as that. No offense, of course. But you seem younger. My grandfather said you could walk for miles, like a teenager.'

I stared back at him. 'It was around then, yes,' I said. My voice seemed to stick in my throat. 'I'm not sure I have a copy.'

He smiled again, friendly. 'Well, I haven't come across any

record of it yet. I've found some other stuff, though. Some photos, paraphernalia. My grandmother kept everything, God rest her soul. I hadn't realized you and she were so close.'

'Yes,' I said. 'That was a long time ago.'

'So. How much rent do you pay again?'

I cleared my throat, wiped my palms on my shirt. 'Five hundred dollars,' I said.

He laughed, then whistled, low and long. 'What a deal, huh? I'll bring the papers by again. Some other things for you, too, that you might be interested in.'

'That sounds fine,' I said. My mind flashed to the bathtub, my bed. Had I cleaned up the feathers? I reassured myself that everything was as it should be.

'Where are you off to now?'

'My job. I work downtown, at a bookstore.'

He looked surprised. 'Oh, I just thought . . .'

'Yes,' I said, smiling. 'I'm old, but I can still hold a job. I have to, even with this rent.'

He looked embarrassed. 'Of course,' he said. 'Well. Have a good day.'

'You, too,' I said, and moved past him, down the stairs. When I looked back, he was still standing there, watching me.

Eighth Avenue was coming to life. The sun was just starting to break and spill over the buildings. Pigeons swooped down from the tops of buildings, attacking garbage on the street. Commuters lined up for bagels and doughnuts at the carts outside of Penn Station, walked by with coffees in one hand, purses and briefcases in the other, cell phones at their ears. Already the tourists were out, whole families stopping on the sidewalks as harried workers pushed past them and salesmen tried to lure them into souvenir shops to buy all manner of I♥NY bumper stickers.

I just walked, trying to shake my anxiety. I had lived in my apartment for decades without problem. Lived in this neighborhood with its garment workers and office buildings and souvenir shops, the seediness of Port Authority just up the street. I was safe here. I couldn't even imagine living anywhere else. I thought of consulting with a lawyer, and my stomach split up in knots. I couldn't possibly afford to pay a lawyer.

Probably it was nothing. In New York tenants had rights. Landlords couldn't just throw them into the street.

I walked past the post office, the lines of people waiting for cabs, the bodegas and Irish pubs and hardware stores that populated this part of the city. As I walked down into Chelsea, past leafy cafés with courtyards, storefronts with sex toys or jewelry in the windows, the steady rhythm of my feet hitting pavement calmed my nerves a bit. Of course I had rights. Landlords can't just throw you out in the street. I breathed out. He was young. He was excited to own a building. That was all.

By the time I got down to the bookstore, I felt okay again. I had my routines. The apartment, the store, the diner. I was lonely, but I was surviving. In the evenings I had my baths, my books, the television. I loved the television, spent hours in my room curled up on the bed, my wings wrapped around me like a blanket, watching anything and everything that flickered across that dull screen. I hadn't always done so well in the world.

I turned onto Jane Street and admired, the way I always did, the trees that swooped over the sidewalks. The bakery across the street already had patrons sitting outside, eating croissants and sipping coffee. A few I knew from the neighborhood. One man had bought a Manzoni novel the day before, and I nodded as he looked up at me, smiling.

I opened the store with the keys George had given me and stepped in, breathing in the scent of must and bark, letting it soothe me the way it always did. Sometimes I thought about how much I would like to live in this space and how I envied George. To think that he could come down here whenever he wanted, wake up in the middle of the night and slip down in his socks and robe. But he never did that. He almost never appeared in the shop before it opened, and often not until after lunch.

I unlocked the case behind the register. Moved my palms over the rarest books, with their covers like saddles, their fragile pages. My favorite on the far right with those words scribbled in the back: *All my old loves will be returned to me.*

Yes.

The girl came in hours later. I spent the morning sweeping and dusting – the dust multiplied every night, as if by magic – and organizing the books George had left in front of his office. Boxes for the store he marked with a large *L* and set by his door; the others he stashed away to go through himself. They were for private collections, libraries, collectors, crazy people, and often just for George himself. I sometimes wondered what George would have been like had he not been born into a family of booksellers, if that passion had been directed toward something else, like corncob art or mathematics, or if he would have found his way to books no matter what.

I was sitting at the register ringing up a college boy when the door banged open and a tall girl strode in, birdlike, balancing a large box in her arms, bags dangling from her shoulders and wrists.

I could not help but stare. She was wonderful. Her mouth was a glossy red bow, her skin so pale it was almost translucent. Her eyebrows arched like the span of a bird's wings over her eyes, which were blue and glittery. Her hair, the color of russet potatoes, streamed from her scalp and towered over her like a strange crest.

'My God these are heavy,' the girl said, exaggeratedly dropping the box on the counter and smiling up at me. The warmth of her smile took me by surprise. 'Do you think you'd take any of them?' She winked at the boy, who blushed as I handed him his change.

'Give me a second and I'll look,' I said.

The boy took his copy of *Transmetropolitan* and turned to leave, smiling at the girl awkwardly as he passed.

'Not bad, huh?' she whispered to me, raising her eyebrows and making a face. He was still in earshot. I laughed despite myself. 'I like them in all shapes and sizes,' she said.

She made me feel comfortable right away. The only other person who'd done that was George, the day I met him, a few years before. I blinked. 'So what do you have here?' I asked.

'Oh, all kinds of stuff,' she said, waving her hands. 'I just want to get rid of it. Start fresh. My apartment's like a Goodwill store right now. I could slap a price tag on everything and open shop. I thought about trashing it all, but you can't throw out a perfectly good book. Bad luck, you know.'

'It is?'

'Sure it is,' she said. She laid her hand on the counter, and

I saw that her nails were black, covered in glitter. She had rings on every finger, and I thought how beautiful her hands were, like peacocks. 'Like throwing away a photograph. How can you own a bookstore and not know that?'

'Oh, I'm not the owner,' I said.

'That's no excuse. Goodness, imagine the havoc you could wreak not knowing that.'

I laughed and started sifting through the box – the novels, the histories, the fashion books with titles like *Vogue Knitting Stitchionary* and *Reader's Digest Complete Guide to Sewing*. I lifted out an illustrated book on botany and a slip of paper fell out of it. The faint scent of cloves wafted up from it.

'Oh!' she said, reaching out for the paper. 'How embarrassing. These books are probably full of my indiscretions. All my illicit affairs, my drug contacts . . . I'm totally kidding. This is probably . . . Yep. A shopping list.' She turned the sheet over and could just barely make out the word *milk* scrawled across it. 'So sad.'

'Don't worry,' I said. 'Your secrets are safe with me.'

'Hmmm,' she said, smiling, squinting at me. 'I think you might be busy enough with your own, missus.'

I looked at her, surprised, but she was smiling. In the sunlight streaming through the window, her eyes looked shockingly blue. *Such a strange girl*, I thought. No one paid attention to me like this.

'You remind me of someone . . .' she said, then stopped herself. 'Wow,' she said. 'Your hair.'

'What?'

'It's, like, pure white. A crazy sort of white.'

I touched it, suddenly embarrassed. 'I guess it is,' I said.

'No, I mean, I love it. Sorry.' She shook her head, pointed at her mouth. 'I need a built-in editor sometimes.'

'Thank you,' I said.

'You really remind me of my grandmother. She was my favorite person when I was growing up. She had this glamour about her, the way you do. And pure white hair. White by the time she was twenty.'

I smiled. 'That's sweet of you to say.' The girl seemed familiar to me, too, but I couldn't place her. There were so many faces in my head, of people I'd forgotten.

The door opened and a man and a woman in their thirties walked in holding hands. 'Good afternoon,' the man said, nodding to us, and the two disappeared into the stacks.

The girl watched after them, then turned back to me. 'She's so going to dump him.'

I laughed and began stacking her books to the side of the register. I felt self-conscious suddenly, standing around talking when she'd come in to sell books. But she did not seem to mind. She even seemed to be enjoying herself.

'I'm Veronica, by the way,' she said. 'Oh, and I do hair. I've got a little salon on Avenue B. Let me give you my card.' She opened her huge black purse and began rummaging through it, peering into it as if it were a mouth. 'Ugh, I can never find anything in here.' She spread the purse on the counter. I was mesmerized by the scattered trinkets inside, thought of a beach covered in gleaming shells. She had makeup, little pots of lip gloss and glitter and eye shadow, a large old-fashioned compact with a line down the center. She had all kinds of sewing and knitting paraphernalia, too: thread, yarn, thimbles. Black knitting needles that clinked together.

I just stood, watching. I suddenly felt as if I wanted to be young like her. Young, alive, with rings like hers. Black nails. An overflowing bag full of a million things.

'Ah!' she said, pulling out and handing me a pink and white card. 'Veronica,' it said, in pink, next to an illustration of a chair with an old-fashioned hairdryer hanging over it, and an address, phone number, and website address.

'Thank you,' I said, studying it for a moment. 'I'm Lil.'

'Pleased to meet you.' She gathered up her purse and slung it over her shoulder, then dropped one of her shopping bags onto the counter. She should have seemed sloppy, I thought, but she had a grace to her that somehow seemed to match her wildness.

'Doing some shopping?' I asked, reaching into the box for more books and stacking them beside me.

'Oh,' she said. 'I was just in the garment district. I'm making a new dress. Ragged full skirt, all these layers that float on top of each other. Laced-up back.' She reached in and pulled out a swatch of lavender fabric – organza, I thought – setting it on the counter in front of me. 'See?'

'It's beautiful,' I said. 'What's the occasion?'

'Oh, nothing special, probably some show,' she said. 'I wish I had somewhere fabulous to go, though. You know what I mean? Some amazing place, like El Morocco, where men wore suits and women swung over the crowds on trapezes. I bet you hit a few places like that in your time, didn't you?'

If you only knew, I thought. I picked up the fabric, let it run over my skin. 'I live in the garment district, but I don't think I've ever gone into one of those stores.'

'They're great,' she said. 'It's a completely unappreciated part of town, don't you think? Someone told me it's the only neighborhood in New York that never changes, where you can walk down the street and feel like it's the nineteenth century. I mean, except for the Gray's Papaya and the White Castle and the triple-X peep shows that cost twenty-five cents. But still. I like that.'

'I never thought of it like that,' I said. 'But maybe so.'

My eyes hit on something then. It was a book, with an old-fashioned sepia-toned image on the cover, a girl with flowers in her hair staring out. But it was the shapes in front of her that I recognized immediately.

'What is this?' I asked, pulling the book from the box. 'Where did you get it?' I never thought I would see such a thing in this world.

'That?'

'Yes.'

Fairies. A group of fairies dancing in a circle, with huge butterfly wings stretching from their backs.

Had she been sent to give this to me? I searched her face but she just stared back, confused at the shift in me. I had an image then, of her, in front of the mirror. The blue silk like water on her pale skin. *Be calm,* I thought.

But I could barely breathe. It was an actual photograph. A girl resting her chin in her palm and staring out at the camera, with that haunted, spooky look that people in old photographs always seem to have, like they're staring out from the beyond. And in front of her: my sister Maybeth, my fairy friends. As if I had left them only minutes before.

'Are you okay?'

'What is it?' I asked again.

She shrugged, still watching me. 'It's just a book,' she said.

'About that fairy scam, you know, those two girls who faked photos of themselves with fairies. They had everyone fooled – all these philosophers, even that writer, the Sherlock Holmes guy. You've never heard of that? The Cottingley fairies?'

'They took photos of fairies?'

'They took, like, five or something, had everyone convinced. But years later, when they were old ladies, they admitted to faking everything. Cutting out drawings and propping them up with hat pins.' She laughed. 'Those photos are crazy, right? I mean, don't get me wrong, I'm open to everything, fairies, werewolves, you name it, but they didn't exactly do a stellar job.'

I looked at her. I couldn't believe she didn't see. But I knew how humans were conditioned to deny all evidence of us, even when it was as plain as day. Right in front of them. Even a girl like her, who could almost have had one foot in the other world already. Still, it was shocking to see firsthand.

The man and woman were now rummaging through the records up front, his hand across her back, holding on to her. A tiny blonde woman struggled through the door, pushing a stroller.

'Sorry. It's just . . . I've never seen these photos before.'

'Oh, I know. Aren't they amazing? Sort of creepy, right? But so beautiful and strange, too.'

I smiled. 'I can definitely buy all these books from you,' I said. 'You've got about forty here. How about a dollar a book? Forty dollars?' I reached in the register and pulled out the money.

'Sounds good,' she said. 'And, please, come visit me. I'd love to get my hands on those tresses. Seriously. Come to my salon, and I will make you *gawgeous*. You got my card, missus.' She made a snipping motion with her first and middle fingers, then brought them to her mouth and blew, as if they were on fire.

*

That night I hurried up Eighth Avenue, clutching the book to my chest. There was a reason the girl had come, I thought, bringing evidence of fairies. Giving me proof that Maybeth and the rest of them were still in the world, or had been within the past century. In the photographs they'd looked just as they had when I last saw them. Perfect. Eternally young and dazzling.

And then it hit me, who the girl reminded me of.

Maybeth. Of course. My fairy sister. I remembered suddenly how Maybeth would dance. On the grass of the fairy court, the elders sitting on their thrones, all of us dressed up in shells and pearls and water lilies. How could I have forgotten? The way she would dance and dance, her hair bright in the water. The way no one could take their eyes off her. I shook my head. Memories seemed to come up on me without warning, but usually it was my human memories that took me by surprise. It was the fairy world that was always clear.

I stopped right at the corner of Twenty-third Street, causing a young woman to crash into me, almost spilling her coffee.

'Fuck!' she said, turning to me like she was about to commit murder. Something in her face changed when she saw me.

'Are you okay, ma'am?' she asked softly.

'Yes,' I said. I hadn't realized I was crying. 'Yes.'

I rushed up Eighth Avenue, wiping my face, my heart bursting. It had to mean something, this. It had to be a message.

I forgot all about Gristedes, my plans to pick up chicken and carrots and celery, make a nice soup that would last for days. Suddenly I was ravenously hungry. This human body, I thought, could never get it right. Always this longing that extended through every cell.

I passed my street and headed to the diner, went in and sat at my usual spot. I opened the book again. The photos took up whole pages. In one a fairy's head was tilted back and her arms were raised above her. I could not make out her face but the shape was unmistakable. In the next picture a fairy fluttered in the air in front of another little girl and held out a batch of flowers to her.

My heart caught in my throat. I could not shake that sick, sad feeling. I had been terrified, for years, that they had all disappeared. But these girls had photographed fairies not more than a hundred years before. I had recognized them. There was proof right there that they still existed. Now, after all this time, all these centuries I had spent in the human world, alone.

Were they coming back to me?

When I'd first fallen to earth, I'd spent years looking for them. My memories were hazy, unclear: just me alone in the forest, wandering by the lake, trying to find them. But they never showed themselves to me, no matter what I did. And then I'd gone to sleep.

The door opened. I looked up without thinking, saw a man pushing through the heavy glass. He was wearing an elegant black suit, and his white shirt stood out, as did his teeth and eyes, against his skin. His silvering dark hair was just slightly too long.

I bent back down to the book. I could almost make out the features on the fairies' faces: the tiny bow-shaped mouths and slanted eyes, the round cheeks and pointed chins.

I must be going mad, I thought.

The man sat a few seats down from me at the counter.

I swallowed hard. I smoothed back my hair. My wings pressed into my shoulder blades.

'I'll have a cup of coffee, black,' the man said. 'And what kind of pie do you have today?'

His voice rumbled through me, and I looked up again. I knew that voice.

'Cherry, pumpkin, apple, pecan,' Mike said. I focused in on the smaller fairy, the way her skirt puffed out below her knees.

'Apple,' the man said. 'With ice cream.' He cleared his throat and looked over at me. I could feel his movements, see his dark outline. It sounded like he had learned English later in life but learned it perfectly. 'Quite some weather today, huh?' he asked.

'What?' I glanced up, tried to look pleasant. His eyes moved over me like hands. I looked up again, and his eyes burrowed into mine. No one had ever looked at me that way, not since . . .

Don't be ridiculous, I thought. *You are an old woman.* I was conscious, suddenly, of my wrinkled, hanging skin.

'It just started raining,' he said. 'You see that?' He tipped his head toward the window, and I saw that he was right. Rain streamed down the glass. People rushed by under large flaring umbrellas.

A woman pushed through the door, and a breeze funneled in, thick with the raw scent of rain and street.

'I love that smell,' he said. 'Where I come from, the best smells are cut grass and new rain.' His voice was so familiar. I knew him. Of course I knew him.

I took a sip of water and realized that my hands were shaking. Immediately I put the glass down. 'I like it, too,' I said.

Mike appeared and set down my bacon cheeseburger deluxe. The fries shone with oil. Suddenly sick to my stomach, I pushed the plate away.

'Excuse me,' I said, and I rushed to the bathroom, where I

locked the door, bent down, and heaved over the toilet. My stomach was so empty that the sickness just seemed to move up in waves from my belly to my throat.

I stood up and looked into the bathroom mirror. My eyes were creased and bloodshot. Tears streamed down my face. The thought moved over me like a blade: Hideous. I was completely hideous. And it was my fault that I had become this. I peered in, stared right into my own eyes. The green was faded. My skin wrinkled, hanging from my bones. My hair – once the color of pumpkins and autumn – was white and thin.

Look closer, I thought. *Under there.* I placed my palms on my cheeks, felt the shape of my face, how beautiful it had been once. I stared into the mirror and imagined my hair growing thick and lush around my face, that same rich color, like spices, like light beating down at dusk. I imagined my gnarled fingers growing long and straight, my neck smoothing down and curving. My shirt turning to green-silver, unraveling, falling down my body in thick folds.

I must have been in the bathroom for fifteen minutes. Maybe longer. That was when Mike started banging on the door, asking if I was okay. 'I'm fine!' I called out, wiping the tears from my face and splashing cold water into my eyes. I rubbed my wet hands on my cheeks and brushed back my hair.

I am fine, I thought. All I needed was to calm down, go home, and get my head together. I would be fine.

I stretched out my shoulders, lifted up my head, and walked out.

'Jesus, Lil, I thought you passed out in there.'

'I'm okay, Mike,' I said. 'Just a little queasy.'

I looked past him and saw that the man was gone. There was

no trace of him. No coffee cup, no leftover dish. A sense of loss came over me so heavily that I felt woozy with it. Mike quickly reached down and grabbed my arm as I stumbled, propping me up.

'Do you need a doctor, Lil?' he asked. 'You're acting so strange.'

'No, no,' I said, pulling my arm away and steadying myself. 'Was there a man here just now? At the counter? Eating pie?'

'Yes,' he said. 'He left a few minutes ago. Are you sure you're okay?'

I was starving suddenly. Ravenous. As if I'd never had food, never had water.

'I just need some fresh air, I think. Just one second. I'll be right back. Do you think you could wrap this up?'

I pushed past him then and practically ran for the door. I stood underneath the awning, watching the rain pound down, looking up the street for a sign of him. I couldn't see anything apart from the stretch of black umbrellas and downturned heads. He was gone. He had been right here, so close I could have touched him, and now he was gone. I stood for a moment, numb and heartbroken at the same time, breathing in the raw scent, listening to the rain slapping against the concrete.

Once I had my food, I raced home. I dropped onto my bed and peeled off my wet skirt and blouse, ripped off the bandage, let my wings spread out behind me. I grabbed a pillow and burrowed my face into it, as sobs moved through my body. I had almost forgotten. All that I had lost. All that I had done. I pushed the pillow down, opened the Styrofoam container I had set on the nightstand. I picked up the burger and a couple of fries and crammed them into my mouth. They tasted amazing. The crisp, greasy taste of the fries mixed with the wet, raw taste of meat and onion and mayonnaise and bun. I couldn't get enough into my mouth at once. After, I clutched my stomach and lay on my side, careful to keep my wings free and outstretched. Suddenly I was so tired I could barely keep my eyes open.

Forget all this, I thought. The room, the bookstore, the garment shops, the hunger, the smell of meat and grease, the garbage-strewn streets, the trucks with the endless bundles and hanging racks and long rolls of fabric.

I shifted on the bed, let the memory rise up and envelop me, one so clear it felt more real than the wet streets outside.

And then it was just his pale eyes and white teeth, his voice in my ear. Fading back and back until it was just him and me, the silk dress in my hands, slipping to the floor. Like water. I moved my hand from my belly, straight down, between my legs. Twisted on the bed, onto my stomach. Remembering. Pain, loss, guilt, desire mixed with the feel of the sheets on my skin, my moving hand, the rain streaking the windows outside.

CHAPTER THREE

went to see Cinderella a second time before the night of the ball, my sister and friends again trailing behind. It was only by surveying the house that I realized what I needed, all the things she needed to get there. A carriage. A coachman. A dress. Shoes.

This time we waited until late at night, when the whole kingdom was asleep and the moon covered everything with silver and mist. The palace gleamed under us, the river seemed to be made of liquid stars, and even Cinderella's manor, as we came upon it, seemed wonderful and enchanted in the soft light. We passed through the walls into a great marble hallway lined with ancient sculptures. Gods and beasts and warriors loomed on every side of us, casting shadows on the marble tile. A large stone lion reared up on its hind legs, its paws swiping the air in front of it. In one corner, perched on a long stick, was a silver face with a seashell swirling from its forehead. The others flew over to it, to examine the closed silver eyelids, the curves of the shell.

I left them behind. I swept up the great staircase to the main floor, with its rich tapestries covering the walls and the many chests spilling over with thick, exotic fabrics and colorful jewels. I passed the chambers where the stepmother and stepsisters lay sleeping, on soft mattresses, under silk coverings, their bodies wrapped in velvet and fur, then slipped up the lone, dust-covered staircase that twisted up to the tower where Cinderella slept in a small garret room on a bed of straw.

I came upon her in the dark. Asleep, with her bright hair uncovered, her skin awash with moonlight, she did not seem like the same girl I'd seen scrubbing the kitchen floor. I had never seen a human so beautiful, even with her hair all tangled and dusty, the straw pressing up into her pale skin and leaving long red lines across the backs of her legs and shoulders. She might have been a full-blood fairy. I knew that she was not like a regular human, but I hadn't thought it possible that she was so much like us. Humans were strange and monstrous and ungainly to us. Even the best ones were. We never would have thought to envy them.

Maybe that is what made me get too close. My surprise. The way her starlit hair spread across the straw. The stark black of the room, and how luminous she was against it. The way she moved in her sleep, dreaming, fluttering her eyes. I wanted to know what she was seeing. Suddenly, I was dying to.

I shouldn't have been surprised like that, taken so off guard. Fairies had talked for years about Cinderella's mother, about how beautiful she had been, how beautiful her daughter was, how important it was for the daughter to grow up and marry the prince of the kingdom and to one day become queen, and how necessary we would be in the union. Others had envied me when I was chosen, but Maybeth and I just laughed and kept playing, flicking water from the lake onto each other's wings. Humans did not matter, we said. Our world is perfect. Theirs is nowhere near. To the two of us, it seemed as simple as that.

I was the one who was beginning to forget.

I landed next to Cinderella's ear. I closed my eyes and leaned in, against her. Her lashes lay on her cheeks like brushes, and her faint almond scent seemed to move around me, wrapping me in. I let her dreams seep into me until I could see them, too. They came in, bit by bit, strange shimmering images. A hand-some man walking forward, tall and dark-haired, his face obscured, the hem of a dress, a large open field. Steps winding up and up. 'What are you seeing?' I whispered, not even think-ing. I let myself sink farther down, felt the sleep pulling at me like a tide heading out. 'Show me.'

I saw the man walking toward me, grass. Light shooting through so intensely that the man and the grass seemed to be transparent. Human dreams were always so strange and unreal, like the world inverted, hollowed out. But hers seemed to be leading me somewhere. I wanted to see the man's face. And there was something else, a feeling that began at my fingertips and moved through me, burrowing into my chest and gut. *Desire.* I focused on the man and willed myself next to him.

He touched me then, in the dream, his face still out of view, his hand moving against my arm and up to my neck. Suddenly it brushed my lips. I jumped up and opened my eyes, but there was just straw there, poking at me, and her pale cheek and long hair. The same small bare room. I looked at her, astonished, and then a feeling of loss came over me so strongly that I almost fell over. I needed to be back in the dream. I moved back into it as if I were ripping open a curtain.

I was immersed in it, in her. I breathed through her lungs

and felt through her skin and fingers. A man's chest pressed against me. My foot pressed into grass. We were outside. I reached for him and lost all sense of myself. Hair brushed against my cheek, a soft breath warmed my ear, so close it tickled me. And all the while, light poured down over us. The color of butter, of lemons. We stepped through haze. I could feel every particle of light touching me, rolling over my face and neck, my bare legs. Like drops of water. My body was disintegrating into light. Moving into his. The look of his arm as it moved toward me, cutting through the haze, creating shadows and splinters of light. I had to squint even as I moved into him.

'Cinderella,' the voice said, drawing out the syllables, lingering over her name, pulling it out as if it were a mood, a pathway to something. And then something else.

His eyes were full of longing, of love. All I wanted was to disintegrate into him. Become pure light. The feeling in my chest radiated through my body. I was not anything else, did not know anything else, but that feeling.

I blinked open my eyes and he was gone. The field, the voice, the hand. I was back in the little room next to a sleeping girl. I closed my eyes and tried to claw my way back in, but there was nothing. Just empty space and that feeling, which was different now. Unsettled. Wrong. Her hand shot up to her face, brushing at me, and I saw that she was awake. I flung myself into the air and dropped to the floor. What had happened? I looked at my hands and legs in horror, fluttered my wings to make sure they were still there. I tried to push off the dream, but it was like a web I was caught in.

She sat up, and it took me a minute to realize she was crying. I stopped moving and watched her, her face in her hands and her hair streaming around them. Her bare arms and the strange burlap shift she was dressed in. I noticed how the soles of her feet were black.

The sun was starting to rise. The longing in her was so strong that the walls seemed to turn yellow with it. It seemed to be turning me, too, into something else. She wanted something she did not have. The man. Of course. She had more desire in her than any human I had ever come across. 'Don't you?' I whispered.

Her longing had saturated her dream, and me. I could not shake it off. That restlessness, like a gaping wound. I had seen countless human dreams, human desires, but I had never felt infected the way I did then, in her garret room. She was so sad. She wanted something, someone she could not have. She wrapped her arms around her knees and pushed her face down, her shoulders shaking.

I was astonished to realize how badly I wanted, even then, to go back into her sleep, to the man, despite her anguish. How much I wanted to hear what he had whispered, the words I hadn't quite been able to make out. I wanted to see his face, his eyes. Tunnel my way in.

There was a faint scratching outside the door.

She sat up quickly, wiped her face. 'Stepmother?' she asked quietly. Her voice seemed to coil through the room and snake around me.

She jumped off the mattress and scurried to the door. She listened for a second, her eyes wide with fear, and then moved back into the room, her shoulders relaxing. As she passed me, where I was hovering, I noticed a bruise on her leg. How tired she was. I could feel the ache in her limbs.

She walked to the window then, the small circle punched into the stone wall. I stayed in a corner, hovering, watching her face. She was looking at something far away. Her face grew soft, as if she were sleeping, and her eyes glimmered and shone. I had never seen human eyes like that.

I flitted from the corner to the window, looked out onto grass and wood. Desperate to see what she saw.

'What do you see?' I whispered. She flinched.

Her eyes grew wet. I slipped up to her neck, her ears, facing the window.

'I love you,' she whispered. 'I love you so much.'

I followed her gaze, but all I could see was empty space. The fields and wood stretching out under the early-morning light, the mountains that seemed to float in the sky, and then, just barely, the tip of the castle, the curve of turrets and towers, in the distance.

I sat up, startled, and looked around. The take-out bag lay crumpled next to my hand, alongside a battered Styrofoam box with a piece of lettuce stuck to the bottom. The storm clashed and banged against the building, the rain like pounding nails. My wet clothes from the night before lay in a jumble at the foot of the bed, still damp; the whole room smelled of them, as if everything had gone rotten.

It was just after five in the morning.

I turned and opened the window, looked out at the water towers, the rooftops, the smudged gray and black sky. The rain pounded down, much more intensely than it had the night before. That raw scent rushed into the room. I reached my hand out the window and let it spatter with rain, watched the raindrops drip down my wrist and across my forearm.

I looked more closely at my hand and wrist. Something was different. I stretched out my fingers. Moved them up to my face. The light was so dim, a pale silver mixed with amber. I leaned over and flicked on the lamp, placed my hand under it as if it were a microscope, and stared.

The skin was smoother, paler. I could have sworn it. It was not the same gnarled, twiglike hand I had fallen asleep with. Was it? I shook my head, closed my eyes and opened them. My eyes dropped to my bare legs. I moved away from the window, suddenly nervous with the light on, and stared down at my smooth skin, my small curving toes. My veinless legs. I could feel my eyes welling over. I stretched back, lifted my arms over my head, and then turned and smiled into the pillow, letting my whole body relax.

It was just past seven A.M. when I awoke again. My hands were wet, I realized, as were the sheets near the window. The rain was coming in at a slant now, causing a huge puddle to form on the wooden floor. Quickly, I sat up and slammed the window shut. I rushed to the bathroom to grab a towel. Slipped into a fresh shirt and pair of pants. I stopped with my leg through one side. My skin. It was wrinkled now, lined with veins. I held my right hand out in front of me, saw that it was gnarled and spotted.

I ignored the feeling that dropped over me then, descending on my body like a dress, falling around me in folds. I was used to that sort of disappointment. In the early days, I had awakened every morning to that same feeling, that same sinking sense of being trapped and hemmed in, the ground pressing up into my spine and limbs. When I camped outside the palace and tried desperately to make my way back to him, it was almost unbearable. No one had recognized me. I could not make anyone understand who I was. It was like losing your sight. I had ripped up whole clumps of grass and earth in frustration, and it had splintered through my entire body, that pain. Now it was a dull ache, as familiar as sheets and air and sun.

I cleaned the floor as well as I could, wrung out the sheets in the bathtub and hung them from the shower-curtain rod. I grabbed the take-out box and brought it to the kitchen, to the full trash bag I needed to drag to the Dumpster downstairs.

I pulled a set of clean sheets from the hall closet and slowly made the bed. Silver light streamed in. The rain thumped on glass and brick. As I pulled the top corners tight, I caught myself again in the mirror.

Now, as always, I couldn't believe that the woman I was seeing was me. I walked up and put my face right next to the glass, looked straight into my sunken eyes, the lines shooting off in every direction. I pulled off my shirt, stared at my grizzled, hanging breasts, my gathering stomach, the feathers that dropped to the floor. My wings twisted out of my back, ugly at the roots, slicing into skin, but with feathers so shining and perfectly white that they made the decay of my body even more stark. Without them I could have been just anyone, any old lady who'd ended up alone.

I was late for work. I sighed, stumbled into the bathroom to wipe the sweat from my body, pour water down the creases of my arms and legs.

Hunger pressed in, gnawing at my gut. Why did I always have to be starving? Once I was showered, I folded in my wings and wrapped the bandage around my torso, then pulled my clothes back on and headed to the kitchen. I hated myself for not having gone to the grocery store as I'd planned. I never took care of myself properly, it seemed. All my refrigerator revealed was the same jar of pickles, the same ketchup. One egg with a crack skidding across the top. A tiny hunk of bread, which I stuffed into my mouth, almost choking on the crumbs that sprayed across my throat. It only made me more hungry. I twisted the top of the jar and grabbed several small pickles, biting down on them all at once, letting the tang of them shock my mouth.

It was then that I saw the book, which I'd left propped open on the couch. *The Cottingley Fairies*. The girl, Veronica, had not thought they were real. 'A scam,' she'd said, two little girls fooling everyone with a camera and hat pins. But I knew my own kind. I knew what was in those photos. Just seeing those flitting bodies made me feel like I wasn't alone, not in the way I'd been before. They had been photographed *in this world*. My sister. My friends. I picked up the book, checked the dates again: 1917. I must have been in New York then, I thought, but my memory was strange, blurry. I had flashes from my years in the human world, all those moments of yearning, of thinking I had found them. I remembered waking up, seeing the clock, the pier, the water, thinking I had gone home before realizing that nothing would be the same again, that I had lost everything. Just one year out of all the years I'd been here. A blur of years, a long haze of sleeping and dreaming and always trying to get back to them. It was only in the past few decades that I could remember my human life with the same vividness I could remember the fairy world. And they had been right there, playing by the side of a creek. With two little girls, rather than me. Had they been watching me? Were they watching me now?

I stared at the main photo, with the four dancing fairies spread across the lower half, looking so free and perfect and complete. Gladys, Lucibell, Maybeth, another I could vaguely remember from the lake. Had she taken my place? It should have been me in the photo. All of them with their insect wings, me with the feathered ones of a godmother. But Maybeth and I had shared the same heart. I traced the photo with my finger. It was her on the far right. The pose of the body, the curve of the wing were unmistakable. Why was she showing herself to me now, after so long?

I felt self-conscious suddenly. 'Are you here, sister?' I whispered. I stopped moving and listened.

I heard rain, cars, voices, the faint stomp of feet overhead.

'Tell me.'

The light shifted in the corner of the room, and I turned my head, trying to catch her. I remembered all the games we used to play: flying along a shaft of light, in and out of a glint on the surface of water. In the corners, just out of a human's range of vision. Our wings folding out like accordions.

'Maybeth!' I said. 'Where are you?'

I closed my eyes, trying to keep from laughing. Then I opened them quickly. Looked all around. But there was nothing there at all, no flicker of wings or moving bits of light. The room was the same as always, with its wooden floor, dark furniture, the yellowed blinds hanging over the windows.

'Why now? Why are you coming back now?'

'Everything they long for, we already have,' Maybeth had said the day I returned to the lake, Cinderella's need consuming me, a new vigor in my work. And the stained grass, the shards of glass covering it.

I shook my head, picked up the book. Something dropped out of it. The girl's card, with its pink old-fashioned script, poked out from under the couch. I bent down, groaning from the crackling in my knees.

I looked around again. 'Did you send her to me?' I asked. 'To help me find you?' I waited one beat, two beats, but there was nothing except silence.

Outside, a man shouted in some Asian tongue.

A sense of hope opened within me. *What occurs in the world of faerie will become manifest in the world of men.*

I had read it in a book once, one of the old, priceless books that sometimes passed through the shop, books centuries old, so delicate that George kept them in a safe in the back office. George had been excited enough by that one to call me in and show me, having no idea whom he was telling.

'This man,' he'd said, 'claimed to know fairies. Elders, he called them, the most powerful fairies. This is a book of their lore. Four centuries old, Lil. Only two copies in the world. Can you believe that?'

We'd looked through it together, in the few hours he had the book before selling it to one of his regular buyers, an elderly gentleman with a traditional library right in his Upper East Side town house. I'd found a small section on fairies who crossed over and became human.

What occurs in the world of faerie will become manifest in the world of men.

I had clasped onto that. Believed that there was still a tie between me and them. That what I had done there affected this world and that what I did in this world affected them. And that someday they would come back for me.

I moved to the window. The rain was stilling now, but the air crackled and hummed with it. The street seemed completely washed out and new, taxicabs moving through the wet streets and spraying the sidewalks. Random people in suits or raincoats or shorts and sneakers dodged puddles and each other as they rushed by. There was something wonderful in all this, I thought, surprising myself. Maybe the world was just opening to me, in a way it hadn't before.

I shook my head. Foolish old woman. I would go crazy if I stayed inside another minute, talking to ghosts. But I was laughing now, and something new was moving through me. Hope and nostalgia mixed together. The image of the lake, all of us buzzing around it.

I grabbed my keys and purse, locked up, and headed downstairs.

My upstairs neighbor Joanne was standing in the foyer by the mailboxes. She looked small and meek, with her blue-gray curls and her cat's-eye glasses.

'Lillian,' she said, turning to me. I had no choice but to stop. 'Can you believe this? Morris not dead a few months and his grandson's gone and sold the building. Not one ounce of respect for what his grandfather stood for.' Her face was like a pot of tea about to whistle.

'I'm sure it will be fine,' I said.

'It's not fine,' she said. 'We're moving to Flushing. The buyout will barely cover the move. After twenty years that we've been in this building. And you, it must be twice that. What are they offering you?'

I thought of the papers gathering on my kitchen table, which I hadn't been able to bring myself to look through. I remembered the day Joanne had moved in, with her late husband, how radiant she had seemed then, starting something new.

'I can't talk now,' I said, gesturing to my wrist. 'I'm late for work.' I didn't know what else to say, only that I needed to get out of the building, into the street.

'We found a decent broker, if you need any help.'

'Thanks,' I said.

Once I was outside, I couldn't walk fast enough. How could he sell the building? Could he do that? I headed across Thirty-sixth Street toward Eighth Avenue. Past the zipper store, past the shop selling buttons of every shape and size and color, past a group of caramel-colored boys slouching in front of a deli, an old woman with a small dog yapping at her heels, a young man with a baby slung across his chest. I turned onto Eighth, heading downtown. The city closed in around me. Four lanes of traffic raced toward me like a river. A homeless man dragged himself down the sidewalk, and a line of bedraggled men stood on the corner of Thirty-fourth Street. Bleating cabs and buildings shooting up, flickering neon signs and a sea of people standing on curbs with shopping bags, looking lost. Up ahead, the blinking lights of Penn Station and Madison Square Garden. Food stands everywhere selling pretzels and kebabs and sausages and fruit and soda. Subway grates looking down over trash and rats. What a place, I thought. What a place for fairies to return to.

I walked downtown along trash-strewn sidewalks, block after block, the city passing on either side of me, with all its life, its filth, but me barely noticing now. If they were here to take me

✳ 55 ✳

home after all this time, I knew there was only one place they would be.

It was eight A.M. I had two hours before the shop opened.

I hadn't gone down to the pier in months, maybe years. I had stopped letting myself hope that I might ever find them again. Now my heart felt like it would burst open and I could almost see them already, telling me it was time to come home.

Eighth turned to Hudson, Jane Street appeared to my right, but with new energy I made my way farther downtown, veering west to the water. The farther I walked, the more my body stretched out, loosened, and came to life.

I crossed over the West Side Highway. The water glimmered under the sun. I moved forward without even thinking, past the piers and the shining glass buildings and the joggers and bikers and people walking their dogs along the thin, curving path that lined the river.

I could forget everything, moving like this. My body blurring into the next moment and the next, until I dissolved into air. It was as close to flying as I could remember. I passed people on their way to work, men and women dressed in suits and looking at me in open disbelief. I laughed out loud as I passed them. 'I'm not an old lady at all!' I wanted to shout, and I became more and more convinced that I would find them waiting for me, all of them, telling me it was finally time to return.

A half-hour later I walked past benches and lampposts and trees, and turned down West Street. I knew the way by heart, no matter how much time had gone by. This is the place I always came back to. The earliest memories I had of this world. I headed down the same path I always had, the water straining against my senses, and turned down to the pier with the small clock tower at the end of it. The water glimmered from behind. Pier A. I came right up on the river. Every cell in my body felt alive, tingling. My breath coming heavy and fast.

Breathing in, I leaned down against the railing and stared into the water. It was almost reptilian-looking, thick, scaly, and green-black, like dinosaur skin; I imagined I could reach out and drum my fingers against the hard surface. Everything was quiet.

'Where are you?' I picked up a pebble and dropped it in, watched it pierce the surface and disappear. I imagined it slipping past Maybeth's face as she slept in a water lily.

I looked around. A few bored commuters stood by the water. A couple was heading up a ramp onto the barge where a crowd of people stood waiting for the ferry, reading newspapers and talking on phones. I walked to the end of the pier and looked out. A clock glowed from the other side of the river, mirroring and magnifying the one I was standing under. I could almost see the silver steps and him on the other side of them, waiting. The way the hands of the clock moved slowly and slowly around, reflecting in the water. Reminding me that in this world, I had all the time I could ever need.

I closed my eyes. Remembered that feeling of descending from the air into the water and down to the bottom of the lake, where the roots of the great tree flared out in every direction, where I could press myself against any vine or leaf and feel the fate of a human pressing back at me. How on certain nights we would all descend into the heart of the tree and gather to hear the elder's decrees. This here; this was our real home, where we all came from.

Something rubbed against my leg and I jumped. It was just a kitten.

I smiled. 'Hello, lovely,' I whispered. It came up to me, rubbed its head against my ankle. I laughed, bent down to pet it. My hand disappeared into its soft fur. It leaped in the air, swiping its paw at a dragonfly that appeared just then. The sheen of the insect's wings made me blink. Then there was a second dragonfly, and a third. I held out my hand as they whirred by.

'You are close, aren't you?' I said to Maybeth. To Gladys and Lucibell. I didn't know what it all meant, except the air, suddenly, felt different. Everything felt different. 'I knew you were close.'

'Are you okay, ma'am?' I looked up into the eyes of a young man, and it was only then that I realized I was crying. Tears streamed down my face. I reached up to wipe them off.

'Yes, thank you,' I said. 'I'm just . . . tired.'

He smiled, his face open. He was so young. Tall, his chest broad and wide, a baseball cap backward on his head. 'I know what you mean,' he said. 'That your cat?'

'No,' I said.

'Ah.' He crouched down and stroked the cat's head, his hand moving delicately back and forth. I thought of Maybeth and the horse, her mouth against its ear as its body softened and the lash marks disappeared. 'Sometimes they just know when you need them.'

'Yes,' I said. 'They are magical creatures.'

The ferry was approaching the slip. 'Jersey City, Hoboken,' the captain called out. The crowd on the barge began to gather by the gates.

'Well, see ya,' the man said, nodding to me, giving the cat one more stroke. 'And, hey. Things never stay bad forever.'

I smiled at his back as he ran down to the barge. Lost in a thousand memories that flickered inside me, each more clear and lush than the last.

When I turned to the water again, I thought, for one second, that I saw a flicker of something. Deep down. Was it the light, the way the sun had hit the surface, in just that instant? I was sure I had seen a wing. A wing in the water.

'Are you there?' I whispered, and I imagined jumping in, letting my body sink until they pulled me to them, until my wings became finlike as they slipped through the water.

I stood and looked, waited. The clock glowed from the other side. I stretched it out till the last minute, but I did not see one more sign of them. They did not return.

With a heavy heart, I turned and headed to work.

CHAPTER FOUR

wasn't sure how much time had passed, how much time I had spent in Cinderella's dreams. She stood by the window. I had to rip myself away from her. *Her tears*, I thought, *are not mine.* Still, I felt as if I were leaving something of myself behind as I slipped down the winding stairs, away from the barren tower they kept her in, down to the rest of the house.

The manor was silent. Up ahead a torch flickered. I peered more closely at the tapestry it illuminated on the wall, which illustrated ancient scenes from myth – Daphne turning into a laurel tree, her arms and legs sprouting leaves and her hair dripping bark; Actaeon becoming a stag, his hounds close behind and baring teeth; Leda's neck stretching out, the feathers sprouting from her skin.

I blinked as I heard the faint sounds of laughter from down the hall. I passed the great bedroom as I moved toward the sounds, peeked in to see Cinderella's stepmother asleep in a room strewn with furs and velvet, the walls covered in intricate tapestries like the one I'd just seen. I wondered if she knew the violence in them, of humans turning to plant and beast at the whims of gods. Curious, I moved into the room, struck by the luxury of everything in it. The diamonds sparkling up from her thick fingers, which clutched the sheets. I could not help being attracted to shiny things, soft things; it was in our nature. I flew down to her, just for a moment, to let her dreams enfold me and erase the longing that clung to me, the image of the man walking toward me in the empty field.

It came up on me like a whirlwind, a dazzling array of images in every color, every texture: Mounds of gleaming coins and jewels, heaps of gold necklaces and bracelets and earrings and pins and rings and barrettes and combs and mirrors, palaces of silver and porcelain and ice and emerald. Peaches and cherries and pineapples and kiwis, all more rare than diamonds, their juice dripping over the lips that consumed them. Weddings with gigantic champagne fountains and vaults of centuries-old wine, servants hauling up bottle after bottle to pour into the mouths of her daughters, commoners made royalty, both of them wives of the prince in this vision, banquet tables covered over with whole roasted chickens and hens and boars and lambs and fish, piles of sweets shaped like hearts and knots and stars. Gold poured down over me in rivers until I couldn't breathe.

I had to rip myself out of her dream. I opened my eyes back onto the room again. The figures in the tapestry leered at me, the stepmother spread out over the bed, saliva gathering at her mouth. The room stank of decay. Shuddering, I flew out of it.

What a place, I thought, for a girl – one with *fairy* in her veins – to live in. I let the sympathy wash over me. It was what I needed: to remember my purpose. Not the man in the field, the need to touch his skin, that feeling of being incomplete without him there. The stepmother's dream was something else entirely.

I came upon Maybeth and my friends in a room down the hall. It took me a minute to realize what they were up to. The closet door had been flung open, and the three of them stood inside, all transformed into human shapes, huge like giants, trying on dresses. Torches floated in the air, making the closet as bright as if it were midday.

I could not believe what I was seeing.

'What are you doing?' I cried. I looked behind me, at the huge bed where the two sisters slept openmouthed, their arms flung over their heads and the unmistakable luster of fairy dust glittering over them. 'What did you do to them?!'

Maybeth danced over to me and pulled me into her hand. My wings beat against her palm. I had never seen my sister in human form looming over me, her blue eyes like lakes. Quickly, I slipped down, shifted into my own human form, my body filling out, becoming hot with blood, until I stood next to her and looked her right in the eye. She was different this way: prettier, less wild, her pale cheeks tinged with rose. Wearing a green gown lined with heavy lace.

'Don't worry, Lil. We're just having fun. Helping you get ideas, right?'

Gladys turned toward me, draped in a deep yellow satin, her dark hair piled on top of her head and dangling down in tendrils. 'This is what she should wear,' she said. 'Have you thought about this, Lil? I think a summer yellow would be divine.' A line of diamonds materialized around her neck as she spoke.

'She'll look like a cornstalk,' Maybeth said. 'That yellow under her white hair!'

'Maybe you should change her hair color,' Gladys said. 'Make it red like yours, or something darker. Imagine this yellow on Lil, May.' She blinked then, and suddenly I was wearing it, too. The thick yellow fabric weighed on my skin, cinching at my waist and around my upper arms.

'Stop it!' I said, waving my hand and switching back to the gauzy dress I'd been wearing before.

'Humans suffer for beauty,' Gladys said. 'Don't you know that?'

'What about this?' Lucibell said, emerging from the back of the closet and wearing a pale blue silk dress. Like water on her skin.

'I didn't see that one,' Gladys said.

'I know,' Lucibell said. 'I conjured it.'

'Let me see it,' I said, reaching out my hand.

A moment later the dress filled out over my body, streaming down my skin. I shivered, turned to the mirror that stood in the corner of the room.

'Lil!' Maybeth breathed. The others pressed in behind me, grabbing at my hands and arms to pull me away. 'Don't!'

'Stop,' I said, and whatever it was in my voice made them obey.

I stared at myself, mesmerized. I had never looked at myself this way, in human form – I had only seen myself out of the corner of my eye, on the surface of a lake or in the sheen of ice clinging to bark. We were not supposed to see ourselves like this.

Now I knew why. As a human I was perfect. My skin pale and luminous. My hair like autumn and fire. My eyes like emeralds, fringed by dark lashes. I pressed my palm against my waist, the silk smooth under my touch, my skin tingling and warm.

'That's the dress you should send her in,' Maybeth said behind me, her voice trembling.

'Yes,' I whispered.

In the canopied bed in the center of the room, the sisters slept on, their breathing jagged in the night air. We could hear the creeping of the servants in the hallways as they moved through the house.

Gladys and Lucibell were quiet now, waiting by the rows of dresses.

All I could think of was the man from her dream. How he would look at me like this. The longing that came from a place deep inside her, winging out and spreading through every cell of her body. Spreading now through mine.

The torches flared and leaped and made patterns against the walls of the closet and the main room.

This is what he would see, I thought. If it were me, at the ball.

I lifted the skirt of the dress. My feet were bare and curved on the stone floor.

'What would you think of shoes of glass?' I said, and turned to see them all watching me, eyes wide in the light of the torches.

'Lil?'

I looked up. I hadn't heard George coming down from upstairs. I hadn't been paying attention at all, I realized, and quickly closed the book I was holding, careful not to harm its crumbling pages. The glass case hung open.

'You seem different,' he said.

'How do you mean?' I covered the book with my palm and tried to push the case closed with my foot.

The store was quiet. Today it had the air of an old attic, somewhere in the country. I noticed then how tired George looked, rubbing his eyes. It was not even nine A.M. yet. I had never seen him up so early. He held a thick book under one arm.

'I don't know. Just different.'

'Oh,' I said, slipping the book under the counter. I was conscious of him staring at me, and I turned quickly to one of the book-crammed boxes next to me. 'I'll just get started on these, then,' I said, pulling out a copy of *Gulliver's Travels*.

He seemed preoccupied. I noticed he was fingering the same pages of his book over and over again.

'Are you feeling all right?' I asked.

'Just a bit tired,' he said. 'I was up all night working.'

'Anything interesting?'

'Actually, yeah.' He smiled, his eyes crinkling at the corners. 'I think I've found a chunk of a lost manuscript.'

'Oh? What is it?'

'A so-called "definitive history of Massachusetts." This governor spent decades working on it. The life's work of a true obsessive.'

'Something you know nothing about, I'm sure.'

He laughed, leaned his tall body down on the counter, his face a few feet from mine. Sometimes it took me by surprise, how handsome he was. 'There's a story that when the British attacked his estate, he locked himself in the study with the manuscript and a rifle. Ignored his family completely.'

'What happened?'

'They all died. At least that's the story.'

'Wow.'

'Imagine, though. Years of your life, all that history, on paper. So delicate, and yet pieces have made their way down to us, after all this time.' He stood up, stretching. 'I need some coffee desperately.'

I saw something pass over his face then. Something more than tiredness. 'What's wrong?' I asked.

'Nothing,' he said, his shoulders relaxing. 'Well, I ran into Lauren yesterday.'

'Oh, I'm sorry,' I said. I took his hand, and for a moment we stood there awkwardly.

'Thanks,' he said, squeezing my hand. 'It's okay. I just wasn't expecting it. I was grabbing a quick lunch on Broadway, and there she was.'

I was almost afraid to speak, as if I would ruin what was happening. George never talked to me about his ex-wife. I had watched his marriage end the year before, and he had suffered quietly, with barely a word. As a fairy I could have blinked my eyes and made him whole, fresh as a stem. As a human there was nothing I could do for him.

'It's hard,' I said. 'It takes time. But you will meet someone else.' I winced at how trite my words sounded. How did I know he would meet someone? Or that he wanted to?

'I just never thought I'd end up like this.'

'I know,' I said.

I wished I could tell him how rare he was, but I couldn't. I'd known that he was the first time I'd met him, when I'd walked into the store on a day so cold that tiny icicles had formed on my wings and fused the feathers together. George had looked up at me, and I knew he recognized me, that there was something in him attuned to the other world. It was the same way I knew that the girl, Veronica, had recognized me.

We watched each other for a moment, and then something shifted in him, something I was surprised I could feel so strongly.

'Do you think a person can get ruined?' he asked then. 'Just tapped out?'

'No,' I said, with more force than I intended. 'No.' My jaw was tight. 'I'm old, I've seen so many things, but I've never seen that. Human beings don't work that way.' I was close to tears. They caught in my eyes like tiny hooks. 'You can always become new.'

I knew I was lying, even as I said it. I thought of my former beauty, the feelings that used to move through me like rivers. A memory knifed into me. A girl on the ground, hollowed out, empty, surrounded by glass.

'Okay,' he said, his voice softer now. He slipped his hand out of mine. 'I'm just tired. I need that coffee.'

'Do you want me to make a pot?'

'No, thanks, I'm heading out in a minute. To Connecticut, actually, to check out a collection.'

'Yeah? Any possibilities?'

'We'll see. An old friend pointed me to it, though, and it looks good. This old man – his great-uncle, I think – has been collecting war books for years. I'm told he's got some first-rate stuff.'

'Great,' I said. I smiled at him.

'I need to get out of here, anyway, clear my head. I wish I could stay away longer. Take a real vacation, you know?'

'Yes,' I said. 'You could use that. Though I'm not sure poring over war books is much of a vacation. You ought to get to a beach or something.'

'Very funny. Oh, damn it. That reminds me.'

'What?'

'This thing I have to go to. I keep forgetting.'

'What thing?'

'The Paradise Ball,' he said, waving his hand dismissively. 'It's this formal shindig every fall at the Pierre. My parents are vice chairs this year. There's no way I can't go.' He paused, sighing. 'I'm a guy who should never be in a tux. Ever.'

'Formal shindig?'

'Yeah, black tie, fancy dinner, hours of mingling with the crème de la crème. I got out of it the last few years, but this year my mother is on a mission.'

I started to feel giddy, despite myself. 'It sounds nice. And I've seen photos of you in a tux. You look rather like Cary Grant, actually.'

'Thanks, but you don't know how much I hate that world, Lil.'

'George, you just spend too much time in dusty attics. A man like you *should* be getting out more.'

'Don't you have some books to put away?' he asked. 'Some . . . I don't know, receipts to file?' He smiled, sweeping his hand over the piles of books on the floor.

'Actually, I am all caught up at the moment.'

'Imagine that. I knew I made a mistake hiring you.'

I laughed. 'So when is it? Who are you going with? You need to bring a date, don't you?'

'It's next month. I have no idea who I'll bring. Lauren will be there, of course. Can you believe my parents invited her? She never misses a society event if she can help it.' He smiled, but I could see how much it pained him.

'But a dance!' I said. 'How wonderful.'

'Maybe you should be my date. Show me some of the dances you used to do. You did dance, didn't you?'

I could feel myself flush. 'Oh, yes,' I said. 'I did. Cheek to cheek, across the floor. There is nothing better.'

'I'm serious,' he said. 'You'd probably appreciate it more than anyone else. We'd have fun.'

I smiled, waved my hand. How wonderful it would be, I thought, to be young and beautiful in his arms. The image flashed up: me in the mirror, the torches flaring around. The gardenias blooming from the balcony.

'No,' I said. 'You need to find some young woman you like and take her. It will be magical. I guarantee you.'

He rolled his eyes. In the early-morning light, the dark bookstore, the dust floating in the air, I couldn't imagine any woman not wanting to go with him. George looked like he was made for the old world. I could see him trudging through the king's forest with a sword, or walking up the palace's silver steps, arm in arm with a nobleman's bejeweled daughter.

'Trust me,' he said. 'It will be the opposite of magical. A bunch of rich old bastards congratulating each other for being rich and old. Women wearing fifty-thousand-dollar gowns for charity. Excuse my French, Lil.' He paused. 'And finding a young woman I like isn't exactly easy. I'll remind you that I'm forty-two. In some states I could be a grandfather.'

'You're so young,' I said. 'And there's a whole city out there! Filled with women. Surely there is someone you could have a glorious night with.'

'Lil,' he said, laughing, 'I think you might be reading too many of those fairy tales behind the counter.'

I looked at the book in front of me and then back at him, my mouth opening to explain.

He put his hand on my arm. 'It's okay,' he said. 'I was only teasing you. I love those tales, too.' He reached down and picked it up. 'This one's a beauty, though, isn't it? You know this was printed in 1835? Right here in Manhattan?'

'Yes,' I said. 'You told me.'

He placed the book gently on the counter. Its bark scent wafting up. He cracked it open slowly, revealing a page of text with leaves cascading down the side, opposite a drawing of a girl cleaning a fireplace. 'These prints. They're exquisite. Look at her face.'

I leaned in. The girl's face was lovely, intricate, infinitely sad. 'It's so emotional,' I said. 'And just a few black lines.'

I was right there. I could have told him, right then. Who I was. What I was. But I couldn't speak.

The moment passed. He was flipping through the book. 'Someone wrote in this,' he said. '*Tous mes anciens amours vont me revenir.*' His French was perfect.

'*All my old loves will be returned to me,*' I repeated. 'It's lovely, isn't it?'

'Yes,' he said, looking at the script more closely. 'Imagine, scribbling in a book and having someone read your words more than a century and a half later.'

'It's incredible.' My voice cracked as I spoke. 'How much is forgotten. I think about it all the time.'

George looked up at me, closed the book. 'Are you okay, Lil? Is something wrong?'

'No,' I said. 'Everything is fine.' I smiled at him, felt a tear drop down my cheek. 'I'm just a silly old lady sometimes.'

'Ah,' he said. 'Aren't we all?' He smiled back at me, and I felt a wave of caring for him. As if I were in my old skin. A new energy moving through me, something ancient but just below the surface. He stood. 'I better start heading up if I'm going to get back this afternoon. I've got another collection to look over tonight, in TriBeCa.'

I did not want George to be alone, the way I was alone.

'Okay,' I said, wiping my face. And after a moment, 'You know, I think your dance will be good for you.'

He shrugged, smiling, gathering up his book. 'Well, at least it's for a good cause, as they say. They also claim that what doesn't kill you makes you stronger.'

An idea was forming. A perfect thought. 'No, I mean I can help you. I will help find someone for you. Someone to take. Someone you'll like.'

He laughed out loud, throwing his head back slightly. 'Well, that is quite a task. Very sweet of you, too, but I wouldn't assign that job to my worst enemy.'

'I'm serious,' I said. And I was. I was! For a second I believed that if I jumped in the air I'd be able to see past his skin, into his deepest heart.

'You want to find me a date?'

I nodded. 'Yes. For the Paradise Ball.'

He looked at me. 'You seriously want to find me a date? You know I'm hopeless at these things, right?'

I smiled. 'I am aware of this, George. That is why I'm offering to help.'

'Desperate times, desperate measures, yes?'

'Exactly. And my help, I might add, is more valuable than you know.'

'I have no doubt.' He threw up his hands. 'And who am I to turn down such a magnanimous offer?' He shook his head, staring at me. 'Now I'd better get out of here before you start threatening to pick out my next wife and name my children, too.'

'That,' I said, 'is not a bad idea.'

CHAPTER FIVE

I opened my eyes in the blue water of the fairy lake, the vines and water lilies looping around me, sparkling with the sunlight that shot through the water. A flurry of fairies was passing, their wings fully spread, translucent. The great tree with its jutting branches grew out of the lake bottom, which was covered in grass and plants and jewels. A flapping red flower opened, and a just-born fairy emerged, blinking her long-lashed glittering eyes. In the distance was the fairy court, the gleaming shell-made seat of the chief elder. Around it the tangled branches of the tree curling down.

It was all so beautiful. And yet, for the first time in my life, my world felt lacking.

'Lil!' I heard, and suddenly Maybeth was swaying before me, laughing wildly. 'Get up!'

'No,' I said, curling back into the water lily and twisting over onto my side. I just wanted to go back. The only thing I could focus on was the image from her dream, an image that had entered my own dreams now, the man standing in the field in front of her, the longing that had moved its way through her, and now me. I pulled the flower petals up to my shoulders and closed my eyes.

Maybeth pressed her face close to mine. 'Come on,' she said. 'What's wrong with you?'

'I'm sleeping,' I said, shaking her off. 'Leave me alone.'

'I brought you a present,' she said, as a tiny seashell appeared in her palm. 'Isn't it pretty? It has red dye inside, to color your lips with.' She made it wink and glitter at me, but I turned away. 'I can show you where to find more.'

'I just want to go back to sleep. I was having a good dream.'

'This isn't like you, Lil,' she said. 'Come on. You've been weird since we came back.'

'I'm fine.'

She sighed. 'You shouldn't have transformed. Something happened to you, didn't it?'

'No,' I said.

'Something is different about you. It's that girl, isn't it? Something's wrong with her. I can't believe she is to be queen.'

'May,' I said slowly, flipping over. I lowered my voice and looked around. In the distance, I could see one of the elders moving his head, his eye rolling toward me. 'Do you ever think of what it'd be like to be human?' I whispered.

She floated next to me, wild, her long purple hair tossing in the waves. 'What are you talking about?' she said, her face changing. 'Why would you wonder that?'

'Shhh,' I said sharply. 'I just wonder. I can't stop thinking about her.'

'About who?'

'Her. Cinderella. And her dreams. She was dreaming of him.'

'So? Of course she was. All humans are like that. Pathetic.

Lil, they're watching us. Let's go. We should at least get up to the pier.'

'But I felt what she felt. The prince was in her dream and all she wanted was to be with him.'

'You've always been good at that, feeling them. I wish I was as good at it as you.'

'You'd hate it. How they feel.'

She rolled her eyes, impatient. 'Anyway, she'll be with him soon. So what?'

'Now I want that, too.'

'What do you want?'

'To be with him.'

'Wait. The prince?'

I nodded.

Her eyes widened. 'Lil. You can't talk like this. You can't.'

'I just want to go look at him. See what he's like.'

'You know what he's *like*! He's the prince!'

'Come with me to the palace, just one time.'

'We can't!' she cried, then clamped her hand over her mouth. Her eyes darted up to where the elder sat, past branches and through the water, past two fairies darting by just then, calling to us to come to the surface, me and Maybeth, my flower sister, and even through all that distance I could feel his eyes slicing through to me. But I didn't care.

'It will be fun. Let's just go and look at him. Don't you wonder about him? They all dream about him. The whole kingdom.'

'Don't talk about him like that,' she said, her voice barely a whisper. 'Don't even think it.' Her clear eyes staring back at me, hard-edged, like diamonds.

It was the first time our hearts hadn't been one piece.

Something had happened to me, I realized then. My own world seemed muted, emptied out. The crystal water, the great tree, the wondrous flowers and gems, the tangle of human fate the elders deciphered, the fairy court lined with shells, the colors so bright a human would have gone blind from the sight of them, the elders moving through the water or sitting at their thrones like elegant, shimmering fish while the young fairies emerged from the water and flew back down again, going back and forth between worlds, the fate of all humanity in their hands: it all seemed to have dried up, in an instant, until the only thing left was him, the field, and his hand reaching out for me.

I had never lied before to Maybeth, but I knew I needed to then. 'I was only kidding,' I said. I made a face at her, then flung myself off the lily.

Her face relaxed. For a moment, the world was normal again. I grabbed her hand and pulled her up with me to the surface of the lake. We passed the elder who'd been watching us, and I smiled over to him, spreading my wings. Water streaming around us on all sides. I lifted my head and tried to forget everything else.

We burst into air. The sun bright above our heads, the air full of the sweet music of our friends, who were scattered on the pier and in the branches of the trees, instruments in their hands and against their lips. Others were returning from the human world, others still disappearing into the line of trees to do their own work there.

I must have been mad, I thought, to dream of the other world, when everything any being could ever want was right here.

I flew into the air, perfect. Whole in a way a human could never be.

The Pierre. Even the name felt like some exotic truffle on my tongue. I had walked past its pale wedding-cake-like façade, seen it shooting like a palace above Central Park, admired its pointed copper roof that shone when the sun hit it. I'd heard stories about its grand ballroom, elaborate and overblown, like something from Versailles. I couldn't believe I'd never been inside. There was so much in the world that I didn't pay attention to, traces of the old world all around.

The Pierre was perfect. The perfect place for the ball. And George was a prince, or as close to one as I could imagine. It was hard to remember sometimes that he'd been raised in a palace overlooking Central Park, that he'd studied at a prep school in Connecticut and gone on to Yale, that one of his relatives was a duke. And now he was going to a ball, just now, at the same moment when a girl showed up with evidence of fairies and just when the prince showed himself to me, too. Theodore *had* had fairy blood, like Cinderella, like all the royal line. Now I was convinced it had been him in the diner. Maybe he had been more than part fairy. Maybe that's why he'd been able to see me the way he had, so long ago, and was able to appear to me in human form now.

And then I understood. Or at least I thought I did. They were coming back to me. Weren't they? They were giving me a chance to change the story. They had to be. George was going to a ball, and he needed a woman to bring, someone he would fall in love with and marry. Didn't he? Didn't everyone? And I knew just the right girl for George. She'd practically been dropped in my lap. There was a reason why George collected fairy stories, why Veronica had shown up with a book showing real fairies on this earth. Even if they didn't know it, I did. I was a *fairy godmother*. Even now I had white feathers on my back, after years of being on earth. I made sure that humans met their fates. If I did this, I could make up for that night so long ago.

Couldn't I?

The thought was dizzying, luxurious: *I could redeem myself* for what I'd done. I could return to my own world, where nothing from this world would matter. Not Leo or the apartment or the bills I couldn't pay. Not my wrinkled, hanging skin, or the ache that seemed to start in my bones and spread out like tree branches.

I tossed in bed that night, imagining the two of them together. George in a tuxedo as black as his eyes, the color of ink, and Veronica in a pale blue dress, her bright hair falling to her neck. I grasped for an image and thought of bright silver walls the dancers could see themselves in. The smell of perfume, of rain. Myself running up the silver stairs, racing through the night with the beating of wings behind me.

I shook my head, tried to rid myself of the memory. The past was becoming the present becoming the past. Everything was happening again and again, until it was set right and all was forgiven.

I sat up in bed. It was only nine P.M.

It took me a second to orient myself. This was not the old kingdom. The silver palace had long ago been destroyed. In its place was a whole city. I breathed in and out, slowly, and concentrated on the sound of cars rushing by, the honking horns and faint sirens, the sound of a television playing upstairs. The footsteps in the hallway as one of my neighbors returned home.

I tried to think of the Pierre, of what was happening now, but my mind kept moving to the past, to everything I'd tried to forget. To me standing on the balcony wearing what would have been her dress, the whole world open and beating like a heart, ready to take me into itself. The clock chiming once, twice . . . The faces of the elders as they bore down on me. I had heard of them leaving the lake only one other time and even now I shivered thinking of it. The terrible sound their wings had made, fully spread and hammering above me. The sensation of falling to earth. My eyes opening onto grass, dirt, and then me standing on the ground, as if I'd been rooted to the spot, my body changed, human now, an enormous, blundering thing. I'd wobbled as I tried to move, to return to them. Hunger, for the first time, pressing into me from all sides. Pressing, physical hunger.

I squeezed my eyes shut, forced myself into the present.

The Pierre, I thought, breathing slowly, concentrating. I conjured its gold-scripted name, its glittering, pale façade. I felt an urge suddenly, to go right then, get out of this crumbling apartment and into the world as it was now. It was only nine P.M. It wasn't too late to go and see the Pierre for myself.

I got ready carefully. I brushed my hair, tried to smooth it, and then pulled it back with a barrette. I patted my mouth with pink lipstick. I looked at myself. If nothing else, I looked like a normal human old woman. Like I should be pinching cheeks and making coffee cakes from scratch. I shuddered.

The city outside was black and draped with lights. The cars flashed in my face. I headed to Seventh Avenue and then uptown, forcing myself to look at the people passing me, to notice the giant billboards in Times Square, the store windows filled with athletic equipment and cosmetics and souvenirs. A whole different New York from the quieter, stranger one I occupied.

I turned right on Fifty-ninth Street, passing the line of fancy hotels across from Central Park, which was a dark forest on the other side of the car-filled street. The doormen I passed nodded as I walked by, gatekeepers to these secret worlds filled with men and women who could afford to pay my entire rent for one night's sleep.

I crossed the street toward the end of the park, passing a row of carriages and horses. All lined up and ready to go. The coachmen waited outside, beckoning for me to sit down. The horses stood perfectly still, their heads lowered, terrifically outfitted in thick leather, like silent monsters.

Across the street was a large spraying fountain, the Paris Theatre, all glimmering in the streetlamps. A red carpet unfurled onto the sidewalk in front of the Plaza.

I shook my head, crossed, and turned up Fifth, trying to focus on the smell of grit and exhaust. The nearby scent of roasting nuts and pretzels from a street vendor. The hard concrete under my feet. The hotel was just ahead, though, and the stone of the façade glittered in the streetlamps. As I passed under the windows, I looked up and saw ceilings painted over and curving with scenes of gods and goddesses, lights hanging down like bits of ice.

The doorman smiled at me and stood back to let me pass through. I paused, expecting to be questioned or pulled aside. The man just smiled and waited with the door open.

I remembered the palace, the complete mastery I'd had over everything in the human world back then. Flying down the great hall and into the prince's chambers, slipping in and out of everyone's thoughts, appearing to him at will, because I wanted to, because I had wanted him to see me in my human form. I was so beautiful then. I could do anything, be anything.

I felt so much. I hadn't felt so much in years. Maybe not ever, not since that night.

I walked into the lobby, close to tears. It was almost entirely empty. Faintly, I registered the shining black-and-white floors, the paintings on the walls, the glass cases. A man sitting on a small sofa looked up at me, then back down again.

Everything felt so familiar. As if I'd been there before. I knew to turn in to a great room with painted walls, a dining area that led into other rooms and had a staircase twisting above it. I knew to turn and walk up the stairs, through the doors, and into a long hallway. Almost no one was around. Upstairs, in the hallway, it was completely silent.

I walked down the hall. Past room after room, all seeming to open into other rooms. Mirrors lined the hallway, so I could not tell what was real, what was being reflected. Above me, glass and crystal dripped down, and the ceiling curved, laced with patterns and swirling shapes, paintings of ancient scenes.

At the end of the hall was a large room and, past it, the grand ballroom. I walked inside.

Huge crystal chandeliers hung from the ceiling, like antlers coated in ice, attached by gold ribbons wrapped around wire, and elaborate bows. Stacks of gold chairs, hundreds of chairs, lined the dance floor. Mirrors and glass reflected everything. At the other end of the room was a stage, framed by curtains. I stared at it, imagined an orchestra spread over it, the sounds of strings and air.

It was eerily quiet, silent except for the dull buzz of lights. I stepped forward, my feet padding along the thick carpet.

I imagined him, Theodore, waiting for me. It was hard to remember, that night of the ball. It had been so long, and I'd heard and seen so many other recountings since. I had had no way of knowing, back then, how that night would live on not only in my own memory but in all the world's. How history would remake it, twist it into a happy tale that would set girls to dreaming centuries after.

It should have been like that.

I remembered the first time I'd come upon George's collection of fairy tales at Daedalus Books, the rows of carefully preserved gilded-edge books he kept in the back of the store as well as in the case up front. I had sat on the ground and pulled out the books one by one, marveling at the drawings inside, which showed small winged creatures propped against leaves, riding acorns, dancing in groups in the grass. They wore caps on their heads and had tight gauzy outfits sheathing their fingerlike frames. I had heard fairy stories, of course, seen the cartoons, but I had never seen the kinds of intricate drawings that filled the old volumes George collected. My heart had burst open. It was as if my past had been scooped out for me like fresh fruit. None of them looked exactly like us, but the fairies were close enough to what was in those books, or at least we could have been. If I had really wanted to, I could have slipped a leaf about my shoulders and let it dangle to my feet like a robe. I could have swept up my hair from my shoulders and tied it back with a flower stem.

Then I pulled down another book with the Cinderella story lavishly told and illustrated, and laughed with my head flung back when I saw the drawings of her, at how absurd it all was, at her yellow hair. It had been years since I'd really looked at how the story had been passed down. I wanted to take the artist aside, talk some sense into him: Cinderella's hair was like starlight, I would say, not yellow like corn. It was just like silk starlight, moon hair that swept down her back and actually glittered. I had been horrified, in the human world, when I'd first come upon the ridiculous fairy godmother so popular in the books and, later, the movies – her plump round body like a sack of apples, the hanging, swinging double chin, the silly upturned smile that pushed out her cheeks like a chipmunk's. She even had gray hair swirled up in a bun.

Fairies were beautiful, I had wanted to explain. Fairies were perfect creatures who could move in and out of human form but who were naturally tiny, so small that a sensitive human would almost always see only a speck of light when we passed, if anything at all. Groups of fairies, gathered around a flower or a lake, would appear to the human eye like a cluster of lights, like the night sky strewn with stars. It was amazing that the girls in Veronica's fairy book had captured fairies the way they had, in photographs, but there was no doubt that the figures in the photos were my own kind. That they had chosen to show themselves to the human world. To me.

I knew I was in New York, in the Pierre Hotel, on Fifth Avenue across from Central Park. I knew where I was, who I was, what I had done, and how much time had passed. I always knew how much time had passed.

Even so, I could almost feel his hand slipping around my waist. I could hear the orchestra starting up, the marble floor sliding under my feet. I felt so full. Like I contained universes inside me. I closed my eyes, twirled around once, then again. I felt his breath on my neck and his palms on my waist.

'Theodore,' I whispered, and for a moment I was right there with him, the scent of gardenia wrapping around me. My heart breaking open. I let myself feel it, the pure beauty and pain of it, of giving myself over to him and leaving my own world behind.

When I opened my eyes, I caught a glimpse of my reflection in the mirror, just a glimpse as I whirled by. My hair like autumn leaves, like flame. The dress flowing down my body to the glass slippers that sparkled from my feet.

The next morning I got to the bookstore at eight. I spent a few minutes tiptoeing about, listening for any sound from upstairs. George had been busy the day before; I saw boxes of books piled by the register for me to deal with throughout the day.

I made coffee in back, smelling the earth scent of the beans as I measured them and poured them into the filter. I swept the floors quickly, gathering the dust at the front of each row, then scooping it up mound by mound into a dustpan. I lifted a stack of books onto the front desk to sort through, and all the while my heart pounded in my chest, my excitement and nervousness mixing together until I thought I would scream.

Having a purpose, something to look forward to. It made everything different. I felt like I was years younger. It was almost a shock to look down at my same wrinkled hands and arms. The other world was so close, just beyond my reach.

When I was sure it was safe, when I was sure I hadn't heard a sound from upstairs and there was still plenty of time before the store opened, I went into the back room and fired up the computer. I'd learned to use a computer a couple years before, when George started listing books online. I liked being online. It was the closest I could come to how I had felt once, when I could dip into any human dream or thought I wanted.

With trembling fingers I pulled Veronica's card out of my purse and typed in her website address. The page loaded, all pink and white and black with swirls along the edges. 'Veronica Searle, Hairdos and Designs,' it said across the top, and underneath was a series of links. There was a photo of her, in black and white, her hair long and wild around her perfect pale face. Even posed and staring off into the distance, she had that fairy energy to her, and I could almost see her spreading wings and flitting over the water.

I clicked on the link that said 'About.' Another photo of her came up, next to the same swirls and colors. Her hair platinum blond in this one, swept up to the side. She was wearing a floor-length dress that flared at the bottom and holding a cigarette in a long holder. She looked aloof, glamorous, until you looked more closely and saw the small smile on her face. I felt like laughing, too, just looking at her.

'I have cut and dyed hair since I was a kid playing with Barbies,' said the words written in curling letters on the side of the page. 'I used to paint their hair with watercolors and clip it with my mother's cuticle scissors. When I was eighteen, I packed my bags and came to New York, and I've been cutting hair professionally ever since. I worked at the Pink Sink for seven years before taking it over and making it mine all mine. I also design wigs, work on photo shoots, and sew and knit like a crazy woman. And I'm obsessed with old things. I love everything vintage. This may make my apartment smell like mothballs, but I can give you the best finger curls or beehive in the city.'

I was riveted. It was like reading a diary.

I clicked on the link titled 'Cut and Color,' which took me to a page with a photo of her in a salon, next to an old-fashioned bonnet hair dryer. On the right were her hours and prices and a description of the hair color products she used. 'I promise to make you gorgeous!' it said. I laughed. 'Your hair is my canvas. I only use the amazing products I use on myself. And nothing but the best touches these tresses!' An array of photos swept by on the bottom of the page, in a mini filmstrip. Photos of Veronica and girls like her. Chameleons, girls who could be anything they wanted, without a fairy to help them.

I clicked on 'Extensions' to see another page full of bright photos. Humans with hair shooting off their heads like geysers. I covered my mouth and laughed. They were so beautiful! I recognized Veronica on the lower right, her hair bright blue and twisted on the top of her head.

I thought about my plan, the one that would bring two lovers together and redeem myself for what I'd done. Their fates, entwined. If I squinted, I could see George there next to her, adoring, a thick book in his hand. They will balance each other, I thought. He will calm her. She will bring him to life. I knew that I was meant to be her fairy godmother, that some-how she had been sent to me, and to George, and that it was my task to ensure that both of them met the destinies I could see so clearly. I knew this. I knew it with a certainty I hadn't felt for years.

The room was dark, the early morning haze just starting to seep in to the back of the store. I felt as if I was in her mind and thoughts.

On a whim, I opened my e-mail program and typed in the e-mail address listed on the website. I typed: 'I am your fairy godmother. I am here to send you to the ball.' I smiled, imagined her bending over a screen the way I was, her face immersed in the pale light. Reading the words the way Cinderella had heard my voice in her ear. My finger hovered over the mouse, ready to press 'send.' I'd only opened this account to buy some items online, shortly after George had shown me how to use the computer, and I loved the idea that I could sit alone in this hushed room and send a message into space, to her. What would Veronica think, receiving such a message from lillian99? Could I make a new account for your_fairy_godmother? I laughed and deleted the e-mail.

There was another link, I realized, at the bottom of the page. 'Journal.' When I clicked it, a new page opened. It took a second for it to fill with a number of diary entries about her life. I scrolled down the page, saw that the entries dated to a month back and that there was a link on the bottom of the page to see entries from before. A few years' worth of archives were listed on the right. How could such a young woman have so much to say, I wondered.

I glanced down at the first one, dated the day before, 10:16 A.M.

So last night on the subway I saw the coolest old man: he had a full-on pompadour that stood, I swear, like a mile high, and swirled around like the top of a soft-serve ice-cream cone. His hair was taller than his body, which was AT MOST three feet tall. And when I walked by him he called me "mami.' Which was not undisturbing and has, more than ever, put me off having chillen of my own. But that hair! I so wanted to lick it.

I laughed and scrolled through the next few entries, reading about a German movie she'd loved, her obsessions with Coney Island and rhinestone jewelry and abandoned buildings, a party she'd been to a few nights before, and how, this summer, the air was so thick she felt it was molesting her. I read about a Pomeranian named Diva that she'd fallen madly in love with when it showed up at her door, and how her heart had broken when the owner came to collect it. Diva, I repeated out loud. I could see the dog panting up at her with its bulging eyes. She wrote about a T-shirt she'd bought – 'Prufrock is my Homeboy' – and included a photo of herself 'glamorously draped over a park bench,' modeling it. In one entry she wrote about staying with a friend's Indian family in California and her fervent desire to become Indian as well, due to the luscious food and colorful garments that really 'complement my skin tone.' I reached the bottom of the page and realized I was smiling at the screen, utterly charmed.

I shifted in my chair. The light in the back of the store was dim, but the computer screen shone out. I was enjoying this. I took a drink of coffee and clicked on a month from the year before, then looked down at the first entry.

I am so sad lately. I'm not sure why. Yesterday I walked across the Brooklyn Bridge at four in the morning. I just wanted to be alone and think. I love feeling that free, suspended over water, leaving this insane city behind. I'd spent the evening with Kara and Melody at the Slipper Room, watching the burlesque show Val's doing, and I think that put me in a weird mood . . . made me depressed, even though we had a great time and Val was hilarious, as usual. But it just felt like we're always trying to imitate these amazing lives that other people had, back when everything was different. Better. We play these old wartime songs and dress in these fabulous old clothes because our own time is so empty. Or something. Sometimes my life starts feeling so small, and I want it to be the opposite of small. I want it to be everything. I think of all the other lives I could have – traveling the world, making art, falling madly in love, playing instruments, taking photographs, living on the water. No matter where I am, there's a part of me that wants to be somewhere else. I don't know sometimes how people choose, make a choice and decide this is what I will be and do, and then they think that it's just natural, that they're just doing what they were meant to do all along.

I scrolled down to an entry from a few weeks before that.

I've been doing a ton of sewing to clear my head. I finished the curtains and started a new sundress, and now I'm thinking about doing a baby quilt for Maureen. I just feel like holing up and getting a ton of stuff done right now. I think I sort of need the rest. I had a dream last night about Ryan. It's been a while since I've had one; I thought they'd stopped for good. In the dream we were driving around through the swamps, like we did that time we went to New Orleans and rented a car for the day. Just driving around in the late afternoon, taking all these little roads. He kept looking over at me and laughing in that way he did. In the dream I felt really calm, like in a way I never do in real life. I mean, completely at peace with the world, like we could just drive around forever that way, with the sun going down and the car filling with shadows. I woke up elated, and then it all came crashing down. I cried for hours. I miss him so much. I keep thinking I'm 'getting better' or 'getting over it,' but it just comes at you sometimes, and you realize it will never be any better. But I'm sort of glad he came back. I can remember every inch of his face again. I was starting to forget.

I kept clicking to go back and back through the months and years, to the journal's first entry. I sank deeper and deeper into her life, reading about her travels – to Mexico and San Francisco and Berlin – and nights out at clubs or shows. I read about the art she loved: Joseph Cornell, photos by Ralph Eugene Meatyard and Diane Arbus and Brassaï. Her soaring passions for misfit men and the sudden crashes after they'd revealed themselves to be cracked and flawed. Her continued grief at the death of her first love, in a car accident several years before. I rifled through her heart, her thoughts.

I couldn't believe that it was all right there, for anyone to see. In the old days, no one spoke what they felt, and what we tapped into was buried deep. Now here was a modern girl, with all the secret desires right up there on the screen. It was the modern way. She had been able to walk into the bookstore and flirt with a young man and talk with an old woman, tell me about her breakup and her life, with no self-consciousness at all. For a moment I imagined what it would be like to be as fearless as that, as open.

What I read confirmed everything I'd intuited about her. That she was, like Cinderella, longing for something extraordinary. That she had been sent to me for a reason.

CHAPTER SIX

never should have seen the prince up close, never even come within eyeshot of him, really. My instructions had been specific, startlingly simple: *Help Cinderella get to the ball.* It didn't matter why, or that she was to go to the ball to fall in love with the prince as the fairy elders had decreed. Of course I'd seen the prince – we saw everything back then, in all the world – but I hadn't *seen* him the way another human would have. The way I saw her.

But I had finally convinced Maybeth to come with me. The lure for her of poking around the royal palace was too strong to resist.

'We'll only take a quick look,' I had said. 'Just to see up close what all the human girls are so crazy about.'

'I'm sure he's as revolting as the rest of them,' Maybeth said. 'I'm going to pull that hair of his and turn it into hay. And then I'll turn him into a cow so he can eat it!'

'May!' I laughed. 'You'll do no such thing!'

We flitted about the royal palace and laughed and squealed, thrilled with our daring. Until I realized – suddenly, shockingly

– that the servants were running into place, bugles were blowing, and carpet was being unfurled across the floor. Just underneath us, Prince Theodore was entering the grand hall.

We should never have been in that palace; I never should have let it get that far. It wasn't officially prohibited, I had argued. It would be fun just to pretend. To flirt with taboos, the other world. And now here he was, the prince himself. My previous encounters with the royal family had been official, regulated by the fairy elders, recorded in the fairy book. This, here and now, was all wrong.

I looked down and saw the spark of his hair. I laughed nervously. He glanced up then, right at me, as if he could see me. But he couldn't. No humans could. Could they?

I was aware of Maybeth tittering and laughing at me, but I just stared down into his blue eyes. It was as if vision had taken on a whole new significance. I had never looked at someone like that, never had someone look like that at me. I forgot everything else.

'Can you see me?' I whispered, just as he turned away.

'Lil, that's not funny!' Maybeth said.

I looked over at her. 'He saw me,' I said.

We were still hovering against the ceiling of the grand dining room. The room underneath us shone with marble and gold. I could feel him moving through the palace, down the great hallway, through to the suites where he slept.

'That's impossible,' Maybeth said. 'You know that's impossible.'

'Sometimes they can see us,' I said, turning to her, challenging her.

She looked down, then back up at me, no longer laughing.

'Lil, you shouldn't be talking like that. And we're late. Come on.'

But I had to be sure. 'I'm taking another look,' I said. 'One more, just to see.'

'Lil, he's promised. He's the prince! *Her* prince!' Maybeth swooped over to me then and grabbed my dress with her tiny hand. Her fingers pinched into me.

'Let go!' I said. I could feel him in his chambers, sitting on his velvet chair with a manuscript open in his lap. All my senses homed in on him, and I could feel his dreams of the hunt the next day, the flush that swept through him. 'He saw me. I can feel it!'

'So what if he did?' she asked, exasperated. 'We have to get back. We shouldn't have come here at all.' Maybeth, my sister, the prettiest, wildest fairy girl, was practically wringing her hands with worry. I almost laughed out loud at the sight.

'Go ahead, then. I'll meet you there!' I said. I was tired of listening to her and her annoying, high-pitched squeal, and with that I tucked in my head and just went. As fast as I could. So that even Maybeth saw only a blur of light, felt a whoosh against her pale skin before I was gone.

I laughed and whooped, my heart racing with the thrill of it. This was my one chance, I thought. I was doing everything wrong, and, for once in my life, I didn't care. I didn't slow down or even think about where I was going, I just darted through the great hall and the gigantic gilded doors and the various ornate chambers until all at once there he was. He looked up from the pages and right into me.

I stopped dead. He was so beautiful.

I was shocked. We fairies were interested in humans; we helped and loved and tormented them. But I had never felt anything like this before. I felt stupid suddenly, and scared. I was used to being invisible and having free rein over the human world. Being able to flit along the curve of a child's ear, playing my harp and tickling the skin with my notes. Sliding myself into a rain gutter. Perching on the tine of a fork. Whispering and singing until the humans dreamed of our world, and longed for it. But I had never been pinned down the way he was pinning me now.

'Hello,' he said. His voice rumbled through me.

I looked back and forth, and slipped my cloak over my face to make myself invisible. Was he one of us posing as the prince? I had heard of banished fairies roaming the earth as humans. But this was the prince. It was impossible. I had been one of those fairies who'd seen to it that he was born, to the queen and king – a woman and man with only a touch of fairy blood running through their veins. I had dangled mint under the queen's nose eighteen years before in human time. In our time only months.

Now I felt time grinding to a halt as his eyes bore through me. Bright eyes, like the water of the fairy lake, the sugar water that moved against you like silk.

'What is your name?' he asked.

No human had spoken to me before. Not in this form, with flitting, flapping wings, hovering in the air.

No sooner did I have the thought than I transformed, right there. Without even thinking about it. My tiny fingers stretched out, my body filled and dropped to the floor. My hair grew in masses down my back. And then, before I knew what was happening, I was standing in front of him, an almost-human, nearly his own height. It was in this form that we had been known to make humans go mad.

I was horrified at my daring, even as the prince stood and walked over to me.

'Who are you?' he gasped.

'Lil,' I whispered, and my voice sounded loud and strange in my ear.

My heart pounded. Run! a voice inside me said, and yet I stood there and lifted my eyes straight into his.

For a second I was sure I heard the voice of the chief fairy elder beating in my ear.

'I have never seen anyone like you,' he said, and then he came so close to me that I could practically taste him. Small beads of sweat formed on his brow, like drops of dew on a grass blade.

I knew at that point I should leave. Pull my body in and swoop away as quickly as possible through that gilded door.

But I could not look away from him. I was sure he would taste of peach juice and dew. Figs plucked straight off the tree.

'I have never seen anyone like you, either,' I whispered, and stepped toward him. I heard the strange sound move through the room. My voice in human form, light as air.

I walked to him. I lifted my hand and pressed my palm against his cheek, in one quick gesture that seemed to have a life all its own. As if the rest of me were still as small as a hummingbird, hovering in the corner of the room.

He looked as if I'd struck him. I stood, tracing the lines of his face with my fingers, staring into his sugar-water eyes. Was this why Cinderella's stepsisters spent their days dressing their hair and painting their faces, to feel like this? I heard all their thoughts, but until that moment I did not understand them. Until now, I thought. These crazy humans, clawing out their hearts when they loved and weren't loved back.

If it had ended there, if I had left, I might have been okay. Though, in truth, it was probably over the moment I saw him in the grand dining room.

But my eyes dropped to his lips, and I could not move. He made me feel as if I'd slipped underwater.

He moved toward me. I pulled my hand from his face and slid it to his dark hair, then ran my fingers back to his neck, where I could feel the sweat gathering. I spread my fingers, moved my palm across his neck. Before I realized what was happening, I'd pulled his face into mine and pressed my lips against his full mouth – quickly, so quickly he could barely have registered it. Not only figs, I thought: apples and strawberries and watermelon, the sweetest in the world. I stopped thinking, stopped listening to the blood rushing through me, pounding through every vein and stretch of skin.

'Lil!' I heard, and the sound crashed through me so that I dropped my hands and covered my ears.

'What is wrong?' he whispered, reaching for me, looking rubbed raw and so soft that I wanted to cry.

But the sound pierced through me. 'Lil!' it cried. 'Let's go now!' I doubled over in pain, and then suddenly the room receded. I felt myself whooshing through space until the blood pounding stopped and the voice went away.

Maybeth hovered in the corner. Her eyes were so wide I thought they would fall out. Tears streamed down her face, glinting and sparkling.

'Maybeth?' I whispered.

I had never seen her like that. I had never seen any fairy like that.

'Don't talk,' she said, rushing to me and grabbing onto my

hand. I felt her nails dig into me. She tightened her grip and then turned and flew as fast as she could, using all her strength to pull me behind her. I flailed out, caught, frantically turning back to him, to those eyes that seemed to bore into me as we fled from the room, from their world, exchanging the gold and marble for pure space.

'No!' I screamed, and I could feel Maybeth's grip tighten even more, and we were hurtling through the air, faster and faster until I was dizzy with it. And then, suddenly, we were back home, next to the lake, resting on two leaves curling from a branch.

Maybeth was shaking, I saw then. Her hands and arms. She stared over at me with wild eyes. 'You can get *banished* for that, for falling in love with a human.'

'In love?' I repeated, as if that were the craziest thing I'd ever heard. But I looked down and saw that I, too, was shaking. I tried to sound nonchalant, but my voice was garbled, strangling in my throat. 'I was just playing around, May.'

'You're lying,' she said. 'You're thinking about him right now. You have to stop. They'll know – they might know already.'

Fear sliced through me. I kept my eyes to the ground, so she wouldn't see. 'I don't think anyone else was at the castle today, were they? Were they, Maybeth?'

I looked up at her, desperate.

'I don't know,' she said.

I dialed Veronica's number slowly, with shaking hands. *This is a normal thing to do,* I thought, trying to calm myself. A normal human thing.

'The Pink Sink,' a voice said.

I forced myself to speak. 'I would like to schedule an appointment with Veronica,' I said.

'This is she,' the voice said. 'Who's this?'

I hesitated. I could feel my face growing bright red.

'Hello?'

'Um.' I cleared my throat. 'This is Lil? . . . I'm from the bookstore. Daedalus Books.'

'Oh, hey!' she said, unfazed. I couldn't tell whether she knew who I was or not. 'What's going on? What time do you want to come in? I'm here most every day.'

'This Saturday?'

'Sure,' she said. 'Eleven A.M., maybe? Later? I'm booked through the afternoon, but could do it later in the day.'

'No, eleven is great.'

'Awesome,' she said. 'You thinking a cut, color, what?'

'I . . .' I had no idea what to say. I hadn't thought that far ahead. 'I'm not sure. I mean, I . . .'

'Why don't we schedule an hour and see?'

'Yes,' I said.

'Great. See you then!'

I could hear voices behind her, the faint sound of music, and then the line went dead. I hung up the phone. I hadn't realized I'd been holding my breath.

On Saturday it took me a second to spot the salon with its little pink awning. I walked over, clutching my purse.

I almost never went to this part of the city. New York was so rich and vast, and yet my whole world seemed to be located between Pier A and Thirty-sixth, up and down Eighth Avenue, and over to the water. But now, within the past few days, I'd gone to the Pierre and now to Avenue B in the East Village. There was so much to see, so much that I never noticed. As a human it took so much work, I thought, to be in the world. Once it had all been spread out before me like a huge feast.

I peeked in the window. The salon had bright pink chairs and curving sinks and old-style bonnet hair dryers arching from the white brick walls. I spotted Veronica, fussing over the head of a young woman with long multicolored dreadlocks hanging from her scalp like snakes. Another woman with cropped purple hair stood behind the counter leafing through a book.

Veronica looked up and met my eyes.

She smiled and gestured for me to come inside. The dreadlocked girl glanced up at me, then away, talking the whole time. Around me the street swarmed with life. I took a deep breath and pushed in.

'Hey, missus,' Veronica called out. 'How are you?' She turned to the girl. 'Lil runs that gorgeous bookstore on Jane Street. Isn't her hair fabulous? Wouldn't you die to get hair this white? It's better than platinum!'

I could feel myself blushing, happy that she remembered me. The girl looked over and smiled, seeming slightly confused. 'It's very nice,' she said in a husky voice.

'I just work at the bookstore,' I said, nodding to her. 'Not run it.' I clutched my purse, not sure what to do with myself. I was suddenly painfully aware of my age.

'We're just finishing up,' Veronica said. 'It's your lucky day! Usually you'd have to wait for hours.' She laughed. 'Just kidding. You can have a seat over there. Want some tea or wine or something?'

'No, thank you,' I said. I sank into one of the chairs, studying her. The girl behind the counter looked up and smiled, then went back to her book.

'So what happened then?' Veronica asked. 'Don't tell me she left him sitting there?'

'Oh, I'll tell you later,' the dreadlocked girl said, glancing at me quickly.

'You can't tease me like that,' Veronica said, shaking her head. Her hands moving through the girl's hair were magical, like she was knitting or crocheting.

'I'm not! And okay, yes, she left him there. Just walked right out and hailed a cab.'

'He didn't follow?'

'Do they ever?'

'Well,' said Veronica, 'miracles have been known to happen. Okay, you're done.'

They made it look so simple: having a friend, talking together about anything.

The girl stood up. Her hair shifted like dominoes, like a lion's mane. 'Oh, my God, V, I love it!' she said, angling her head back to see herself from the side. She did look wonderful. I thought of Cinderella, locked in her garret, covered in dust, filled with dreams. The way these girls lived now! The freedom they had!

The girl slipped out of her smock and shook her head. Veronica turned to me. 'So are you ready?'

'Yes,' I said. 'And she looks . . . amazing. Really beautiful.'

'Thanks!' the girl said as she handed her money to the woman behind the counter.

'What can I say?' Veronica said, shaking her fingers and then blowing on them. 'Some of us just have the gift.' She gestured at one of the sinks, touching me lightly as I passed her to sit down.

The dreadlocked girl left, trailing a strong scent of herbs behind her. A few minutes later, Veronica was tilting my head back into a small tub.

'So do you live around here?' she asked.

She turned on the faucet, and water streamed down my scalp.

'Midtown,' I said.

'Oh, that's right. Garment district, you said. That's a cool area. I live right down the street from here. God, your hair is gorgeous, so thick. Do you have something specific in mind, or are you going for it? I mean, I *am* an artiste. We could do a cupcake pink, put in some extensions, shave it up the sides . . .'

'Umm.'

'I'm totally kidding. With you it is all about the *glamour*.'

I laughed. 'I just want . . . a new look,' I said, warming to the idea. 'Yes. It would be impossible to mess it up, I guess.'

'Just relax,' she said. 'You're in good hands. You'll be *gawgeous*!' She giggled. She had a giddy, coltlike energy to her, as if she could run off at any moment.

Her black nails and ring-covered fingers smoothed the shampoo through my hair. The water streamed and bubbled down my scalp. I closed my eyes and enjoyed the feel of her fingers, the water pouring down my neck.

'All done,' she said too soon, wrapping a towel around my head. She propped me up so that I was looking into the mirror that covered the opposite wall, then led me to a second chair. She slipped a smock over my head and whirled me around so that my reflection was a foot or two in front of me. When she whipped off the towel, my hair fell past my shoulders, damp and white. I looked down. Then up again. For a moment I saw my face as it used to be, with my hair streaming down like liquid fire.

She hummed as she lifted my hair and began pinning it up in chunks.

'How is your dress coming along?' I asked when I caught my breath.

'Oh, I screwed it up,' she said. 'I was experimenting, but it looked terrible. I can't pull off something so frilly. I'm making some pillows out of the fabric.'

'Have you always made things?'

'Oh, yeah,' she said, her scissors flickering in the mirror. 'My grandmother taught me how to do all that kind of stuff. I never appreciated it when I was a kid, but now I make most of my own clothes. And I sell stuff sometimes, too. Dresses and bloomers, little bags.'

'I wish I could sew, make things with my hands,' I said.

'It's so easy. I could teach you in one afternoon, I bet. If that. Hey, relax.' I hadn't realized I was tensing up. She put her palm on my shoulder, soothing me. 'I'm not going to take too much off. I know this can be as bad as the dentist's office for some people, but not in my chair.'

'I trust you,' I said, as her thin silver scissors slid coldly against my neck. Inch-long bits fell on the floor around me. I looked up again, stared at my face, my pale green eyes. I could not help feeling giddy the way I had once, so many years before, when I'd seen myself in the light of the palace torches. As old as I was, the sense of possibility and transformation was still there.

'You must have been fabulous back in the day,' she said. 'I

would love to have lived in New York in the forties and fifties. My grandmother used to talk about how things were back then. She told the best stories. I wanted to be an old woman even when I was five. Did you always live in New York? Are you from here?'

I stared at her. 'No,' I said. 'I mean, yes.' As she cut my hair and let it drop to my shoulders, it curled out lush and shiny, like hair from a magazine ad. I was mesmerized.

This couldn't be right, I thought, what she was doing. She had to be using magic of some kind. Again I thought of Maybeth. But I could see that Veronica's back was as flat as an expanse of prairie, that she was a regular girl. I smiled despite myself. A flicker, behind me, in the mirror: Was it her? I turned suddenly, but there was only the salon behind me, a window to the quiet street.

'Hey, careful!' she said. 'I'm creating art here.' She laughed. 'My grandmother used to talk about the grand old buildings, back in the day. I still love going to the places that remind me of her stories. Like the Algonquin Hotel, the Russian Tea Room, the garden at Barbetta with the stone fountain. Those places will wipe you out, though. Drinks at the Algonquin are fifteen bucks.'

'What about the Pierre?' I asked.

'The hotel, you mean? By Central Park?'

'Yes.'

She scrunched up her face. 'I'm not sure I've ever been there.'

'I think you would love it,' I said. 'You should go by it one of these days.'

'I will,' she said. 'God, you must have a ton of stories.'

I blinked, shook my head. 'I have a terrible memory,' I said, smiling. 'I just remember fragments.'

'You are one stingy broad,' she said, laughing and touching my arm. 'There's no way you didn't see some amazing stuff in your time. You must have gone to movie palaces, gone to dances, dated guys who looked like Brando. I can just see you breaking hearts left and right.'

I thought back, concentrating. I had vague memories of a different time, a different city. I could remember parties from fifty years before, the way we all used to stand around in our gowns, martini glasses in our hands and jazz wafting out of the open windows. The dresses I wore once. A dress I had loved especially, white rimmed with black around the sleeves, the hem, the collar, the waist. The skirt had flared out over my hips and would pop up when I twirled around. I remembered someone else, a friend, in a soft, long gown.

'Oh, please,' I said. 'I'm just an old lady. I can barely remember my own name sometimes.' But still, her words thrilled me, as my mind went back further in time. I *had* been fabulous. I had been one of the most gorgeous and wispy and long-red-haired fairies in existence. Over the years I had appeared to countless poets in glimmers on the surfaces of rivers or in panes of glass, inspiring some of the most famous love poems throughout history.

She laughed. 'You are a wily one,' she said. 'I am an *aesthetician*, you know, a beauty connoisseur, not to mention an artiste. You don't think I can see how gorgeous you were once? I mean, not that you aren't now.'

'You can't see that,' I said slowly. 'All my beauty is long gone. Trust me. Vanished without a trace.'

But maybe it hadn't, I thought now. Not quite. I moved my head back and forth. My hair swung down to my shoulders, thicker, I was sure, than it had been before. And he, in the diner, had looked at me as if I were beautiful. Something was still there, some power inside me, trying to come out.

'Your hair, for one. It's like snow. Were you a platinum? You had to have been.'

'A redhead,' I said.

'No kidding. I would love to see a photo.'

'Well . . .' I said, reaching up and touching my hair self-consciously. 'I don't think I kept any.' I had a dim memory then: of smoke and flame, a face crumpling into ash.

'You don't have any old pictures?' she asked. 'You gotta have one or two around, some box stashed somewhere that you look at late at night.' She winked, goading me. 'Come on. I know you've got locks of some hot dude's hair stashed away. Some rose pressed in a book. Or something far more scandalous?'

'You are mad,' I said, laughing.

She leaned over and pulled out a plastic bag, took out a cushiony pink curler.

'I haven't seen those in years,' I said.

'I know,' she said. 'I love them. I'm a sucker for everything retro, I have to admit. It's a bona fide problem of mine. I can't even believe sometimes that I was born in the eighties. It seems so criminal.'

'Your life seems exciting enough, even so. This is a wonderful time to be young.'

She snorted. 'Ha!' she said as she rolled up a section of my hair and snapped the roller closed. Her fingertips brushing my scalp, sending tingles through me. 'There's no romance to anything at all anymore.'

'Oh, I think you can find some here and there still. Don't you?'

'Well, it doesn't find me,' she said, waving dismissively. 'You know, I always fall for liars. Isn't that right, Kim?'

The purple-haired woman, silent before now, looked up and laughed. 'Oh, hell yes,' she said. 'This girl's dated every loser in the city. Seriously. Every one.'

'I just fall easily, I guess,' Veronica said, sighing. 'I'm what you call a *romantic*. Unlike Kim here, who had the misfortune to be born without a heart. She's like out of *The Wizard of Oz* or something.'

'She falls in love in two seconds,' Kim said. 'Next, next, next!' She snapped her fingers.

'No heart at all. A real shame,' Veronica said, turning to me. 'You believe in love at first sight, Lil?'

The question took me off guard. 'Yes,' I said immediately, without thinking.

She paused with a roller in her hand, midair. 'You've totally fallen in love at first sight, haven't you?'

I looked at her in the mirror. I could feel my pulse quicken, my cheeks flush red. I had never spoken about Theodore to anyone. How wonderful it would be to tell someone after so long, I thought. What could it hurt? It felt right, speaking it out loud, to her. I had never felt that way with a human. She was so much like Maybeth, but not even Maybeth had understood what had possessed me that day I kissed the prince.

'Yes,' I said, my voice quivering. 'It was so long ago, but yes. When I was a girl.' I paused. I found myself tensing up, expecting something terrible to happen.

'What was his name? What was he like? Tell me everything!' Her eyes glittered with interest. She plucked another roller from the bag.

'Well,' I said. 'His name was Theodore, and he was very beautiful. Like a prince.' I warmed to the topic. 'He had black hair and just the most . . . interesting face. Kind eyes, very intelligent. Everyone loved him. I mean, every girl I knew wanted him, to be with him. But not me, not at first.'

'So what happened? Where did you meet him?'

'I was out one day, with a friend, and then there he was. He looked up and saw me; and that was it. I kept staring at his lips, his skin, his eyes. But it was more than that. It was the way he looked at me.'

I could see him, right there: his dark hair falling in his face, the curve of his mouth, his pale eyes looking straight into me.

'I felt like I already knew him but at the same time like I had to know everything about him. I didn't realize how much it had affected me until I returned home and he was all I could think of.' I remembered it: the ache in the pit of my stomach, flowering like a wound. 'He saw me. No one else could. I mean, when he looked at me, I felt like I'd been invisible until that moment.' It was the first time I'd tried to explain it to someone else, and I could not find words strong enough to contain those moments, the freedom I had felt in them.

'Oh, gosh,' Veronica said, wistful, lifting her hand to her face. Her rings caught the light and glimmered faintly. 'I'm so jealous. I just have the worst luck. Or I just pick all the wrong dudes.' Kim nodded at the second choice to me in the mirror. 'How'd you two get together? Tell me everything! I love knowing that things could be like that – at least once upon a time. I was so born in the wrong era.'

I stared at her for a moment, my heart racing, but she only looked back at me, smiling and expectant. Warm, open to everything. *Go with it*, I thought. We were in forbidden territory now, things I had never said before, to anyone. 'It took me completely off guard,' I said. 'Of course, you never expect it. But then there was a dance. I wasn't supposed to go to it, but I went anyway, to find him.'

Veronica did a strange shimmy then, and her striped skirt flared around her knees. 'Such a rebel you were,' she said. 'I knew it! So great.'

'It was great,' I said. I remembered the excitement burning through me, the feel of the silk touching my skin. 'I made quite an entrance, too. Everyone stopped dancing, the band stopped playing, he stepped out of the crowd and extended his hand to me. It was straight out of a fairy tale.'

'Ahhh,' she said, exaggeratedly swooning. 'Why don't we have these things? Dances, nights like that. So what happened? What happened to your prince?'

'God, you are a nosy bitch,' Kim said, but when I looked over, she was smiling and leaning forward in her chair, rapt.

'It wasn't meant to be,' I said, almost shaking with excitement. The words felt like sparks coming out of me. 'We talked and danced for hours. It was the only time I knew how wonderful it is to dance in a man's arms, to just feel like you could fly, but it's him, all him, who's making you feel that way.'

'Yes,' Veronica said, her hand on her heart. 'I can see it like I was there. It breaks my heart. Nothing is beautiful now, the way it was before. With me and my friends, it's all getting drunk and making out in back rooms, you know?'

'No kidding,' Kim said.

I looked at them both and saw how vulnerable they were behind the masks of makeup, the elaborate clothes and hair.

'How long did it last?' Veronica asked. She paused with a lock of my hair in her right hand, a curler poised beside it.

'I only saw him twice,' I said. I could feel myself flush. I was too aware of how hollow the words sounded.

Her face fell open. 'Oh, Lil,' she said. 'Why?'

I was surprised by her reaction, and even more so by mine: the clutch in my chest, the ache at the back of my throat. 'It wasn't meant to be,' I said. 'It wasn't allowed. It was a different world then.'

'Ah.' Veronica reached out and touched my shoulder. 'You couldn't run away together or anything?'

I shook my head. 'Something . . . happened. There was an accident.' I paused. 'It's hard to explain. It might sound foolish to you – I mean such a short thing, meaning so much.'

'It doesn't sound foolish at all,' she said, and I saw the sadness in her that I had read in her journal. It was so close to the surface, I realized. 'I had something like that once. I wish I could find something like that again. I don't care if it's only for one night. I just want to feel alive. Really alive.'

'You know,' I said, feeling the excitement rise up in me, flowering out through my chest, 'there may be someone new coming along for you. A new love. I have a feeling about you, in fact. That maybe there's a dance in your future, too?'

'Ha!' she said as she started spritzing the rollers with some sort of spray. 'No guy interested in me would ever go near anything like that. Trust me. Unless you're talking about a lap dance.'

Kim guffawed.

'Well,' I said, smiling, 'I think the one coming along will be different. Much quieter, a poetic soul. Maybe even a business owner to boot.'

'Hmmm,' she said. She narrowed her eyes and looked at me. 'Are you trying to set me up, Lil?'

I shrugged. 'Maybe.'

She turned to Kim. 'Why is everyone always trying to set me up? Am I that hopeless?'

'Yes,' Kim said. And then to me, 'Please set her up. I am begging you.'

'Hey,' Veronica said. 'My taste may be bad, but it's my taste, and I'm very attached to it!'

'Well,' I said, 'I might just happen to know a fantastic man, very brilliant and handsome, who has' – I could barely contain my excitement now – 'a ball coming up. That he needs a date for.'

'You've got to be kidding me,' she said. 'A ball?'

'Yes,' I said. 'At the Pierre Hotel.'

'What kind of a guy goes to a ball? Seriously.'

'A rich one,' Kim said. 'One who is not a loser. And were you or were you not just lamenting the fact that these things don't exist anymore? If you don't go, V, I will personally strangle you.'

'Well . . .' Veronica said. 'I didn't mean in New York.'

'You're going.' Kim looked at me. 'She is so going!'

'Great!' I said, clapping my hands.

'I don't know,' Veronica said, speaking more loudly as she took a blow dryer to the mass of curlers. 'The last time someone set me up, I spent an entire hour of my life hearing about video games.'

'I'm not sure this person even has a television,' I said.

She snorted. 'Probably too busy with his comic-book collection.'

I closed my eyes, listening to the hum of the dryer, not even minding the heat of the rollers against my scalp.

When I opened my eyes a few minutes later, she was unfurling my hair from the rollers. It dropped in huge, bouncing waves to my shoulders and flipped up at the ends. She brushed through the curls with a wide, flat comb, a can of hair spray in one of her hands.

'I hope my hair is half this gorgeous when I get older,' she said. 'Look at yourself.'

I turned to the mirror. My hair looked like pure snow, sparkling in the sunlight. It swirled and swooped along my face and then swept past my shoulders.

A grin broke out over my face, erupting like boiling water.

Veronica jumped up and clapped. 'I'm so good!' she said, dancing. 'A genius!'

Kim shook her head. Veronica stuck out her tongue at her and looked down at me, ebullient.

'Thank you,' I said, and squeezed her hand. 'You are an artist.'

'An artist who's going to a *ball*,' Kim said. 'What could be cooler?'

'Stop with that,' Veronica said, pointing to each of us with the bottle of hair spray in her hand. 'The both of you.'

'Don't you want to know the name of your prince?' I asked. 'His name is George. He owns Daedalus Books. And he's a book collector. He likes old things, too.'

Veronica made a face. 'Sounds like a prince, all right. I'm getting allergies just thinking about it.'

'Oh, come on,' Kim said. 'Who are you kidding? How many dresses do you have hanging in that closet of yours, with no place to wear them to?'

'Listen,' I said, standing up, watching my hair shimmer and

gleam in the mirror, 'why don't you just stop by the store? Sometime soon? I'm almost always there, and George is there at least half the time. Just come see what you think. I'll even give you a book or two, on the house. What do you have to lose?'

Veronica rolled her eyes, defeated. 'Fine!' she said. 'Fine, fine, fine. This is all I need. One *more* person convinced I'm a romantic failure. And you haven't even met any of my beaux!'

'You should thank your stars for that, Lil,' Kim said, as I handed her my money.

To my surprise, Veronica threw her arms around me and kissed my cheek. 'I'm so glad you came in today,' she said, stepping back. 'And I do need some help, I ain't gonna lie. So thank you. I will totally come by the bookstore.'

'Me too,' Kim said.

'Well,' I said, taken aback. Feeling, for a second, tears beating at my eyes. 'I very much look forward to it.'

I was so close. So close to setting things right.

I walked into the street again and headed down Avenue B, letting my hair swish against my neck. If I spread out my wings, I thought, I could fly over and above all of this, stretch out my arms and hurl myself into empty space, feel the clouds dipping into my skin as I stared down at these streets, these faces, all of them as small as stars sprinkled over the night sky.

The street was alive. A slim-hipped, slouching boy with hair to his waist walked by, and I let my eyes roam down his neck and arms and jeans. I felt more like my old self than I ever had. *If I blink*, I thought, *I can make the boy feel anything, be anything.* I could feel my old powers coursing through me.

I felt as if he, Theodore, the prince, could be around any

corner, waiting for me. Surely that had been him in the diner. Surely none of these things had been a coincidence.

I peered into the restaurants I passed, glanced into the boutiques and coffeehouses and the huge self-service laundry on Seventh Street. I was struck by a pile of wonderful junk bursting out of one of the storefronts, just off the sidewalk: a faded white hatbox, a bright red Formica-topped table, racks of colorful clothing. In the window I saw boxes spilling over with fake pearls and rhinestones and gold chains. I ran my palms down the sleeves of the dresses hanging from the rack.

I was suddenly conscious of my dull shirt, the tattered skirt dropping down my legs. I picked out a purple-striped dress and went inside, barely able to stop myself from laughing. The fabric shimmered in my hands.

In the shop it appeared that every vase and knickknack and piece of clothing in the world had been crammed onto the shelves and racks and boxes. I wandered through the aisles and touched everything: a lamp in the shape of a stretching ballerina, a painting of a smiling pit bull, beads that looked like miniature Easter eggs. As I approached the glass case in front of the cash register, I nodded to the woman behind it as she sat folding scarves into a box. And then my eyes fell upon the most wonderful thing, something that could have been crafted by fairies: a scarf with every color in the world in it, that seemed to change color under my gaze. I reached over, ran my fingers across it. The scarf seemed to glitter and spark under my touch, and for a moment I couldn't look away.

'Don't you love that?' the woman behind the counter asked.

'Yes,' I said, picking it up. It was large and diaphanous, as big as a shawl. 'It reminds me of something, a place I used to love.'

The woman was tall and thin, like a column, and her hair was held back with chopsticks.

'Ten dollars and it's yours. Would you like to try on that dress?'

'Yes. Yes, please.'

She led me back to a space that was barely big enough to stand in and then drew the drapes closed around me. I checked that not a sliver of the space was showing to the room outside it, then carefully removed my old clothes and slipped the dress over my head and let it fall.

I turned to the mirror. I was transfixed by the image in front of me: It was me but not myself, the dress snug against my body but not too snug, just right, and the purple stripes gleaming against my skin.

'Do you have a pair of shoes that might go with this?' I asked, peeking my head out. 'In a six?'

'Let me look,' the woman said. A minute later she brought me a pair of shiny pumps. I slipped my foot into one. It fit perfectly. Just like the glass slipper, I thought, laughing to myself.

When I left the store with my old clothes and tennis shoes squashed into a shopping bag, the heels felt strange on my feet. I loved the clacking sound they made as I walked down the street. I twisted my shoulders to feel the dress shift and trickle along my skin.

I knew that George and Veronica would fall madly in love, live happily ever after, the way she had been supposed to so long ago. *What occurs in the world of faerie will become manifest in the world of men.* This was it, I thought. The mistakes of the old world corrected in the new one. A new beginning.

I started heading uptown. Almost as if my body had a mind of its own. I craved something. The water. Trees. Flowers. Something from the other world. *All my old loves will be returned to me.* The sky felt so close I could have reached up and touched it.

You should just go home now, I told myself. *Go home and rest. Take a bath. Watch television.* On a Saturday afternoon there was always some old movie on, something with a Carole Lombard or a Marlene Dietrich.

But I didn't feel ready to go back. My feet made a steady rhythm on the sidewalk. I could walk for hours sometimes, despite my creaking bones and soft body, as if I were in a trance. A remnant of my fairy existence, I supposed. That day every street felt like a revelation. I had to warn myself not to stare too hard at the people I passed; I wanted to touch them all, talk to them, stare at their faces, ask about their violin cases or leather portfolios or the books peeking from their bags. I wanted to pet every single dog I saw strutting or slinking past.

I thought about going to the pier, but I found myself heading north instead. Eventually I turned on Twenty-eighth Street, and I realized then what I had come for. Pots of flowers and tall, gangly trees lined the streets on either side. It was like entering a forest, the only street in Manhattan where you had to brush past leaves and branches to get down the sidewalk. I breathed it in. The buildings were dilapidated, hardly changed from the century before. I paused in front of a bamboo tree and ran my fingers up the side.

A sense of calm entered me. The heady scent of the flowers – every kind of flower, lining the streets and filling all the shops – swirled around me.

I stepped forward, into one of the shops. A dark-skinned man nodded at me from behind a cash register. Strange, exotic blooms sat on the shelves in the front of the store. Behind them were bursting small trees and plants. I walked up to one with leaves so dark they were almost black. The curves of the leaves were so pronounced they looked as if they'd been carved with scissors. *This*, I thought, *right here.*

Wet-leaved tropical trees hung and bent into the aisle and over the damp tile floors. I moved to the back of the store, breathing in the moist, pure scent of soil. The leaves tapped my head as I walked through them, and I put up my hands to clear a pathway. If I squinted, imagined my feet making soft dents in the tiles, I could be in an ancient forest, in the old world. The forest behind the palace that we had looked out over that night, from the balcony. I breathed in. The smell of rain. *I love that smell,* he had said.

I let the leaves brush against my face and hands as I walked to the end of the aisle and back up again, emerging into the main space. I felt fantastic.

'We have some new blooms in,' the salesman said, approaching me. He pointed to a refrigeration unit with glass doors.

'Those are beautiful,' I said.

'Harvested yesterday morning in Holland.' He leaned in and opened the door, revealing flowers so red they were like open cuts.

I left the store and started walking. I almost ran into a couple of men hauling boxes from the back of a truck parked at the curb. I passed by piles of baskets held together with strings, stacks of clay pots and crates filled with small flats of pansies and cacti. Ahead, a group of men were lowering pots on ropes and pulleys through cellar doors. The air was heavy with water, the pungent scent of plants, soil.

Billboards rose over the street, from Sixth Avenue. My head was spinning. I walked past silk-flower shops, warehouses over-flowing with plants, stores that sold every sort of gardening paraphernalia. Men loitered outside every doorway, it seemed. Down the block a profile flashed into view, a man ducking into a store. I recognized him immediately.

There! His dark hair curled over his collar. I pushed my way past the junipers and spruces, the shop owners and the working-men shouting out to one another, bending down and taping up plants for delivery. I turned in to the store.

Maybe it was the flowers that convinced me he had actually come back to me, that he was there right then, looking for me. I had the sudden, sharp memory of him plucking a flower and holding it to my face, slipping it behind my ear. What kind of flower? I stopped walking. *Gardenia*, I remembered suddenly. The balcony had been covered in flowers. He had leaned down and snapped one off for me, a glowing white bloom. The smell of it had seemed to penetrate my skin.

A man shoved past me, and my elbow pushed against a bamboo tree, the long stalk jutting up, pressing my skin. I stumbled forward into the store.

I focused in. The flowers shot up all around me, in every color and shape. The place seemed to specialize in orchids. Perfect, deformed-looking blooms covered with spots, flapping out like parachutes, twisting and curving up, dangling in threads toward the soil. I caught my breath. The large trees were in the back, just as in the last shop.

I walked toward the sprawling greens, bending down and

pushing my way through. With each step I could feel my wings loosen, my skin pull and tighten, my eyes grow more clear and bright.

'Theodore?' I whispered.

I could feel the silk of the ball gown. Like water.

I reached the back of the store. Saw a man squatting down in front of a tree. His black hair curved over his collar.

I could smell the rain, the gardenias. I heard the music from the ballroom, drifting out onto the balcony. I felt the glass slippers cradling my feet.

For a moment I was so close. It was as if he'd always been right there, in front of me, ready to take me back. Then he turned his face to me.

'Can I help you?' a strange man asked.

'No. No, thank you,' I said. I felt a feather rub against my arm and slapped it off. I stumbled as I moved to the exit, veering past the two workers, careful not to bump up against the flowers.

I pushed my way down the street as if I were swimming and moved back to Seventh Avenue. I kicked over a pot of soil, not meaning to. I almost stepped into a box full of daisies. I squinted ahead, the strange mixture of forest and city, the lush green and the concrete, the skyscrapers. I focused on moving forward. By the time I reached my own door, I felt as if I'd been walking through the city for days.

I let myself in the front door and dragged myself up the stairs. Once I was in my apartment, I breathed out, let my whole body slow down.

The room closed around me, and a feeling crept in, gnawing at my guts and bones. A howl formed, then swept out and broke through my eyes and mouth and into the air.

I was ridiculous. I spit out the word: 'Ridiculous.' An old, desperate woman. I hated my swirling hair, loathed my own skin. I deserved all of it, for what I'd done. I could not suck enough air into my lungs.

I pulled the dress over my head, then tore off the bandage that bound me. Desperate, as if I were on fire. Then, leaning forward, I let my wings spread out on either side of me and began to slowly pull them in, until they blanketed me completely.

CHAPTER SEVEN

After Maybeth and I returned from the palace, I tried to forget what had happened there. Everything I had done. How I had felt in my human body, the way my heart had pounded as blood rushed through me, the feel of the marble floor pressing into my feet. The air changing weight and shape and tingling against my skin. His eyes right on mine, seeing into me. As if he, and only he, could see who I really was.

No.

I needed to buckle down and start focusing on the task at hand. *Cinderella.* I had so many things to do: Go to her. Dress her. Get her to the ball, so that he could fall in love with her and make her his wife. This is what was written in the great tree, what the elders had decreed.

Once she arrived at the ball, my task would be complete. The moment he set eyes on her, he would love her. It was his destiny. What she was made for.

'Lil!'

I glanced up. Gladys swung above me, laughing and sticking

out her tongue. She threw up her hands and swooped down, pretending she was falling.

'Help!' she screamed. 'I'm drowning!' She plunged into the lake so hard that sprays of water leaped up, drenching me.

'Gladys, what are you doing?' I slipped into the lake next to her, tugging at her hand, and gasped. There, past my hand, two of the fairy elders slid by underneath the water, about a half mile below the surface. They seemed giant through all that water. Their bright purple robes made them glisten like sea-fish, their wings spread out like giant fins.

I pulled back and leaped back onto the pier.

'Get out of the water, Gladys,' I hissed.

Just then her head burst through the surface and her laughing face was below mine. Gladys was the most beautiful of all of us, and even I had to blink sometimes when I saw her up close, to be sure I wasn't dreaming.

'Why such a grouch?' she asked, shaking her head and sprinkling water droplets across the surface of the water. 'I was just playing.'

'Well, you're not funny,' I said. 'I'm trying to work. Do you even know what that is? And of course you have to come bother me at the exact moment that two of the elders are passing by.'

Gladys stopped laughing. Her face paled. Suddenly she was right next to me, crouching on the pier. 'What? When?'

'Just now.' I looked down into the water.

Her body slumped into mine, and I thought I could feel her shaking.

'Here,' I said gently, putting my arm around her. 'Just let's not do anything to get into trouble, all right? This is an important time in the human kingdom and we all have so much to do.' I felt bad for her. And for me.

'Yes,' she said. 'You're right. I have some vines to tend and humans to visit. I need to find Lucibell. Yes, yes, yes.' She sat up. I could see tears glistening on her lashes. 'But did you and Maybeth really sneak into the castle?' she asked. She looked up at me slyly, her eyes peeking out from under her thick, tear-speckled lashes. 'She said you actually showed yourself to the prince.'

My heart almost stopped altogether. I would kill Maybeth, I thought.

'Gladys,' I whispered. 'Don't ever say that again. Please! And of course it's not true. Why would you even think such a thing?'

Her face shifted and a smile cracked her face wide open. 'You love him!' She laughed, and then leaned right over and kissed my cheek before leaping back into the air. 'But I won't tell anyone.'

'Gladys, please!' I was desperate now. 'It's not true!'

She laughed again, fluttering above me. 'Whatever you say. I don't have time for you or your love affairs, anyway, Lil. I've got so much work to do. Maybe *you* should go see Cinderella.' Squealing with laughter, Gladys swooped up into the air. 'Or better yet, the prince!'

With that, she was gone. I felt the guilt clenching my neck, burrowing its way through my throat, up to my mouth and tongue. I pulled into myself and tried to think of her, Cinderella, everything I had to do to help her meet her fate. Instead, all I saw was him. I longed to be in that body again, to feel that sensation of giving myself over to such a force.

The sun beat down overhead, and in front of me the branches

of the great tree rose glimmering out of the water, the leaves rippling in the breeze like a school of fish shimmying past. Fairies fluttered all around me, leaving the water and diving back in again. Everyone had their job to do, as I had mine.

But I sat back for one second, two seconds more. Letting the memories sink into me. The shape and weight of his body pressing into air, and then against me. The feel of his skin under my palm, soft and slightly damp at the back of his neck. The way I had grown so large and yet felt so fragile and strange, delicate. I had loved the feel of the marble floor under my feet. The scent of gardenias from outside. The faint scent of the meat being roasted in the castle's kitchen, down the stairs and past the gilded doors.

'Theodore,' I whispered at the air, liking the sound of it, and I closed my eyes and imagined the way a flame had seemed to overtake my whole body in an instant when I touched him. The way it had her, when she dreamed of him, but now it was all me. Before then I had not experienced desire in any form – it wasn't part of our world, wasn't anything we even understood – and I took to it.

It suited me.

Over the next week, I found myself looking for him everywhere. I had seen him twice, in the diner and outside the flower shop – the signs were there. But he was elusive. I went to the diner each night, dressing carefully, taking time to brush out my hair. I couldn't afford whole meals, so I sat at the counter with books from the store, slowly eating cups of soup and nursing mugs of black coffee, my head snapping up every time someone walked through the front door. I sat there for hours some nights, convinced he would arrive any second. But he didn't come back, and I became more and more convinced that Theodore had come to this world as a sign. A sign that they were ready to forgive me. That I had a task to do. That we would meet again in the other world.

In the store I found it hard to concentrate on the work in front of me. I seemed to spend all my time trying to remember, as if understanding all of it would bring him back to me sooner. What was it about him? I just remembered the way he saw me, the way he made me someone new. He hadn't only seen me. He had recognized me. What had he recognized? What was it?

My mind circled back and back to that moment, trying to burrow in.

We could see humans back then. We could pass by them and feel their thoughts, their suffering, the parts of them that were closed off to the world, the parts of them that ached for it. But none of it ever touched us. We used to laugh at the mess of human life. But standing in the prince's chambers in human form, staring up at him, I had seen everything with the eyes of a fairy and a woman. Everything, from the tiny beads of sweat above his lip to the fear and desire that gnawed at his gut. I remembered how I had tasted it when I leaned in and touched his mouth, how I had wanted to take him into me. It was a dangerous way to see a person. I knew every moment of his life, every feeling passing over him, every fear and memory, and I saw it all right as he was seeing me, as a woman, alive to the world.

My mind beat up against it.

Everything had seemed different inside that body: His hand running across my waist. The flame in the center of me. And the smells. Of course. Had there been smells before? I couldn't remember. That night on the balcony, the palace. The smell of rain and flowers and lush grass. The smell of champagne as I brought the glass to my lips and felt the bubbles pop against the tip of my nose. The perfume the women wore, gliding past me. The smell of silver and waxed marble and his jacket, as we spun across the floor. It had felt as if the entire world had just split open. As if I'd lived, until then, on the surface of things, never knowing that you could hack through to something else. How could the fairy world have compared afterward?

The ball was a few short weeks away, and I had heard nothing from Veronica. I'd told George not to ask questions, that it was all taken care of. I knew I needed to call her to make arrangements, but there was a part of me that just wanted to forget everything and wallow in the past, the way I'd been doing.

Then one afternoon she appeared, as if I'd conjured her.

I was counting the register for the day when the front door banged open, and she stomped over to the counter. 'Hey, Lil,' she said. 'Are you busy?'

She was a mess. Black lines ran down her cheeks, and it took me a second to realize she'd been crying. I hurried out from behind the counter.

'What's wrong?' I asked. 'I was just closing up. Let me get you some tea.'

'Thank you.' And then, 'Do you have any gin?'

'No.'

'Whiskey?' She laughed, and her face crumpled into tears.

'What is it?' I moved toward her and put my hand on hers. I tried to see into her, the way I might have once. 'Are you hurt?'

'No,' she said, her voice ragged, black tears streaming

down her face. 'It's just . . . I'm sorry, I just can't get myself together.'

'Let's go sit down, okay?'

She nodded. I locked the front door, then led her to the office in back, gesturing to the chair at George's desk. I pulled out a stool from the corner of the room and sat across from her, taking her hand in mine.

'What happened?'

The sobs were moving up and down her body. 'I'm so embarrassed,' she said, 'to be crying like this over some guy.'

'Ah,' I said. Relieved it was only that.

She looked around the office, self-conscious. 'You're working, you have things to do. You must think I'm completely psycho, barging in on you like this.'

'No, no,' I said. 'It's okay.'

She looked at me then. 'I guess I feel like you know things. I don't know why. I felt it right away when I sold the books to you and then even more when you came to the salon.'

I waved my hand, trying to mask how anxious and glad her words made me. 'It's because I'm so old,' I said. 'It gives one a certain *wizened* air.'

But she just looked at me, her eyes bright blue from her tears. Water eyes. 'No,' she said. 'It's something else.'

I smiled nervously, then looked away. 'I'm sorry you were disappointed by this boy,' I said. 'I know how much it hurts.'

'Thanks,' she said. 'I wish I wasn't like this. But I feel like someone ripped my heart out. I don't know why, but I can't ever just be normal about anything.'

'I know.'

'I don't know why I'm this torn up about it, though,' she said.

'I mean, it seems totally out of proportion to what happened. So something didn't work out. I just wanted so badly for it to work out. And I know in a few days I'll be fine, but it doesn't change how broken I feel now.'

I could almost feel the longing in her. I wondered if she dreamed of him, the way Cinderella had dreamed, so long ago. I thought of the man in the diner, his eyes burning into my skin. My heart clenched in my chest, despite myself.

'You're one of the most vibrant girls I've ever seen,' I said. 'I had a sister once, like you. You remind me so much of her. She's been gone a long time, and you bring her back to me.'

'Really?'

'Yes.' It was true: Maybeth was more real to me in that moment than she had been in years. She might have been right there.

'What was she like?'

I smiled. 'Wild,' I said. 'Always screaming with laughter and getting her nose into things. But she was also very kind, gentle. She could heal animals, in fact. She had a special connection with them.'

'What happened to her? Or is that something I shouldn't ask?'

'Oh, she . . .' I paused, unsure what to say. 'There was an accident. When we were young. A long time ago.'

'I'm sorry,' she said. She leaned back into George's chair. 'I like that I remind you of her. That's funny, I forgot you told me that. And you remind me of my grandmother. I mean, not that you're . . . Well, she was just amazing, Lil. She was an actress when she was young, in Berlin. Just the most glamorous lady you could ever meet. She'd stand over the stove cooking in heels and red lipstick, whip up a strudel or some schnitzel like it was nothing.'

I laughed. 'She sounds *just* like me.'

'Hey, I can totally see you doing that. She made everything so fun and romantic.' She picked up a framed photo from the desk: black and white, George and his father in suits, standing side by side in front of a tall building. 'Who's this?'

'That's George with his father.'

'Ah. He's handsome, isn't he?'

'Yes,' I said. 'He is.'

'So . . . gentlemanly. A bit like Gary Cooper or Cary Grant.'

'Oh, absolutely. I've even told him that, but he will have none of it.'

'And he's the one with the ball? The one who owns this place?'

'That he is.'

'How long have you worked for him?'

'A few years.'

'What'd you do before that?'

'I was a . . . kind of guidance counselor,' I said, 'for a long time. I've done all kinds of things for extra money, but I always loved to help people reach their potential.'

'I can see that,' she said, smiling. 'So were you serious? I mean about George?'

I smiled. 'Deadly.'

'Hmmm. Sounds ominous.' She looked around the room at the piles of books and papers, the bound manuscripts with faded, crackling edges, a poster from an Antonioni film on the wall. I watched her taking it all in. 'He's a huge reader, huh?'

'He reads all the time,' I said. 'He does a lot of interesting stuff. He just discovered a bit of manuscript, a history of Massachusetts from the nineteenth century.'

'Hmmm. I see.' She picked up a book from a stack on the desk. 'Silent films. I love these women! Garbo, Theda Bara, Clara Bow. My grandmother met Dietrich once, back in Germany when they were young.'

'Your grandmother sounds fascinating.'

'She was.' She flipped through the book. 'Louise Brooks,' she said, stopping. 'I forgot! I saw that *Pandora's Box* is playing at Film Forum. I've meant to see that for years. Do you want to go?'

'Oh.' I was taken aback. For a moment I wondered if she was joking with me. 'To the movie? With you?'

'Yeah.' She smiled, arching her eyebrows. 'Why not?'

'When?'

'What about tomorrow? Are you free in the afternoon, for a matinee?'

'What about Wednesday?' I asked.

'The four o'clock?'

'Great,' I said, my heart pounding. I felt ridiculous, like a schoolgirl.

'Maybe we can get a drink after, or grab some dinner. That cool?'

'That sounds fine,' I said. 'Perfect, actually. I'd love to.'

'Awesome. You know, I really appreciate you being so kind to me, Lil. Most people would have just thought I was nuts, showing up like this.'

'No, they wouldn't have,' I said. 'It happens to everyone. But *not* everyone gets to go to a ball with Cary Grant.'

'Well. That is a good point.'

I clapped my hands together. 'Oh, you'll have a wonderful time. The time of your life. I just know it. And you'll need a dress, of course. Shoes.'

'And a horse-drawn carriage?' she asked, teasing me, her face sweet and open.

'Of course,' I said. 'Just bring me a pumpkin.'

It felt good, laughing with her. It occurred to me that in a way this was what I had longed for back in the other world: the kind of affection and love that flickers into being out of nothing at all.

'You know, there is something that comforts me,' I said, 'that you might like to see. Come.' I motioned for her to follow as I walked to the front of the store. I opened the glass case and reached in. Wondering still if it was safe to show her.

She bent down and looked at the line of books. 'Such beautiful old things,' she said. 'My grandmother, she had rows of books like this in her bedroom. I have this fetish for ink and parchment, you know? It's all her fault.'

'So does George,' I said. 'I think he has some quills somewhere he bought in Italy, quills and ink and wax and seals.' I pulled out the Cinderella text. 'This one is my favorite. Isn't it something?' I handed it to her. 'It's very, very delicate.'

She took it as if I were handing her a piece of thin glass. She flipped slowly through the book, enchanted. 'Yes,' she said. 'This. This is the kind of world I want. You know? This.' She looked up at me, and her face was radiant now. 'It's strange, isn't it? The world can seem so small, and then you see something and remember how much there is in it. Do you know what I mean? I love this book. I love it.'

'I thought you would. And then look. Here, in back.' I read

the French out loud to her: ' "*Tous mes anciens amours vont me revenir.*" '

'Tous what?'

'It means, "all my old loves will be returned to me." '

' "All my old loves will be returned to me," ' she repeated. 'Do you think that's true?'

'I don't know,' I said. 'Maybe. I hope so.'

It felt as if everything was coming together. The next day I could barely contain myself, I was so excited. I spent the morning dealing with NYU students and two young women selling fifties records and a man looking for a first edition of On the Road. George came downstairs just before noon.

'Good morning!' I called out cheerily as he poured himself a cup of coffee and ambled up to the front desk.

'Morning,' he said. 'What's the story?'

'You ever see *Pandora's Box*?'

'Louise Brooks? Sure I have. My first crush, in fact. Some might say my first love. I always had crushes on girls with bobs because of her. Still do.'

'Oh, yeah?' I laughed out loud. 'That doesn't surprise me at all.'

'You've seen the poster in my living room, right?'

'I've never been to your apartment,' I said.

He looked shocked. 'You haven't?'

'Never.'

'In all this time? These . . . what is it, three years?'

'Almost.'

'You're kidding me,' he said, shaking his head. 'I'm not very polite, am I?'

I laughed. 'George, it's where you live. It never even crossed my mind.'

'True, but in all this time . . .'

He was looking at me strangely, confused. I knew he was seeing me in a new way. He probably had no idea why, but I did.

Because I was changing. Changing back. They were coming for me. He could see it, sense that something was different.

'Anyway, I have a vintage Louise Brooks poster over my couch that I got at an auction years ago. I'll have to have you up soon for coffee.'

'That would be nice. The film is playing at Film Forum. I'm going Wednesday afternoon. I wish you could come with us.'

'Well, unfortunately, due to my incredible generosity, it seems my sole employee has the day off.'

'That *is* unfortunate,' I said.

'Who are you going with?'

As casually as I could, I said, 'My friend Veronica.'

'Veronica? Have you mentioned her before?'

'No, but . . .' I hesitated. Wondered if I should tell him about her and what I was thinking. *She was made for you,* I wanted to say. Thinking it made me feel whole again, almost. But what I said was 'She's a new friend. Very beautiful, smart. Different. I think you'd really like her.' And then, my heart racing, 'I was thinking she might be a good date for you.'

'Oh, you do?' He looked at me, amused.

'For the Paradise Ball. She's already agreed to go, as it happens.'

'Oh, has she?' He sighed, shaking his head. 'You sure you don't just want to come yourself? It will be great fun.'

'George,' I said. 'You need to find someone. Someone you want to be with. Trust an old lady.'

He lifted up his hands. 'I hear that all the time. But I'm not at all convinced that everyone is made for relationships. I'm not sure I'm made for one. I sometimes think I would have been better off never getting married in the first place.'

'You just haven't found the person you're meant to be with,' I said automatically. 'Believe me. You and Veronica will have a wonderful time.'

'Well, we'll see,' he said. 'Bring her on, then, if you insist on breaking my heart yourself. Who is she, anyway? How do you know her?' He looked over and seemed to notice me then for the first time. 'You look great, by the way. Your hair is different.'

I blushed. 'Thanks,' I said. 'Actually, she did this. She does hair, and she sews, and she writes . . . She's something of a force of nature. Owns a darling little salon in the East Village, all pink and white. And she's stunningly beautiful, but not at all self-conscious. And, more than anything, she's just so . . . *alive*.'

'Well,' he said. 'A girl like that might find me a bit . . . on the dull side, don't you think? I mean, aside from my obvious charm.'

'Don't be ridiculous,' I said. 'She'll be mad about you.'

'If you say so.' He smiled, pointing to the book I'd left open beside me. 'So what are you reading?'

'*The Cottingley Fairies*.' I picked it up and showed him.

'Let me see.' He took the book from me and slowly flipped through it. 'Oh, yes, the two little girls. You know, there's a movie that came out a while ago. And I know I've seen those photos in person. At the Frick, I think. They're pretty interesting, aren't they?'

'The photos are here, in New York?'

'I think so. Well, at least they were at one point. I don't know, really. There are a few fairy-themed pieces at the Frick, as I recall, so I might be confusing them with something else. Actually, I think they just have a few paintings they recently acquired. From the fairy craze in England. The *Times* had a piece on it.'

I looked at him carefully. Could he know what he was saying? 'I don't think I've ever been there,' I said.

'Never been to the Frick? Really? I thought you were from New York. You should go. I think you'd love it. It's the private collection of an old steel magnate. A mansion full of art. You can feel the ghosts in that place.'

'Oh, yes,' I said. I laughed, self-conscious. 'I have heard of it. Of course. Things get a little jumbled when you get to be my age, George.'

'You act like you're a hundred years old, Lil.'

'It sure feels like it,' I said.

He paused, then shook his head, looking at me. 'So. Louise Brooks, huh?'

'That's right.'

'Remember, Lil. I'm no good at this.'

'Lucky for you,' I said, 'I am.'

CHAPTER EIGHT

he sun was dropping in the sky, melting into the mountains. The palace spread out under me like a silver river, the sun hitting the thousand steps that led to the front gate and the great clock resting on top of it. Turrets pierced the sky, flags waving back and forth at their tips.

I flew above it, slicing through the air, my arms outstretched and my wings spread to their full span. The clouds like mist against my face.

I could feel the excitement that afternoon as the whole kingdom prepared for the ball. It was the night everyone had looked forward to for months, during all the flat, ordinary days that made up their lives. No one had ever experienced the kind of breathless anticipation that had erupted when the king sent out a batch of engraved invitations a few months before – invitations the servants carried from estate to estate and girls hid under their pillows and inside their corsets and some families even had gilded, knowing it was the only royal invitation they'd ever receive – announcing that his son was ready to pick a wife. Every household in the kingdom had been thrown into a frenzy of preparation. Every daughter had been starved and fitted with corsets and made to dance for hours each night so that she might be the most graceful girl there. Mothers and fathers dreamed of the favors a royal marriage would bring upon them – the spoils of war, the increased land allotments, the invitations to royal hunts and festival day celebrations – and consulted astrologers and witches over which gown should be worn with which pair of shoes. Even the peasants were excited, as the king had arranged for troubadours and musicians and players to visit each village, and for vats of wine and all manner of delicacies – candy-covered nuts, roasted pheasants, flowers sculpted out of sugar – to be served in the village squares.

It was a night to burst forth in the world, to let yourself shine like some sort of star in heaven, to make men and women and even the king or queen laugh at your wit and admire your carriage and beauty. The kingdom's children were all drunk with music and drink and promise, and most would stay until the very beginnings of the dawn appeared on the horizon.

The peasants dreamed as they finished their day's work, imagining the palace's dazzling walls that were said to be coated in diamonds and pearls.

'The pearls are as big as apricots,' mothers whispered to their children as they sat in circles and cleaned wheat. 'And the chandeliers are like thousands of icicles hanging from the ceiling. It is like the most beautiful winter day, when the fields are full of snow angels, except the snow and ice are diamonds and it's not cold at all.'

Noble parents told their children about the prince, how he was the most handsome man in the world and could defeat fifty men in battle while composing love poetry that would make a hardened criminal weep. Still more told stories about the palace balls: the endless dancing, the way the women would whirl over the shiny marble floors while the men pushed them out and gathered them back up again. They described the heavenly sound of the violins and trumpets, the pianos that sounded as delicate as little raindrops falling on glass. 'And tonight you will see it all for yourselves,' they would finish.

I listened to them, and their longing.

I dropped down to earth, to the palace. Below me, well-wishers streamed in and out of the front gates, and the cooks hauled slaughtered chickens and pigs and hens and vats of wine and ale into the kitchens in back. Servants floated lit candles into the moat and seamstresses flew up the steps for last-minute adjustments.

I thought of Maybeth and Gladys and Lucibell and the other young fairies, all of them scattered through the kingdom to do their parts, whispering into the ears of young men and women, guiding them to their fates. The prince was not the only one destined to find a spouse this night. And here I was, tasked with the most difficult and prestigious job of all, and I wanted no part of it.

I knew he was standing in front of his mirror, adjusting his suit. I felt him inside of me. Thinking of me. He had spent nights tossing in his bed, wondering at the way I'd appeared to him, wondering if he would see me again. 'I am right here,' I whispered, and let the words make their way into him. I could taste him. I could feel him just as clearly as I could feel the air pushing against my face, the water droplets forming on my cheeks.

I could see myself in his thoughts. My human, physical self

and the way I'd appeared before him and lifted my lips to his. I was giddy with happiness, despite everything, and I let myself sink into his thoughts more deeply, until I could feel the way his blood moved faster as he imagined holding me, dancing with me at the ball, tracing a line down my neck with his lips. I knew it was wrong, but I just wanted one more moment with him. Soon enough I would go to Cinderella and fulfill my duty, return to my own world.

I did not want to move, even when I knew it was time, when I could just start to hear the clip-clopping of the horses and squeak of the carriages as they raced through the early evening toward the palace, carriages in which splendid young women sat dressed to the nines, their hearts pounding and cheeks flushed, their fluttering hands smoothing their hair and eyebrows and dresses.

Finally, I forced myself away from the palace, from his thoughts, and into the air. Over the fields and past noble estates, over forests and rivers, my heart breaking as I moved from him to her, rushing toward fate . . . until I landed on a branch outside her window. My palms against the bark. The air chilly against my face, excitement and energy rushing from the house in waves.

For a moment I was suspended between worlds, selves.

And then I bent down and peered into her room.

She stood in front of the glass. Tears on her face as she heard doors slam, her stepsisters and stepmother rushing down the stairs and to the carriage outside. She had spent the last few hours helping them get ready. Carrying dress after dress from the closets to the bed, helping her sisters step in and out of each one. She had helped them string jewels through their swept-back hair and around their necks. She had brought them tea and water, listened as they dreamed about the night in front of them – who would be there, which girl the prince would choose to marry. She had told the stablemen and coachmen to prepare the carriage, ordering that they leave precisely at 7:30 P.M., one hour after the ball was set to begin.

I fluttered about the windows, slipped through the tree branches, and waited.

I watched her stepsisters and stepmother emerge from the house. Like exotic birds in their elaborate gowns and jewels, their hair stacked on their heads like layers of cake. The older sister in bright gold and purple, a brocaded dress that flared out at her hips and trailed behind her for several feet. The younger, more beautiful sister in a diaphanous light green, the mother festooned with diamonds and rubies, which wove through her hennaed red hair and dripped down into her impressive cleavage.

'You all look ravishing, ladies,' the coachman said, smiling, as he held open the carriage door.

'Really?' the older sister said, stepping into the carriage, glowing with more happiness than she would ever feel again.

The mother swatted her backside with a jewel-coated fan. 'A young lady never sounds desperate for a compliment,' she said. 'Not even from the king himself.'

The younger sister snickered as she followed her mother into the carriage, the coachman shutting the door behind her.

As they passed under me, I felt their longing so strongly I became dizzy with it.

I rested my back against the bark, recovering, peering through the leaves, watching the carriage turn off onto the path that led to the castle, and all the while, a lump in my throat. A feeling like I couldn't breathe.

Finally, I left the branches and the tree, and passed through the window into her room.

'I am your fairy godmother,' I said, as my body transformed and filled out.

She turned. A strange cold feeling ran through me as I watched her. I could taste the sadness on her. And yet she was made for him. He was her destiny.

Her face dropped open. She was luminous, even then. 'You,' she whispered.

'I am here,' I said, 'to send you to the ball.'

I spotted her on the corner of Sixth Avenue and Houston, unmistakable with her tall boots, her bright, sweeping hair, the shimmering dress and pale skin that looked even paler in the sunlight. Her sleeves were short and I could see colorful designs snaking down her arm. As if she were from another world. She was standing in front of a food cart, gesticulating to the man behind it.

'Veronica,' I called out as I approached.

When she turned, her face lit up, and she smiled widely. 'Lil!' she said. 'You caught me. I'm starving.'

The man was loading a pita full of falafel, onions, and white and red sauces.

'I can't believe you're going to eat that,' I said. 'You look as if you live on air.'

She shrugged. 'Well. Pregnancy does that to a gal.'

I looked at her in shock.

'I'm kidding!'

The man wrapped the concoction in foil and handed it to her. 'Mmmm,' she said exaggeratedly, taking the food and paying him. 'I love sloppy street food. One of my favorite things about this city. Where I come from, you'd have to make a real commitment to get food like this.'

'It does smell good,' I admitted.

We walked slowly toward the theater as she took a big bite and handed the overflowing pita to me. I took a small bite, trying to be delicate.

'I don't think there is any better way to bond,' she said. 'We might as well be blood sisters now.'

We ate half the pita before she tossed it in a trash can, then bought our tickets and entered the theater lobby, with its coffee bar and black-and-white posters on the wall. I felt swept into it suddenly, and I remembered how much I had loved the movies once: the glamorous men and women glimmering from the dark screen, the thick velvet curtains that pulled back on either side. I hadn't been in a theater in years.

'I'm so glad you asked me to come today,' I said. 'You have no idea what a treat this is for me.'

'Oh, me, too,' she said, handing her ticket to the young usher and giving him a flirty smile.

He blushed back at her.

We went into the theater and sat down side by side in the dark and hush of it. Veronica kicked up her boots onto the seat in front of her and slid down, clasping her hands in her lap.

'Look at how many people are here,' Veronica whispered. 'In the middle of the day. I love that. Everyone bailing out on the real world to see some old flapper film. Awesome.'

I looked around the theater, then back at her. I felt as if I were seeing the world through Veronica's eyes, the power of her vision was so strong. It was the same world, but brighter and more colorful than it had been before. There was no trace now of the sadness she'd felt only two days before, but I knew she occupied each moment fully, perfectly, and that the next time she felt pain or disappointment, she'd weep just as openly.

It was this that I had envied once. Exactly this.

The film began, but it was hard to pay attention. Gorgeous images flickered over me, sumptuous, as if from a dream. I lost track of time, let them lull me into an almost-sleep.

'Lil.' I opened my eyes, and Veronica was leaning into my ear, whispering. 'Are you into this, Lil?'

'Yes,' I said. I sat up to clear my head. 'Yes. It's beautiful.'

'Oh, okay.' She sank back down in her seat.

After a moment I leaned in toward her. 'Why?'

'I don't know, it's a little slow. I was just seeing what you thought.'

'Shh!' A woman in front of us turned and looked at us sharply.

I lowered my voice. 'Well. It is pretty slow.'

She looked up at me sheepishly, her eyebrows raised. 'Do you . . . maybe want to go?'

'Do you?'

She made a face, then nodded. 'Unless you don't.'

'Oh, I do.' I stood, and she followed, and we made our way out of the theater, stumbling over people's feet and purses to get to the aisle. The moment we were in the hallway again, we both burst out laughing.

'I thought I was going to die of boredom,' she said, taking my arm and pulling me to the exit. 'That was beautiful to look at, but my *gawd*! I like a bit more plot with my well-coiffed dames.'

'I know,' I said, gasping for breath. I felt a part of things. A part of things!

We erupted onto the sidewalk, almost colliding with a man walking a fluffy little huge-eyed dog. Veronica stopped in her tracks, and the dog bounded up to her.

'Aren't you precious!' she cried out, dropping to her knees and reaching out to the dog, who immediately turned and tried to jump up onto my body.

'Oh, it likes you!' she said.

'Yes,' I said. I bent down and looked at the dog, its melting black eyes. I thought of my sister and the horse, how it had looked at her. I wondered if she was nearby, if the animal sensed her.

I patted the dog's head, my hand disappearing into its fur. I could hear Veronica and the man talking, but as if from a distance, about Pomeranians and the dog's strange habits and a dog named Farrah that Veronica had kept as a child.

The animal kept blinking at me, staring up at me as I ran my hand through its fur.

'You see her, don't you?' I whispered.

The animal blinked and let out a small bark, and then Veronica was kneeling beside me, taking its face in her hands. 'Look at how pretty you are,' she said. I looked up at the man, his smooth young face.

'Have a great night, girls,' he said, nodding at us. 'Come on, Janet.'

'Janet!' Veronica repeated as the man and dog walked away. 'I love it! Lil, if that man weren't gay, I'd totally date him just to be near Janet. I think I'm in love with her.' She sighed dramatically and clutched her heart as we headed along Houston and then up Sixth Avenue. I watched men's heads turn as she passed, following her tall, slinky body.

We wandered up Sixth for a while, then turned west onto the zigzagging streets of the West Village. Talking casually about whatever entered our minds. It was a day of playing hooky from everything, and I was surprised at how well my body behaved, how good I felt.

'I love this part of town,' Veronica said. 'I always wonder who lives in these gorgeous places. Probably investment bankers and fashion models, but I imagine all kinds of romantic doings behind these doors.'

'Yes,' I said. 'I love them, too.'

She stopped suddenly and turned to me. 'You're really cool, Lil. You know that?'

It was disarming, the way she could come out with things like that. 'Thanks,' I said.

'There's just something . . . different about you. Like I said before. Like you know things. Do other people see that?'

'Actually, most people your age don't see someone like me at all.'

'That's terrible! Don't say that.'

'No, it's true. It's easy for people to miss things.'

'Well, there's something about you,' she said. 'It feels like you're just . . . wise. I don't know, I know it sounds flaky, but I totally believe in all of that stuff – like past lives, like if someone hits you in a certain way, then you have to figure out why. I feel like I was meant to meet you.'

'To go to a ball?'

'A ball?' She laughed. 'Maybe.'

It was growing dark, and the full moon had come out, rimmed by clouds. I pointed up at it. 'There's always a beautiful moon here, isn't there? No stars, but the moon over the city is always so beautiful.'

'Yeah,' she said. 'I miss it, though, the sky full of stars. You can forget about it, living here.'

Leisurely, we walked back to Sixth. The world seemed glowing, magical: the streetlamps just clicking on, the lights draped across windows and awnings, the people strolling past as if, for once, there was no specific place to go. I breathed in and smiled up at the sparse treetops, the night sky.

'Lillian?'

I heard my name once, then a second time, a bit louder. I turned, surprised.

A woman walked up, shaking her head. 'I can't believe it, after all these years.' She looked like she was in her late fifties, with dark gray hair falling in short waves around her face. Well kempt.

Veronica looked back and forth from me to the woman, her face open and expectant. Suddenly my back ached, my wings pressed against the bandages.

'I'm sorry,' I said, 'I don't . . .'

'You don't remember me? Come on. I may be an old lady now, but I don't look so different, do I? You don't!'

'I'm sorry,' I said. I wasn't sure what to think or say. Did I know her? Had she been sent to me? She couldn't be a fairy, not this woman.

We were stopped right in the middle of the street, crossing Tenth. A bag banged my arm as a young woman rushed by. I moved closer to the curb, and Veronica and the woman followed.

'It's Audrey,' she said. 'Remember me? I was friends with you and your sister.'

'Oh, you knew Maybeth!' Veronica said, clapping her hands together.

'Maybeth?' the woman repeated.

'I don't . . .' And I realized then what was happening. My powers were returning. My sister was close by. Of course it would affect the occasional human, even cause some to know my name.

'I don't have a sister,' I said gently. 'Not anymore. I think you're confusing me with someone else.'

'Your name is Lillian, though, right? You know, I did know your sister.' Her face clouded over, looked serious.

'I'm sorry,' I said. 'We're in a hurry. You're making some mistake, I think.'

The woman just stood there, watching me.

'Again, I'm sorry,' I said. 'But we do have to go.'

I started walking then, letting Veronica follow.

'You didn't know that woman?' she asked tentatively, after a few minutes had passed.

'No.'

'But she knew your name . . .'

'I think she knows me from the bookstore. She's probably just confusing me with someone else.'

'Oh, that could be,' she said. 'We're just a few blocks away, aren't we?'

'A few blocks from your future?' I asked, winking at her. I forced myself to smile, and she rolled her eyes at me, laughing. 'Why, yes, we are.'

CHAPTER NINE

recognize you,' she said, her eyes filling with tears.

'Yes,' I said, as gently as I could. 'I'm your fairy godmother. I came to you before, many years ago, but you may not remember.'

'Why have you come now?'

There was something of the scared animal about her. I looked down the length of her body. The pale bruises on her arms. Her skin dusted with ash. The rags she wore, stained with dirt.

'Child,' I said, reaching out to her. 'I'm here to send you to the ball.'

'The ball?'

'Yes, the ball that the king and queen are throwing tonight, in the palace.'

She just stared at me, her eyes blue and glowing. 'My stepsisters are there,' she said. 'I helped them prepare. They spent weeks preparing. It's not a place for someone like me.'

It was hard for me to speak. It felt as if something in my chest was on fire. For a moment we stood and watched each other.

'That is why I'm here,' I said finally, reaching out and touching her arm. 'We'll get you all ready, and you will be the most beautiful girl there.'

She shook her head, unbelieving. 'But my chores ...' she said, flailing her arms. 'I have so many things left to do still. You don't know what happens to me if I don't finish my chores. I should be doing them now.'

'Child,' I said. 'You don't need to worry. I can take care of everything.' I took her hands in mine and was surprised to feel how cracked and callused they were. She didn't try to hide them.

'I'm sorry, Godmother, I do not mean to be impolite.'

'It's fine, child. But we need to hurry. The ball is starting even now.'

'Thank you. Thank you. I'm all alone here.' Something in her softened then. She fell into my arms, clinging to me. For a moment I just stood there, in shock. The only human I'd been this close to before was the prince. Strands of her hair floated up into my face, tickling me, smelling like powder.

'You're not alone now, my dear,' I said. 'You won't be alone again.'

I smiled, but I was disoriented by the feelings moving from her to me. An emptiness, like a black hole. Right from her and into my chest. It was strange, but not unpleasant. I wanted that, the space in her that he would fill.

I extracted myself from her and took her face in my palm. 'Are you ready? The clock is ticking, you know, and look at you.'

'Yes,' she said. 'I am a mess, Godmother. Thank you for helping me.'

She looked at me with such love then. I could do anything to her. I looked away, uncomfortable.

'Now, you'll need a dress.'

She laughed like a small child, lifting her hand to her face. 'Am I really going to the ball? A ball at the palace?'

'Yes.'

'What will my stepsisters and stepmother say? They've been talking of the ball for months. Oh, Godmother, you have no idea. They've ordered hundreds of dresses that I have ironed and washed in the river and let air in the gardens. They've refused to eat for weeks. They all believe that the prince will love them.'

A stab of annoyance moved through me, listening to her.

'They will not recognize you. But the prince, he will, the moment you walk in. He has been waiting for you. His whole life.'

She shook her head, put her hands to her head. 'I am not worthy of a prince.'

'You are his destiny, just as he is yours.'

The sun was just beginning to turn, melting over the line of trees outside. The room smelled like dust and grass and flowers. How could she be sad in such a world? She should be embracing all of it, I thought. All of it.

'I don't think I have a destiny, Godmother.'

'Everyone has a destiny. And I am here to help you meet yours. Now, let's get started. Let's see. What do you need?'

At that moment I felt him. The prince. In his chambers, thinking of me. In the middle of the dance floor in his suit. Something broke in my chest, and I gasped with pain.

'What's wrong, Godmother?' She rushed forward, put her hand out on my arm.

I took a breath, let the pain spread through me.

'Nothing,' I said, gently pushing her hand away. 'You'll need a beautiful dress. You'll need to be the most beautiful girl there.'

Her face seemed to change in the light. A flash of pleasure moved across it. She had dreamed of him, in the field. Longed for him as she scrubbed and mopped and hung wet clothes in the sun.

'Now, hurry. Go into the garden and bring me back three berries from the silver tree that grows in the center.'

'Oh!' she said. 'The one the robins live in?'

I nodded, unable to speak, and with delight she turned on her heel and left the room. I heard her slight step on the twisting stone stairs.

I sat on her bed, suddenly feeling as if my chest were collapsing in on itself. I was astonished at what happened next. My throat opened. Hot liquid ran from my eyes and down my face. Droplets moved down my chin to the silk of my dress. I stood and walked to the glass, peering in at myself. I had never felt anything like it. That ache! The tears that wet my skin. My eyes were bright green and filled with water.

What was happening to me?

I knew that in this form, in human bodies, we took on human attributes, but I had never felt anything like this. It consumed me. Her pain had become my pain. All I wanted, *all I wanted*, was him. I was convinced suddenly that the only thing that could heal me was him. Was this how she felt all the time?

I smoothed my hands over my human body. Down my wet face, my long neck, my breasts and waist and belly. Is this what he would feel? Is this what he was imagining, even now? I moved my face in the mirror, the line of my cheekbones catching the light, my thick lashes dotted with tears.

I felt so full!

I leaned my head back, imagined his mouth on my mouth,

the palm of his hand sliding across my spine, the way it had felt to breathe in his breath, feel his heart beating against my skin.

I heard her rushing up the stairs. For an instant I imagined leaving her here, going in her place. Me being the one in the dress, me walking into the palace and not having to hide, not having to be invisible, no longer fluttering in the corners of the room, whispering thoughts and dreams into them, but standing right there in the center of everything, my full beauty unmasked, being able to take all of it up into me until they were blinded from it and he could not see or feel anything except my hand on his, my eyes watching him.

'Godmother?'

It was like she'd slapped me.

I whirled around to face her.

She dropped the branch of berries she'd been clutching in her hand.

'Come here,' I said, stretching out my hand to her, and she shrank back, toward the door.

'Who are you?' she breathed, and I knew that something in my face had changed, scared her.

And then something in me snapped off, and I loved her again. 'I am your fairy godmother,' I said. 'As I told you.'

'Why have you come?'

'To send you to the ball.'

'But why? Why me?'

'Because it is your destiny. Your mother was a friend to the fairies, and for that reason her child is to be queen of all of this kingdom.'

'Oh. My mother! My father buried my mother under a silver tree that robins live in.'

'I know. I was there. All of us were.'

'You were there?'

'Don't you remember? You were a child. We were covering you. We were all over you.'

'No,' she whispered. 'I don't remember anything. Just the silver tree and the hole my father dug under it.'

'Bring those to me,' I said, pointing to the berries on the ground. My face was dry now, though I felt remnants of what had passed over me before.

She bent down and picked them up, handed them to me.

Staring straight at her, I plucked off the first berry, then flicked it out of my hands and toward her. She blinked, and in that moment her soiled smock disappeared. In its place appeared a long pale blue silk dress that nipped into her waist and flared down to the floor. Her skin and hair gleamed, and her feet were bare.

She held up her arms and stared in amazement, then rubbed her hands down the silk that covered her body.

'How did . . . ?'

'Shhh,' I said, silencing her. I held out the twig. 'Pick two more.'

She looked at me, her eyes wide, and then reached forward and touched one berry, then another. I plucked them off, opened my palm and let them drop to the floor. As they hit the stone, they transformed into a pair of sparkling glass slippers.

She gasped. 'Oh!' she said. 'They are so . . . I can't believe it.'

'Yes,' I said. Outside, the sun was sinking into the mountains, and I knew they were all already dancing. She was beautiful and would be there soon, and whatever heart I had was broken. 'Put them on.'

She stepped into the shoes, leaning into the wall to balance herself. They fit over her feet perfectly, curving them into arches.

'What are you doing now?' George asked a few days later, pulling out his keys and gesturing for me to leave the store before him. I stepped outside; the early evening was balmy, still light, with a breeze moving through it.

'Heading uptown,' I said. 'Going home.'

He smiled. 'I'm headed that way, too. Stopping by a friend's barbecue. Why don't you come along?'

'Oh,' I said. I had been looking forward to slipping out of my clothes, the bandages. 'I don't know. I'm feeling a little tired.'

George clicked the last lock shut and turned back to me. 'At least walk with me,' he said. 'And see how you feel in a bit.' He raised his eyebrows up and down.

'I am an old woman, George,' I said, smiling now. 'I can't be showing up at barbecues.'

He grabbed my hand, folded it up in his. I pulled away, instinctively, but he held tight. 'It's a beautiful evening, Lil. At least take a walk with me. Okay?' The sky behind him was silver, and the sun spilled through. 'Hey. I'm letting you set me up. I don't ever let anyone set me up. Ever. You owe me.'

He looked right at me, his dark eyes pinning me to the spot, to the sidewalk in front of the store. *He senses things*, I thought. I watched him standing there, so beautiful with his dark hair flipping about. Almost like Theodore.

'Come on,' he said, pulling me by the hand.

It was nice, walking with George. I closed my eyes for a second, feeling my hand in his, imagining I was a young woman walking these streets with someone like Theodore, just a regular young woman on a summer afternoon, heading to a barbecue with her beau. I giggled.

'What is it?' George was watching me, a half smile on his face. 'What are you thinking about?'

'Oh, nothing,' I said, quickly shaking my head, embarrassed. 'Just remembering something.'

'Tell me,' he said, dropping my hand and gesturing in the air. 'You've been working in the store for a few years now, and I know hardly anything about you or your life. You should tell me some things, don't you think? It's good for the soul.'

'What do you want me to tell you?'

'Well,' he said, swerving around a woman pushing a stroller and then veering back to me, 'why don't you tell me what you were remembering? You always seem to be remembering. Right?'

I felt self-conscious suddenly and was grateful for the movement of the streets, the people. 'I just was remembering how things used to be,' I said. 'Being young. How different things were.'

He smiled. 'I know. You need to get out more, Lil. Don't you think? Not that I should talk.'

I looked at him and saw he was being sweet. 'Maybe.'

'I remember a lot, too,' he said. 'I mean, I spend a lot of time remembering the past. It's not healthy, but I do it.'

'What do you think about?' I asked. I looked at him differently then, and it was as if I had a way in: I saw him as strange, a little melancholy. The thought popped into my head: He needed to fall in love. He would fall in love. With her.

'I don't know,' he said. 'When I was young, I thought I'd be a poet or a writer. I was going to write novels hunched over an old typewriter, move to Paris or something. That kind of thing. But now look at me.'

'What do you mean, look at you? You're doing so well!' I thought of the bookstore: its crowded shelves and musty smell, its glittering cases, filled with treasures. I couldn't think of anything more beautiful.

'The store's okay, but I guess I just thought my life would be . . . bigger. Bigger than what it is now.' We were crossing Fourteenth Street, heading up toward Chelsea. The city felt fresher, more open. 'You're coming with me, aren't you?' he asked. 'We could both use some time among people, don't you think?'

I smiled. 'Yes,' I said. I looked around, at the wide street, the people, the fading sky. 'Yes, I could.'

'Great,' he said. 'I've got to drop something off real quick first. Do you mind? I promised my friend a book for one of his clients.'

'Okay.'

We turned onto Twenty-third Street. He gestured to our left, and I looked up at a brick building with lacy wrought-iron balconies jutting out, a HOTEL sign swooping down.

'He's just in here,' he said. 'Has his own gym, if you can believe it.'

George pulled me through the swinging doors and into a lobby, where various people were scattered about on the mismatched couches and clashing paintings hung on the walls. He led me past the desk and to the right, past an elevator and through a creaking doorway, then up a set of marbly white stairs with filigreed iron banisters. We reached a landing, and the stairs swung around and kept going.

On the next floor, George led me down a corridor, with more hallways shooting off it. We stopped in front of a black door and walked in.

I was surprised by the incongruity of the scene: a gym, radiating healthfulness, stuck amid the crumbling, faded beauty of the rest of the building. The array of workout and weight-lifting equipment, the heavy fan blowing air through the room, the mirrors on the walls, a woman riding one of the bikes and a man sitting in an elaborate machine with his arms stretched out on either side of him.

I wanted to cry out with delight. In New York you could find almost anything behind a closed door.

'Hey!' A muscular blond man walked up and slapped George on the arm. 'What's up?'

'Not much,' George said. 'Heading up to Jennifer's with my friend Lil. I brought your book.' He pulled out a copy of *Tropic of Cancer* from his bag and handed it to the man. Then he looked at me and winked. 'First edition,' George whispered.

'Thanks,' his friend said, taking the book. 'I'm Mark, by the way. George always hooks me up. My client's going to go crazy over this. How are you doing?'

'Good,' I said.

'Lil works with me,' George said. He looked at me. 'Mark's a trainer.'

'Oh, yeah,' Mark said, to my surprise. 'I've heard about you. George says you've straightened the place out.'

'He does?'

'Hell, yeah,' Mark said.

'He is very generous to say that.' I kept watching the man on the machine. His arms spread out like wings, in and out. 'What's he doing?' I asked. 'What is that machine?'

'Oh, you can do all kinds of stuff on that. Right now he's working on the muscles around his shoulder blades and upper arms.'

'It looks like he's flying,' I said.

'It's a great exercise, a great machine. You want to try it?'

George laughed, rolled his eyes. 'He never stops. He's like a preacher.'

'It wouldn't hurt you to use it, either, my friend.' He looked at me. 'I'm always trying to get him in here, but he's always coming up with some lame excuse.'

'I'm not exactly a jock,' George said, shrugging.

'You're telling me,' Mark said. 'Lil here could probably run you into the ground.'

I was excited suddenly. I was changing, and I wanted to see what my body could do. 'I'll try it,' I said. I had a vision then of myself: Hair flowing like autumn leaves, my body smooth and soft. Young again.

George looked at me in surprise. 'I'm impressed,' he said. 'You might actually shame me into doing a push-up.'

When the man on the machine finished a minute later, Mark led me, carefully but firmly, over to the looming contraption. He motioned for me to sit, then stood above me and pulled down the arms of the machine, locking them in place. From them he pulled out two long cords with handles on the ends and motioned for me to put my hands in.

'Go on, take these. Grab hold,' he said.

I slipped my hands through.

Mark cupped his palms around my hands. 'I'm going to let go,' he said. 'Just hold this here, keep holding it. Don't let go. I'm not even putting weight on this, okay?'

He released his grip then, and I felt a strong force pulling on me from either side. The pressure of it slid up my arms, burned up to my shoulders. I could feel my wings rustling behind me and pushing into my skin.

'Pull,' he said, leaning into me. He tapped my forearm, the fleshy part underneath, and I moved my arms, following his lead until they were stretched out on both sides of me.

'Good,' he said. He stood back and watched me, keeping his hands out, hovering on either side of me. 'Now press back in again, to where you started, and do it again. You're doing great.'

I let the pain of it rip through my arms and into my blood. It moved into my back now, the burning, stretching from my shoulders and down my spine. It hurt, but it felt wonderful, too. I was using muscles I hadn't used since I'd been able to fly.

It flared up in me in a second: the desire to fly.

Sun streamed in through the window, reflecting onto the mirror in front of me. I glanced up, but I could not focus in. All I knew was the stretch of the cord, the scraping sound of it pulling back and forth.

I felt a hand on my shoulder, and a moment later the movement stopped. My body became solid again. I looked up. It was only then that I noticed the feathers drifting in the air, fluttering down to the floor. Mark's eyes met mine. The sound of the bike had stopped. The burning ran up and down my arms.

'It really is like you're flying, isn't it?' he whispered.

'Yes,' I said.

George walked over then. 'Have you had enough yet, Lil?' he asked, rubbing his hands together and then slapping Mark on the back. 'I think you've tortured her sufficiently.'

I looked back at Mark, who just stared at me. 'Good job,' he said. 'You should work on those muscles, get them going. Come by anytime.'

*

We walked back up Eighth Avenue. Every cell in my body was alive and pulsing. I could feel my shoulders, still in that movement. I reached up my arms and stretched them back.

'Sore?' George asked.

'A little,' I said, dropping my arms to the side. 'I was not expecting that today.'

It was a restless energy moving through me. The world was so bright. I was tired, I realized, of spending night after night in my apartment, watching television, eating, being alone, punishing myself.

'Sorry,' he said. 'I hope that wasn't uncomfortable for you.' He was shy suddenly, unable to meet my eyes.

I looked at him, surprised. 'No,' I said, touching his arm. 'I loved it. Thank you.'

'I'm glad,' George asked. 'Are you okay, though? You look like you're not feeling well.'

'Yes,' I said, turning back to him. But he was right; I didn't feel okay. I felt as if my arms and shoulders were on fire, as if I wanted to tear down the street, screaming at the top of my lungs.

George just looked at me, squinting his dark eyes, and then swerved to miss a tall young man elbowing past.

We walked up the blocks, silent. There was a gnawing inside me that was becoming a steady ache, and I kept hearing the scraping back and forth of wire and metal, feeling that pull in my back.

I watched an old man walk by, cradling a small dog in his arms. A young Asian couple were wrapped together like lettuce leaves, their arms around each other's waists and their hands touching. I wondered how they managed to move.

I shook my shoulders, stretched out my arms. The whole day seemed to have shifted over and tilted on its side. As we passed the Fashion Institute, a blonde woman with her hands full of shopping bags rammed into me, one of her bags pressing into my thigh. I found myself reaching out and smacking it away as she passed.

George laughed. 'I hate this part of town,' he said. 'And we're not nearly in the worst of it. People everywhere. You can't even move.'

I did not want him to see how out of sorts I was. My shoulders ached no matter what I did. I extended my arms in front of me and pulled them back. I loosened the tension in my back, shook myself out.

A clump of feathers drifted into the air and fell around us. One landed on George's cheek, and he brushed it off, barely noticing.

'You ever been inside the Garden, Lil?' he asked. The round dome of Madison Square Garden loomed up ahead. 'My brother got comp tickets to a Rangers game last year, and we sat up in those boxes up top, these suites with couches and refrigerators. It felt like you could reach down and touch the ice from up there.'

'No,' I said. 'I don't think I've done that.'

I shifted again and noticed more feathers popping into the air. My heart lurched after them.

'You like hockey?'

'I guess,' I said. One of the feathers landed in a woman's long dark hair. I was tempted to reach out and pluck it off. I had no idea what George was talking about.

'I love it. I'm not much of a sports guy, but I love hockey.

We used to play as kids, my brother and I, when the lake behind our house froze over. Great times.'

'That sounds nice,' I said. 'Your brother and you.' I tried to hold my shoulders still, clench in my muscles, but my body was absolutely at odds with me.

'We had a lot of fun as kids,' he said. 'I think about going back there now.'

'Back where?' One of my wings began to unfold.

'Illinois,' he said. 'That's where we grew up, though our family is from New York, and we always had the business. Let's cross. She lives right there.' He pointed to a tall apartment building across the street. I looked around frantically for somewhere to hide. We were only a few blocks from my apartment, but I wouldn't make it till then.

I will be okay, I thought. I just needed to be alone. To unclench my wings and stop the pain coursing through me.

We stood at the corner of Thirty-third and Eighth Avenue, staring out over the traffic at the post office across the street, with its long columns and leisurely sweep of steps. I could barely breathe. Sweat dripped from my hair and down my forehead. My other wing unclenched. Cars whizzed past. About a hundred yellow taxicabs with their lights blinking. The drone of the cars, the honking, the sounds and the yelling and the *whoooosh* as they zipped by over lanes and lanes of traffic . . .

I want to fly, I thought then. *I have to fly.* My muscles were burning. My wings coming undone.

When the 'walk' signal finally came on, we crossed the street and entered the building. It seemed to take hours for us to move from the front desk, where the doorman called up and announced our arrival, past the lines of mailboxes, to the elevators. Feathers were popping into the air in whole clumps. I could feel the tingle of air against my skin, rushing up my back. The tickle of feathers. The ache in my muscles, yearning for release.

George caught a feather in his palm and spread out his fingers. 'Look,' he said, his voice full of wonder. 'How strange.'

I nodded and clutched my stomach. A spurt of feathers leaped into the air, then began to drift slowly down.

'My God, Lil,' George said, peering in at me. 'You don't look well at all.' He reached out to touch my shoulder.

'No!' I said, reeling back from him. He looked down at his palm and then back at me. He had touched a wing. I had felt his hand on the feathers and bone.

I looked at him, but the ache in my back was too strong for me to focus in.

'I think we need to take you to the hospital, Lil,' he said. He reached into his bag. I shut my eyes, and a steady line of white flared in front of me. My wings strained at my shirt. I was tensing my muscles so hard against them that I could feel them knot and pull, twist into circles and back out again.

I opened my eyes to see George, sheet white, his cell phone in his hands. 'I'm calling an ambulance,' he said. 'Right now.'

Just then the elevator doors opened and a small blonde woman walked out carrying a gym bag.

'Please,' I said, terror bubbling up in me as I pushed into the elevator. I clutched my stomach. 'Let's just go up there, okay? I feel nauseous, that's all.'

George stopped for a second, then snapped to attention, following me into the elevator and frantically pushing the button. 'Only eight floors,' he said. 'Hang on.'

We stood together, not talking, staring at the illuminated line of numbers on top of the door. I stepped back and felt a wing hit the wall behind me.

'Almost there, Lil,' George said, startling me. He was afraid to even look at me. Confused by the white feathers swirling in the air, all around us. I watched them land quietly on his black shirt, like snowflakes drifting down, and I felt my wings loosen more.

The doors opened finally, like an enormous sigh. George grabbed my hand, and we ran down the yellow hall, trailed by feathers and by the strange bony shapes pushing out from my back, straining my shirt, which had already begun to tear.

The running seemed almost to be the final straw. I was in searing, unbearable pain. And yet this was the closest I'd come to flight in years. I felt the feathers unfurl and my feet strain to leave the ground . . .

George stopped and started banging on the door. I held on to the wall to steady myself. A moment later a young woman answered. I could not even see her, just the shape of her and the shapes of several people behind her, scattered about, but I could feel the shift from friendliness to horror, the people gathering around and crying out, and then George pulling me through a hall and into a bathroom.

'Leave!' I cried, twisting from his grasp and pushing him out of the room. The moment I slammed the door shut, I heard a terrible rip. My bandages and shirt finally gave way, and my wings sprawled out on either side of me. I held out my arms and shimmied from the shirt, then sunk to the floor. My wings were like two separate bodies dancing above me. I heard them wreaking havoc: Sweeping along a shelf filled with cosmetics, which tumbled to the floor. Pushing past the plastic shower curtain and slapping the tiled shower wall. I glanced up, reached up to make sure the door was locked.

And then I was on my knees, retching into the toilet and letting out huge, racking sobs that used up all the air in my lungs and left me gasping.

'Lil!' I heard. Banging on the door.

'I'm okay,' I gasped. 'I'm okay!'

I fell back down and pressed my cheek to the tile floor. I heard another crash as my wings somehow unhooked a shower tray filled with shampoo and bath salts.

And then, quiet. I closed my eyes and let everything fade out, concentrating only on my body, releasing the pain and relaxing every muscle. My wings fluttered frantically, then finally settled and stilled. My muscles unclenched. The searing pain began to fade down to a dull throb. I wanted to fly so badly, from such a deep, deep place, that I ached and moaned with it. But the immediate pain was gone. Then the unbearable desire to fly moved to someplace buried within me, tamped down, back in its place. My wings were out and open, slowly flapping to and fro. The tile was cold against my cheek. The relief flowing through me was almost overwhelming.

'Lil?' It was George, followed by more rapping on the door.

I didn't answer. *It's okay*, I thought, *everything is okay now*. My wings fanned back and forth. The air streamed through them, the feathers, and they were weightless. Beautiful. I smiled into the floor, allowed myself that moment of relief, the joy of release. *If every moment*, I thought, *could be like this*.

'An ambulance is on its way,' George said through the door. 'You'll be okay. Everything will be okay. Don't be scared.'

I sat straight up, not even wincing when my right wing smashed into the shower rod and the curtain came crashing down.

'A what?'

'I know you don't like doctors,' he said, his voice low, soothing. 'But they'll take good care of you, I promise.'

I looked around wildly. I was in a small bathroom, no windows, nothing. A pain came into my stomach and the back of my throat, beating behind my eyes.

I shook it off and stood up. With every ounce of strength I had, I concentrated and pulled my wings back in, ignored the ripping as they folded in like an accordion, feather by feather, and clamped down against my skin. Grinding my teeth, smashing my lips together, I focused in and made one last push, until my wings folded in and lay flat against my back.

I bent down and picked up my ripped shirt – a loose black shirt, in tatters. I looked around frantically for something else, seeing only a stack of towels. Then I caught sight of myself in the mirror, standing there with my breasts hanging down, my skin wrinkled and shining with sweat, my face panicked, afraid. I flipped the shirt around and slid into it so that it was open and ripped in the front but my back was covered. I pulled the shirt in on both sides. There was enough fabric to cover me, if I had a way to hook the material.

'Lil, are you okay in there?' George again, his voice high and tense.

'I'll be right out!' I said, trying to sound normal, forcing my voice to stay low and still.

I pulled open the medicine cabinet, then slammed it shut again. I surveyed the shelves, the pots filled with Q-tips and creams and cotton balls. No safety pins, nothing I could use. I leaned in and pulled the two sides closed as far as they would go and knotted them together. I looked in the mirror again, my wrinkled soft stomach visible but the shirt covering me, my breasts and – I turned to see – my back.

I looked around the room, and at last I noticed the feathers everywhere, spread across the floor and the shelves, in the sink and tub. Panic moved through me as if it were a physical thing, and instantly I was on the floor again, gathering them with my hands, whole fists of them, almost crying out when they slipped from my grasp and back into the air.

'Lil!'

Under the sink I found a small broom and dustpan and grabbed at them, tried to sweep up as many feathers as possible and throw them in the toilet. They flew into the air and scattered onto the floor again. I dropped back onto the floor and swept desperately, keeping my hands on the piles. They seemed to be multiplying, growing. I grabbed at them, handful after handful, and pushed them underwater.

When I finally opened the door, George was practically beside himself. 'My God,' he said. 'I thought you were dying in there. Are you okay? What's going on?'

I watched him step back and look me over. A few people were lingering in the area; I could feel their eyes on me. I held a towel over my stomach.

'George,' I said, as calmly as I could. 'I'm fine now. I was a little sick, that's all. Food poisoning, I think.'

He just stared at me.

'What happened to your shirt?'

From the street I heard sirens. I glanced back into the

bathroom and saw feathers lying on the sink, on the floor, the toilet.

'I need to go home,' I said. 'I'm sorry.'

He didn't say anything. His eyes were wide and dark.

I caught sight of a terrace where people sat around a large table that had an umbrella jutting out of the middle, talking, eating, and laughing. Behind them the sky was fading, purplish, and the buildings rose in layers, their lit-up yellow windows like wounds in their sides.

For a moment it seemed so beautiful, like the night of the ball, like everything I could not have – either then or now – because of what I'd done.

'They're here, Lil,' he said. 'Just let them look at you.'

'I have to go,' I repeated, squeezing his arm, and with that I moved to the door, pulled it open, and ran down the hallway to the stairs.

CHAPTER TEN

She was ready. My work was done. I stood back and looked her over. I had outdone myself, I thought. But I didn't feel satisfied. Not even close.

Her face was radiant, perfect. The smudges of dirt were gone, the circles under her eyes disappeared. Her eyes were almost shockingly blue. Her starlight hair lay piled on her head, with long tendrils hanging down her neck. The gown nipped in her waist, flared out over her hips, and shimmied along her as she moved, stopping just above the glass slippers that shone like diamonds from under the hem. The dress's soft blue color lit up her skin, making it luminous and pale, almost iridescent. I looked at her and thought of pearls, the insides of shells.

We were rarely moved by human beauty, but I found myself frozen in front of her, with my heart caught in my throat. I loved her then, despite the ache in my stomach. She seemed absurd in the dusty stone room, standing in front of the cracked mirror, next to the straw mattress on the floor. I thought of her mother, her fairy blood. No matter how much magic I had worked on her to sweep up her hair and brighten her cheeks, it was clear that her beauty was something inside her, a gift she'd been given.

'Does it suit me?' she asked. 'Do I look right?' Her voice was so hushed that it seemed like the rubbing of silk against the stone floor.

I forced myself to smile. 'You look beautiful,' I said. 'Like a princess. No one will be able to take their eyes off you.'

Gently, I touched her shoulder and turned her to the glass. 'Look,' I said.

I stared at her face as she watched herself. The shock in her eyes that turned to wonder. The happiness and anticipation that seemed to bleed off her and color the room. I could feel it moving up over me, and I winced, resisted the urge to slap it off.

This is what you are supposed to do, I told myself. *This is who you are.*

'Thank you,' she breathed. 'I can't believe it.' She turned her head back to me. 'You have no idea how much I have dreamed about this.'

'Oh, I think I do,' I said, smiling, trying to keep my voice kindly but hearing that same sharp edge creep in. I glanced forward, into the glass, and caught my own face next to hers. My human face, with its hair like autumn, its green-gray eyes. The face *he* had seen. Oblivious, she leaned back against me in a gesture of caring and thanks. I put my hand on her shoulder. Maternal. Soothing. I breathed her in, that same desire and longing, and when I closed my eyes, her thoughts became my thoughts. The feel of glass on marble as we walked up the silver stairs. Toward him. His arm circling around.

She was so close to me, I thought. I could reach up and snap her neck.

I opened my eyes and looked in the mirror. *This is who I am,* I thought. And then, *It should be me.*

I stepped back and breathed in. I needed to get her to the carriages, I realized, as soon as possible. Stay focused. I thought of Maybeth's words: *Everything they long for, we already have.* I thought of her voice at the fairy lake, her wings spreading out in front of me as we raced along the shore. How happy I'd been, before the day we went to the palace. How full I'd been, how complete. Maybeth was right. It was human need that had infected me.

But the thought kept rankling, creeping up and sliding against my neck. *You don't have everything,* it said. *You don't have him.*

'You don't want to be late,' I said, trying to shake it off, all of it. 'Not too late, anyway, just late enough. Your sisters left an hour ago, though. There is nothing to be afraid of. This is your destiny.'

Destiny. I held the word on my tongue and rolled it around, memorizing it, willing it into my blood and bone. I reached back to her and gestured for her to move forward.

'Down we go,' I said.

She smiled shyly and walked past me, lifting her gown with both hands and watching her slippers as she moved. 'I have never worn shoes like this,' she said. She tapped them against the stone, like a little girl. She stepped forward, thrusting her ankle forward and swiveling her foot so she could see the heel. It sparkled up at her like a piece of ice sculpture.

Child, I thought. I watched in disgust, feeling my resolve crumble. 'We don't want to be late,' I said then. 'We still need to get you a carriage.'

It took every bit of willpower for me to not make my voice a knife and lash her with it.

She looked back at me. 'Sorry,' she said, giggling, and I watched the dress move against her curves as she walked ahead. Her body looked lush and languorous under it. I thought of the way his face would change as she entered the room. She had been made for him, they said. She was everything he'd ever wanted. That's what they had told me.

She was growing more at ease in her new clothes, her new self, with each moment. Becoming who she was meant to be. This is what I had been brought to her for. Each human had so many selves, they said, and so much confusion. They do not know how to be who they are, who they were meant to be. That is how we help them.

She moved toward the door, started down the stairs. I followed her, watching her hair glow in the dark stairway, the tiny diamonds I had sprinkled throughout.

I could have ripped her apart with my bare hands.

I just wanted her out of the house, at the front steps. Just minutes, I thought. It had all come to this, and all this was was minutes. I had lived for hundreds of years and would live for hundreds more. This was nothing. Just get Cinderella to the ball, to her destiny. That is what they had said.

I reached the first floor, my wings straining against the fabric holding them down, and pushed my way through the lobby and into the street.

With one hand I kept a grip on my shirt in front so that it wouldn't fly open; with the other I clutched the towel to me. A group of pigeons leaped into the air and took flight before me, and suddenly it seemed that the air was full of feathers: gray and white mixed together, hurtling in the breeze and raining over everything.

I couldn't control the images in my mind, the memories so real and immediate I could taste and smell them, feel the way the air changed, hear the flapping of wings when they came upon me.

The sky was deep purple now. I began walking as fast as I could up the street, across Thirty-fourth Street, past the pizza parlors and fast-food places. Past my apartment and up into Times Square. I wasn't sure where I was going, why I was passing the safety of my own apartment, but it was as if an invisible string were pulling me.

Everywhere I looked, I was sure I saw birds swooping over us, their feathers drifting down to the street. *They're not real*, I thought, and all I wanted was to outrun the terrible battering wings, the feeling of reaching out for the glittering golden door as the coachman opened it, lurching for the red velvet seat with them just behind me, closing in.

Lights glowed all around, from the neon signs and marquees, the hundreds of cars moving past like fish in the water.

The air smelled of garbage and food and cold. There was a parking garage, a Blockbuster. I clung to them as if they were anchors. I touched my black shirt, fingered the knot in front. I touched mailboxes and lampposts as I passed. Just ahead, Broadway swerved over Eighth Avenue, the streets curving into a circle, and right in front of me, as I crossed, was the bright golden statue, angel-like, that guarded the southwest entrance to Central Park. Behind it lay the lush dark green of grass and trees, of forest.

I could feel my wings spreading. I understood, then: I was going to fly. They were coming back for me, were forgiving me, and I was going to fly.

My wings began to unfold, but it was okay now. I moved past the statue and through the gate and into the grass, leaning down to pull off my boots and then letting my feet sink into the ground. Normally I would have avoided Central Park at night, any exposure to danger, but as my wings began to rise up like baking bread, like a breath, I did not care. I moved through the dark, and I felt a smile take over my face, something I couldn't control. I walked and walked, plunging into the park's secret, dark places. The air was cool and smelled of grass.

No one can hurt me, I thought, and for a moment I felt powerful, otherworldly, proud. I was a fairy, I thought, and laughed out loud, stretching out my arms. I was so beautiful I would have made everyone mad with it, everyone on this earth.

When I'd been walking a good while, passing through an underground passageway and past statues and small, strange buildings, when the park seemed to be empty and the lights gone, I stopped. I looked around again and stood stock-still, listening. I could hear cars, shouts, but from a great distance.

Once I was convinced I was safe, I reached down, untied my shirt, and pulled it off. Let my wings unfold right into air, feather by feather, extending to their full span. Leaned back my head and stretched out my arms. There was no feeling like it. The tips of my wings curled toward each other, forming a giant heart.

The air slid along my bare breasts, through my feathers, seeming to smooth out and erase everything. The ache in my back and legs seemed to disappear bit by bit until there was only this, this moment with my wings flapping back and forth, slicing through the air. I breathed it in and let it move through me. I felt young again, smooth and beautiful.

Suddenly I could not bear it for one more minute, being confined to the earth. There was a power raging through me, and though I had no idea where it came from and why it had come now, I felt it flare up and through each feather, each quill and barb filling me until I could no longer even see straight. All I saw before me was an expanse of green, and sky. And then I closed my eyes, and I *remembered*: the earth far, far below as we swooped and glided or just drifted along on our backs, the way every color pierced and burned, and how the sky was every kind of blue and purple and pink as we streaked through it. This is what I had lost.

I started walking, more and more quickly. Back then it had been my world, I thought. I had had no idea that I could lose it. That he would come along and make me believe that love was more important than she was, than any of it was. I walked faster, and before I knew it, I was running, racing, my arms out to the sides and my wings pushing the air in waves on either side of me, cutting right through and propelling me forward.

How could anything have been more important than *what I was*? I jumped up and came back down again, my feet sliding along the grass. I could barely breathe, but it didn't matter. How could one feeling have been more important than this? I sped up, sped up until the entire world blurred, and then, with one lunge, one breath, I leaped right up into the air and folded my legs underneath me. I looked up at the sky, *reaching* for it. I felt it. I was flying. The air became a waterfall, streaming down my sides.

And then, before it could even register, I was on the ground, on my side, one of my wings smashed and twisted between my body and the grass. I looked around and realized: I had barely moved. I stared up at the sky, and for a moment I was sure I saw a flicker, a glance.

'Help me,' I whispered. 'I'm sorry. Come back to me.' I blinked, and the sky was dark again, completely still.

I tried again. I pulled myself to my feet and ran forward, letting my wings spread out on either side and lift me into the air.

But they didn't. I couldn't go anywhere. I ran forward and pushed myself into empty space, only to end up on the ground again, my cheek pressing into earth.

I must have stayed there for hours, curled up, the dark like a blanket over me and the grass pressing into my arms. The pain in my back moved up and down in waves. When I shifted, there was blood in the grass. I pulled my wings in, close to my skin, but they jutted out all wrong. Pain shot through me, like needles, where wing met bone. Feathers fell to the ground. I moved my body. Feathers covered the ground, mixed in with grass and blood. I closed my eyes. Sobs racked my body, and I just pushed my face into the earth, let them pass through me.

I did not want to ever move, ever get up again. *I could not fly*, and yet the memory of flight was inscribed in my bones. I thought of the photographs of the fairies, pale and ghostlike, fluttering in the frame.

I lay on my stomach, clutching the ground, and let all the memories wash over me. All of us sitting around the fairy lake, the leaves sprinkling down over us, the water the color of berries. How all I could think about was his face, the feel of his skin on mine. How I had longed, for the first time, to be somewhere else, to be someone else entirely.

There was a pain in me as heavy as a universe, it seemed, as I remembered. I did this, I thought then. I had entered her dream, taken on her desire until I forgot my own place completely. Who I was, and was meant to be. What I was supposed to do. I wanted to stop everything, and die. I had done this to myself. There was no relief for me.

Get up, a voice said. I lifted my head and looked around. Even that movement sent pain shooting down my back. *Get up now.*

I thought I heard voices, in the distance.

'Maybeth?' I whispered. I listened, but all I heard was a faint sound of wind. And then, from far away, voices again.

'Lucibell?'

I tried to pull my body up. Gasping with pain, I burrowed my palms into the earth and pushed, inching my back into the air. But all I could think was, *There's someone here.*

I felt something wet trickling down my back. My wing jutted out and brushed my arm in a way it had never done before. There was a searing pain, a feeling as if I'd been ripped through.

I blinked and felt someone there, dashing past me. 'Hello?' A wing to my right. I turned my head but saw only empty space and blackness. I stopped and listened again. 'Maybeth?' The wind whooshed through the leaves and grass, my bent feathers. Tears streamed down my cheeks, but I forced myself to ignore the pain and sit up. I had no idea how long they would wait for me.

'I'm here!' I said, making my voice as loud as I could. 'I'm ready to go home!' As if they couldn't see me. As if I couldn't remember what it had been like, fluttering next to someone's ear and whispering into it. How the whole earth was like a musical instrument that we could play effortlessly. Sliding down leaves and through people's hair. Flipping from a stone to a fingertip to a peach. Making the wind shift with our wings, a heart swell or break with one whispered word.

'I'm right here!!' I shouted. 'Maybeth! I know you're still here! I saw you in photographs!'

I grasped the tree next to me, a branch poking out, and pulled myself to my feet. Wobbling, I leaned into the bark to steady myself. The breeze pushed past again, and I shivered, startled to realize that I was almost naked.

It was beginning to grow light. I heard a thumping, thumping and then breath. A jogger was close enough for me to hear the rhythm of his feet and heart.

I could not fly. My sister was not there. My heart was broken.

Steeling myself against the pain, I pulled my wings in and in again, tightening all my muscles, and then reached my hand back to feel the damp feathers. My left wing seemed to be okay. My right one was twisted and wrong, angling out and hanging down. I crawled back through the grass, feeling for my towel and my shirt.

I wrapped the shirt around me the way I'd done earlier, but this time I had to force my right wing down, wrapping it in the shredded garment. I had never felt so raw in my life, my wing mangled and throbbing under the fabric. I tied the shirt in front and reached for the towel, pulling it across my shoulders.

I looked around one last time, but the presence I'd felt a few moments earlier was gone. In the tree above me, I thought I caught a shadow, a flicker of white, but I realized a moment later that it was only a bird returning to its nest.

I stumbled into the open then, out from under the tree, and surveyed the park in front of me. The hills and pathways in the distance. I moved toward them, and it was as if there were razor blades tied to my shoulders, cutting into my back. *Just get to the street*, I kept saying to myself, and I moved in what I hoped was the right direction, toward the twisting pathways.

When I finally caught a glimpse of concrete, I started to run. All I could think of was getting home. A salt bath, I hoped, would heal me.

I stepped out into the street and lifted my hand into the air. A taxi stopped, and I climbed into it, slid onto the leather, and winced as my back hit the seat. 'Thirty-sixth, between Seventh and Eighth,' I said. I tightened the towel around my shoulders. Outside, the park whizzed past, a blur of green. I tilted my head against the glass and looked up at the branches and leaves, the benches and railings in front of them, the people stopping to talk or browse at one of the sidewalk displays of photographs or drawings. A carriage clomped by next to us, and I watched a man and woman inside, laughing, with their arms around each other.

Leaning forward, I pressed my forehead into the clear plastic window and shut my eyes.

'Are you okay, lady?'

'What?'

I looked up. I hadn't realized I was still crying.

'You don't look too hot. Maybe you need a doctor?'

I sat up and focused in on his face in the rearview mirror. His black eyes stared back at me.

'You're bleeding,' he said. 'It's not any of my business, but you look like you need help.'

I looked down then and saw that blood had caked along my forearms, was sticking to my neck and dripping onto the leather seat.

'I'm okay,' I said, wiping my face. 'I just need to get where I'm going.'

'If you're sure,' he said, flicking his eyes from me to the street ahead.

I sat back and closed my eyes again.

CHAPTER ELEVEN

e circled down and around and came to the upstairs hallway, which led to the main stairs and front entrance. The rest of the house was ornate, heavy, imposing, in sharp contrast to Cinderella's barren quarters. I almost felt a twinge of sympathy for her, but there was too much else happening inside me. The emotions running through me felt like rivers, like changing seasons, like entire worlds. I felt as if I would be sick. Suddenly I longed for the fairy lake. How calm we all were there. The flat surface of the water and the smooth feeling as we pressed in.

Rushing now, we passed the open doors to her stepsisters' chambers, glimpsing the opened drawers and wrecked wardrobes, the gowns strewn across the elaborate beds and carpets, the servants rushing around, desperately trying to clean the ephemera that clung to everything. I took it all in at a glance: stray buttons and fake jewels, the powder sprinkled across the vanity, the open vials and spilled beads and discarded shoes and hair clips. The house was still buzzing with the excitement and hope that had occupied the room, the fierce, beating hearts now rushing across the kingdom to the giant silver palace. The house was full of their dreaming, of him.

We came to the front stairs.

She looked back at me and smiled. 'I hope he will like me,' she said as she stepped down.

'Of course he'll like you,' I began. 'I've made you—'

Distracted, she started to fall. I watched, in slow motion it seemed, as her heel caught on the side of the thick Oriental runner that led down the stairs. I watched her face change, the look of fear that passed over her.

I could have reached out and stilled her. I could have put out one hand in plenty of time – my reflexes were far beyond those of humans. Or I could have just willed her to stop. But I didn't. I stood in place and stared at her as she slipped down. *Help her*, a voice said inside me, but something in me froze. I waited to step forward until she was already down.

And in that moment my heart opened, slammed open, as if someone had punched right through it. Everything I wanted was right in front of me, I thought. I could put on a dress and conjure the golden coaches, go *right to him*. I could pull the glass slippers from her feet and put them on my own. I don't know that I had ever felt anything close to what I felt in that moment. Not happiness. Triumph. Desire. Hate.

She only slid down a couple of stairs before she came to a stop, grabbing the banister and pulling herself up, looking back at me and laughing. It seemed to take a whole hour, those few moments. It was as if someone had raked their nails across my face.

Her laughter tinkled up to me. 'I am so clumsy!' she said, stilling herself. 'I have to be more careful in these shoes!'

I shook with anger. I did not say a word. I walked ahead, down the stairs.

'I'm sorry,' she said, rushing after me, nervous now, her hands running along the railing, careful to stay upright. 'I'm not deserving, Godmother, I know. Please don't be mad at me.'

I ignored her. I reached the bottom of the stairs and strode out into the wet night. The wild tangle of plants and flowers outside the door – her mother's work, long ago – infused the air with perfume. The night was warm, sultry. Soon enough I would be back in the cool air of the lake and leave all this behind. I would ask to stay away from humans, I thought, from now on. Angrily, I leaned down and plucked a huge bluebell from a stem, then tossed it to the ground. In its place appeared a gleaming golden coach.

'Oh!' I heard her stopping behind me. She was not afraid anymore.

I turned and glared. 'Hand me a batch of leaves,' I commanded, pointing, 'from that bush there.'

She leaned down and obeyed, passing me the leaves with shaking hands.

I threw them in front of the carriage with all my strength, and up sprang a quartet of horses, tied to the carriage with long, ribbonlike harnesses that glittered in the night air.

'Now,' I said, stepping closer, grabbing her wrist with my palm, so hard it might have snapped off – I could *feel* it, how delicate her bones were – 'I want you to hand me a twig. From the ground.' My teeth were gritted, my free hand in the shape of a fist. '*Now.*'

She stood and stared at me. Her eyes huge and wide.

The moment opened up, and waited. It seemed to stretch the length of the palace steps, the forest leading to them. And then she dropped her eyes and rushed away.

'Here, Godmother,' she said, what seemed like seconds later, and I turned to her, almost surprised. I could feel that my cheeks had flushed, my body gone warm.

She was staring at me nervously, holding out a twig. Her face was radiant, despite the worry that creased it. I snatched the twig out of her hand.

'Have I made you angry, Godmother?' she asked then, her voice low and trembling.

'No,' I snapped. And then, more quietly, 'No.'

I tossed the twig to the ground, and a coachman sprang up in its place. Without a word he took his place behind the whinnying horses and grabbed the reins. *This is destiny*, I thought. *This is how it is all supposed to happen, just like this.* The gleaming coach ready to whisk her into the night.

'It is time for you to go,' I said softly. 'It's your time.'

She didn't move. Her eyes were filling with tears.

'Go,' I said. I reached out my hand and touched her face. 'They are waiting for you.'

'Are you sure it is okay?' she asked. 'Are you sure it is right for me to go?'

'It's the wish of the fairies,' I said, smiling at her. I felt, then, all the grief that lay buried in her, and my heart softened. I was supposed to be her guardian. I had been made to feel her pain, her lost, grief-stricken nights, the straw mattress that dug into her back and left red lines across her skin. I had been made to feel all of it, the same way she had been made to fall in love with him.

I could barely hear her when she spoke next. 'But why me, Godmother?'

I touched her shoulder. 'You were chosen,' I whispered. I ignored the sliver of pain that shot through me. I forced my hand to stay gentle and light. 'For him. He is going to pick a wife tonight, and you, my child, have been chosen.'

I watched my words wind their way into her, making her whole face shift, her expression go soft. My own pain widened then, to a long stream. It was hard, I realized, to know where my pain stopped and hers started. I could feel it coming off her, as my words sank in.

It slipped into me then: All those nights she'd spent by herself, with no one to talk to. The grief she felt when her mother drowned herself in the lake, when her father remarried, when her father died soon after, leaving her, a girl who was all light, in a dark sprawling house where she was hidden away from the world, where her beauty was wasted, and where her dreams grew so intense that she practically lived inside them, never quite knowing what was real and what wasn't. I felt her callused hands, the ache in her body, the future that yawned before her in that house, waiting on her stepmother and stepsisters hand and foot, never knowing what beat within her, what other selves she could be and worlds she could live in. Never knowing that she had been made to be a princess, to go to a ball that people would still talk about centuries later, one that all girls would dream about when they dreamed of falling in love.

She deserves this, I thought. Suddenly I wanted, more than anything, for this girl to find relief. She had been made for him. I was a fairy. I could close my eyes, stretch out my wings, and be back by the lake within moments. The coach was ready, the horses stamping their feet furiously, anxious to fulfill the duty I'd conjured them for. The coachman sat with the reins in his hand. And Cinderella radiated pure light. She would be the most beautiful woman at the ball.

Everything was in its place.

I closed my eyes and breathed in. 'It is time,' I said. I ignored the pain pounding through me. In a few more minutes, it would all be over.

I snapped my fingers, and the coachman jumped to the ground and opened the carriage door. Inside, the velvet seats were as red as blood. I turned to Cinderella and watched the dying light on her face, her skin, the ice blue of her dress.

He would take one look at her and forget me.

'Come,' I said.

She did not move. My own emotions were too strong, too ferocious, for me to read what was happening within her. *Just go,* I thought. *Go!* I forced myself to think of the fairy lake. The water that wrapped around me like a pair of arms. The way we never felt anything at all resembling longing, because our world was already perfect, so full it brimmed over. In moments I would be there.

Cinderella still stood, and I saw she was shaking.

She reached up just as I was about to go to her. She ripped her hair out of the swept-up bun I had conjured for her. I watched, unmoving, as the diamonds scattered down into the grass. Watched her kick off the glass slippers. They tipped over into the grass. I couldn't take my eyes off them.

'I am not going,' she said.

*

The next morning I woke up slowly, painfully. My wings were bunched up behind me in my bed. There was a burning in my shoulders. Every muscle hurt.

The sun was bright on my face. Hazy images, of trees and grass and forest paths, scattered across my mind.

I remembered then, and it was like a blade cutting through me: I could not fly. The desire stretched from my wings down into my bones, into every vein. But I could not fly.

I curled up, into myself. My face burned with embarrassment, even though I was alone. *George must think I'm out of my mind,* I thought.

Was I? After so many years of wandering the earth, had I finally lost it completely?

I had thought the prince was in front of me, leading me into the flower shop. I had seen him at the diner. The same voice. The same way of looking at me. It had felt as if no time had passed at all, as if I were a fairy again and he was the only one who could see me. Me, who had always fluttered above humans, made my way into their thoughts and dreams, whispered advice into their ears, changed their hearts. I who was a wisp of a thing, dangling in the air and floating above them. Always on the outside, in the periphery. Invisible. To be in that body pressed up against him . . . Tasting his lips, feeling his tongue and hands, his eyelashes as they tapped my cheeks.

He had seemed so close. My world had seemed so close. How could I feel flight through every inch of me, have these appendages that ached for the air, and not be able to fly? Maybe they were never coming back. Maybe they had abandoned me to this world for what I had done and were never, ever planning to forgive me. The photos, the prince at the diner . . . Was it all just in my head? Wishful thinking, as they say?

I was homesick. My chest ached. So many years, I realized, I had been quietly waiting, wishing I could change history, suffering but not putting a name to it. It was amazing how a person could opt out of his or her own life. Follow a routine. Go to work in the morning, come home in the evening. Turn on the television, take a hot bath. Forget. You could get through so many days and nights that way. I had done it for years, barely acknowledging the terrible emptiness inside me, like a tide always trying to pull me out to sea.

I looked down at my wrinkled, ragged hands. I was so old. Once I had been one of the most stunning creatures in the world.

It had been three hundred years in human time. Cinderella and the prince had been dead for centuries.

I shifted. Where they met skin and bone, my wings ached.

It was seven A.M. I needed to get to work. I knew that George would be sick with worry. My answering machine had been blinking when I got home. I had heard the phone during the night.

George. Despite everything, a shiver of pleasure sparked through me, a glimmer of hope. I *would* be redeemed. I knew it. Today I would call Veronica and let her know that everything was set. And then I could go back.

I sat up. My wings didn't hurt so badly, I decided. Suddenly I was filled with energy. It had just been too early, I thought. I couldn't fly *before* sending them to the ball. I was a fairy godmother! That was who I was. It didn't matter that my wings didn't work and that my hands were covered in wrinkles. Nothing mattered but getting her to the ball.

If only I had understood that back then.

I washed as well as I could, careful not to hurt my wings further. The banging on my door started as soon as I stepped out of the bath.

I wrapped a towel around me and crept into the bedroom. It was already eight-thirty. I had no time for visitors. Quietly, I dried myself off, then slipped into a skirt and blouse.

Just then I heard the front door clicking open, the little bell I'd strung to the top of it tinkling against the wood. I froze.

'Ms. Lillian? I'm coming in.'

Leo. A moment later I could hear him moving around the front room.

I thought back, to all those other moments when people had crept up on me in the dark, rifled through my things, noticed the occasional feather drifting through the birdless air. All the times that people had changed, one second open and normal, the next their faces clenched like fists. I knew that look, the faces people made when they pointed and called me 'witch' or 'devil.' It had been many years now, but I knew it. You could almost forget, sometimes, how much threat there was, past the locked door.

I pushed into the main room. 'What are you doing?' I asked. 'How did you get in?'

He raised up his hands and just stared at me. 'I'm sorry,' he said. 'I came by to talk to you, is all. I've left you messages, notices. I can't seem to reach you.'

'But how did you get in?' I said, hearing my voice rise.

He held up a rusted key. 'I've been going through my

grandfather's things,' he said. 'Mainly, I just wanted to see if this still worked. I'm really sorry. I didn't mean to scare you.'

I stared back at him, my heart beating wildly.

'I just . . . I really need to talk with you. It's urgent. I brought a notice here to leave for you. I wanted to make sure you got it, that you were okay.'

'I'm fine,' I said. 'I'm very busy, that's all. I don't appreciate your coming in this way.'

'I'm so sorry,' he repeated. 'Here, I'll just leave this.' He placed an official-looking document on my table. I refused to look at it. 'I do need to talk to you. And again, I am sorry to have barged in like this. The thing is, I've sold this building. The new owners are planning to turn it into offices. So you will need to move. I feel terrible. I know you've been here a long time.'

'I can't just move,' I said. 'You can't do that.'

'Actually . . .' he said, coughing, not quite meeting my eye, 'you don't actually have a lease anymore. I found an original agreement that hasn't been valid in at least three decades. And even with a lease . . . Well, even with a lease, buildings get sold. I feel terrible. I know how close you and my grandmother were. I'm offering a nice deal for all the current tenants, which will help you get settled somewhere else.'

I was sick. He didn't seem to know where to look. I just stood there. Where could I go? How could he do this?

'Like I said, we are offering a very generous buyout. Just read the papers.'

In a few more days, it will not matter, I thought. My mind latched on to the ball, clung to it. They would be coming back for me by then, once I'd set things right. None of this mattered.

'I'll read them,' I said.

'Okay.' He stepped back. Awkward and sheepish. 'Again, I apologize.'

'Fine,' I said. 'Now I have to get to work, if you don't mind.'

'Yes, of course,' he said. But he was hesitating.

'Is there something else?' My mind flashed to the bathtub, the feathers that would be floating in it, the same feathers that would be scattered across my bed, through my room. I couldn't remember the last time someone else had been in the apartment. *I should be more careful*, I thought.

'I——'. He stopped himself. 'Well, I've got a bunch of photos. My grandfather had just boxes and boxes of stuff. I found some old photos of you, even.'

I shook my head, confused.

'You were something,' he said. And then, embarrassed, 'I mean, you were really beautiful. No disrespect intended.' He coughed again. 'Anyway. I thought you might want some of them. You and your . . . family.'

'I think you're mistaken,' I said. 'They're not mine.'

'Well,' he said, looking at me strangely, 'I mean, I saw the other stuff. I just . . . Well, I can come back with them. If you change your mind.'

'I really am late for work,' I said.

'Yes, okay,' he said, turning to the door. Then, as he was leaving, he looked back at me. 'I'm just really sorry. I guess I never quite realized, and . . . You're a strong lady.'

The moment he was gone, I locked the door and pulled my living-room chair over, shoving it under the knob. I stood for a moment, realizing how loudly my heart was pounding. It throbbed in my forehead and ears, up and down my legs and arms. His words had disoriented me. A sick feeling crept over me, one I could not explain. An image of shattered glass entering my body.

There was nowhere for me to go. The ball, the gala at the Pierre, was in less than a week. I knew that it would change everything, but still I felt a terrible, gaping fear. What if I had misunderstood everything? And there were feathers everywhere. I thought of the bathwater, the feathers floating on top of it and sticking to the tiles. Evidence.

The feathers gave me a purpose. It seemed imperative suddenly that I get rid of every shred of evidence. The last thing I needed was to be found out when I was so close to leaving this world forever.

I pulled a cardboard box from my supply closet and went to the bath. The tub had partly drained, but the surface of the water was covered in long, gleaming white feathers. I reached down and swept my palms across them. They were softer than fur, whiter than snow. Even floating on the water, they curled and stretched like living things. Sad, separated out, but still vital, perfect.

I released the drain in the tub and began scooping up the feathers, letting the water run off them. I dumped clumps of wet feathers into the box. Wisps of them stuck to my palms and wrists and fingers, but I kept scooping and dumping until the tub was empty and only a few soft white strands clung to the sides. After, I wiped the tub down, careful to pick out the feather remnants from the sponge and add them to the box.

I walked through the rooms, stopping at my bed. I raked through the bedsheets to pick out all the other feathers that had accumulated. When I was done, I walked into the main space with the feather-filled box – they were all dry by now, magically, shimmering and glacial – and, again looking around to make sure I was alone, removed the iron cover from the right-hand front burner and lit a fire. The blue flame flared up and turned yellow.

One by one I dropped the feathers into it. Despite myself, despite the fact that I had performed this ritual for years, my heart ached as I watched the feathers flare up. The fire took hold of them, turned them white hot, made them burn so bright I had to cover my eyes. And then, two seconds later, gone, without a trace. Just a faint smell of vanilla and smoke. It took me fifteen minutes to get through the box. Then I lit a match and wiped it against the sides, letting all the bits and pieces flare up and disappear.

It was already 9:30 A.M. I locked the door behind me and headed to work.

George was waiting for me when I arrived.

'Lil!' he said. 'What the hell happened? I've called and called. I went by your apartment. Are you okay?'

'I'm fine,' I said. 'I just ate something bad. I was ill. I'm so sorry I reacted that way and made you worry.'

'Lil, you went crazy! Are you kidding?'

'I don't know what came over me. Really.'

I had a hard time meeting his eye. He knew. He had to know. There had been so many feathers, they had blown all over him.

'Are you sure?' he asked more quietly. 'I've been worried about you lately. You seem to get distracted so easily. And just . . . I worry about you.' I glanced up at him, saw his face knotted with worry. I couldn't help but notice how handsome he looked, with his flushed cheeks and dark eyes. He and Veronica would be so handsome together.

I mustered all my concentration, to look as sweet and innocuous as possible. 'George,' I said slowly, 'I didn't feel well and maybe overreacted a bit. It can be scary, getting old. You lose control of your body in ways you never thought you would. It can be very difficult.'

I knew I had succeeded in making him uncomfortable. The specters of age and decay always did that to the young.

'Yes,' he said, looking away. 'I'm just sorry I couldn't be more help to you. Maybe I overreacted, too. I don't know.'

'It's fine,' I said, touching his arm. 'I appreciate how concerned you were. And for inviting me. I hope I didn't embarrass you too much. Your friends seemed lovely.'

'I am not embarrassed, Lil,' he said. 'You are a dear friend. Don't think I don't appreciate what you're doing for me, too.'

'That's right,' I said. 'And when you meet your date and have the best night of your life, you'll be in my debt eternally.'

He laughed. 'Let's get this place open,' he said. 'There are millions of aimless book lovers wandering around out there needing a fix.'

'Yes, sir,' I said.

He had no idea, I realized. All those feathers, his palm on wing and barb, and he had no idea. It was astonishing. Maybe in New York nothing could surprise anyone anymore.

I unlocked the front door and switched the Closed sign to Open.

*

I called Veronica just after lunch.

'Okay, my friend,' I said. 'I think someone needs a proper ball gown. An ice blue silk, maybe?'

'And what is it that you are suggesting?'

'Aren't you some kind of gifted seamstress?' I asked. 'Or is that just a rumor?'

CHAPTER TWELVE

er hair fell into her face and over her shoulders, glittering in the fading light, shifting from white to cream to a pale gold. Her feet were bare, delicate. I watched the silk of her dress rubbing into the grass, the wrinkles creasing it, the straps slipping over her smooth shoulders. She was a mess. Tears fell down her reddening face. The glitter I had spread over her, the kohl around her eyes, her red lips – it was all rubbing off, streaking her face in lines.

I looked away. Then back again.

She hunched down on her elbows, her legs crossed, her hands buried in her hair.

'I'm sorry,' she wailed, wiping her face even as more tears streamed down it. Next to her the shoes lay in the grass. The sun hit them as it sank and turned them briefly to flame, then back again. Behind, the horses flared up, growing impatient, their muscles rippling under their smooth black coats.

I knew I should be fixing it all: the horses, who threatened to bolt away at any moment; the coach that was losing its luster every minute that went by; her. But it was so beautiful, all of it, the mess of the human world. I couldn't understand the feelings moving through me. How full I felt.

For a second the world stood still and I could see my future – her future – stretching in front of us, wide open, like fate didn't matter, like anything at all could happen and the future was a giant wave carrying us both forward.

She stretched her arm in the grass and I saw then, just barely, the red line etched across her wrist. A scar.

'Don't be sorry,' I said, but my voice seemed stilted and false. My words hung in the early night air. 'What happened to you? Who did this to you?'

She didn't look up. I wasn't sure if I'd even spoken out loud. I needed to move into her, understand her, fix her, but the feelings moving over me were so new and acute. The hatred and jealousy pierced into and through me, a long line, like silver. At the same time my heart opened to her. I wanted so badly to erase the pain that racked her body. The line across her wrist. She didn't deserve any of it, not these moments, not all the moments she'd been made to suffer.

And then part of me wanted something else. To bend down into the grass, and feel her silk starlight hair, smell the ash on her, all the days huddled under the chimney with a broom in her hand. I wanted to touch her pale, perfect skin, her fragile wrist, the line snaking and twisting across it, her wound.

I didn't know what to feel or think. I watched the tears run into the grass and stay there. She dragged the back of her hand across her face and looked up at me.

'I feel so stupid,' she said. 'I ruin everything.'

I stood there, hesitating. All the feelings passing through me. I felt as if I could stand there forever, watching her.

'Please don't make me go,' she whispered.

Before I knew what I was doing, I dropped down next to her. For the moment, sympathy won out, erased the other emotions seesawing through me. She was *supposed* to go. It was supposed to be the night of her life.

'It's your destiny,' I said. 'Don't you understand? It will be everything you ever wanted.'

She was sobbing now. I didn't know if she could even hear me.

'It's the ball,' I said. 'It is all arranged. He will see you and fall in love with you. Do you hear me? You were made for him. It's your destiny.'

'No,' she said, into her hands. 'I can't go. Look at me. I am not supposed to go to balls.' She kicked out her foot, and I watched one of the slippers fall to its side. She pulled the diamonds from her ears and dropped them into the grass. I watched them sink into the ground.

'Why are you like this?' I whispered. I was truly stunned. The ball, the prince – it was all I had thought about for weeks now. His hands on my waist and his mouth on my neck. The way I had felt whole, fully myself, when I was near him. I thought of the prince from her own dreams, standing in the field, walking toward her. Toward me. I knew he was all she had been thinking of, too.

She pulled her hands from her face and just looked at me.

'I know you dream of him,' I said. 'I've seen what you dream of. And now it's here. This night. It's what you've always wanted.'

'No,' she said, staring at me. 'I just want to be alone. I want to be someone new.'

I leaned in and touched her face. A wave of tenderness passed over me. I couldn't tell where I began and she ended. 'He will make you into someone new,' I said. 'He can make you whole. He can make all this disappear. The hole in your gut. This.' I picked up her hand, ran my fingers down to the scar on her wrist.

'Hello!' Veronica called out, her knee-high vinyl boots clacking across the wooden floor. She walked up to the counter, smiling. Her features were delicate under her multicolored makeup, and her eyes were like flowers, large and thickly fringed. A dark, glittering blue. I heard George draw in his breath. She looked stunning in her forties-style burgundy dress, her bright orange hair pulled back from her face.

I thought of Maybeth shrieking, hurling herself into the lake and then up out of it.

She noticed him then, stopping in her tracks. 'You're George,' she said. 'Aren't you?'

'Yes?' he said, looking from her to me.

'I'm Veronica,' she said, extending her hand to him, batting her eyes. I couldn't believe it: for a moment, she looked almost bashful. 'Your date to the ball.'

'Veronica,' he repeated.

'I recognize you from your photo.'

'I didn't realize . . .' George stumbled closer to the counter and bumped into it. When he reached out to shake her hand, she laughed and tilted her wrist, bending it up farther so that he had no choice but to kiss her hand.

'I showed her the photo of you and your father,' I said to him, 'back in the office. The Cary Grant one.' I smiled, enjoying his embarrassment. 'We're actually going shopping so she doesn't show up to the ball in rags.'

'So . . . you actually go to balls, then?' she asked. 'For fun?'

He looked horrified. 'It's a charity event my parents are involved in. It's not really my . . .'

'I'm kidding,' she said. 'It sounds nice. The idea is growing on me, I'm not gonna lie.' She smiled, her blue eyes glowing, and I could feel him relax beside me.

'George owns this place,' I said. 'He's a real book lover.'

'Oh, I am, too,' she said. 'I read all the time, always have. You know what I studied in school?'

'What?'

'*Franch litrature*,' she said, making a silly snooty face.

'I was a French-lit major, too,' George said. 'I was obsessed with Mallarmé and Proust.' He paused, self-conscious. 'I was a bit of a nerd, I suppose.'

'I don't believe it for a second,' she said, winking. 'I, on the other hand, dropped out. In my senior year. I'm smart like that. And I barely even remember French. Lil showed me a line in one of your books here and had to translate for me. I should never admit all this, should I?'

'Let me guess: *All my old loves will be returned to me.*'

I turned and looked at him – at his flushed cheeks, dark hair and eyebrows, his hands stained with ink. I wanted to clap out loud and felt a laugh rise in my throat, but I restrained myself. He will calm her, I thought. And she will make him feel alive. All of a sudden I could see them: their thin, pale limbs twisted together, the two of them sipping cider next to a fire, the snow falling outside.

'Yes, that's right,' I whispered, the way I used to whisper back when I was the fairy godmother, at that exact moment when the eyes turned soft and mouth cracked open and I had those humans right where I wanted them. I practically laughed out loud, remembering.

'What did you say?' Veronica asked, turning to me. She smiled, raising her eyebrows at George, and mouthed 'Thanks,' even though he could see what she was doing.

'Did I tell you that George is an amazing cook?' I asked, reaching out and tapping his back affectionately. George looked at me. I didn't know where the words had come from. It could be true, I thought.

He cleared his throat, and his hands flew to his mouth for no reason at all. The next second he threw them back down at his sides and then, a moment later, onto the countertop. 'Well, I can make soup, lots of soups,' he said. 'Squash, broccoli, split pea.'

My heart twisted up for one second, and then Veronica said, 'Mmm. Butternut squash soup is my favorite. It's almost that time of year, isn't it? Squash and apples and pumpkins. I love it.'

Despite everything, every ounce of fairy blood still in me sprang to life. I hadn't forgotten the pleasures of bringing together two young lovers, of figuring out exactly what one human needed from another. Not once, even after all these years and years of human life. I too can be a genius sometimes, I thought as I grabbed my purse. Even now. I walked out from behind the counter. 'All yours,' I said to George.

Veronica smiled at him. Then she reached down and plucked George's right hand off the counter, pulled it to her mouth, and kissed it, leaving a dark red stain. I could hear his throat catch.

'So I'll see you soon,' she said, waving at him sweetly with her black-nailed hand, turning to the door. 'I can't wait.'

I walked out behind her, then acted as if I'd forgotten something. 'One second,' I said.

'Where did you meet her?' George asked as I walked toward him. 'My God.' He looked as if he'd just seen a mermaid. His face was red and ragged, as if he'd been smacked.

'You don't think I get around?' I asked, indulging myself. 'Well, I have news for you. I do get around. I get around a lot!' I looked at him, smiled, and let the world settle back into place. 'She's a great girl, George.'

'Well, I . . . I look forward to getting to know her.'

As I walked out the door, onto the street, Veronica grabbed my arm and squeezed.

'Lil, he's adorable,' she said. 'Totally my type. At least, he is now.'

The way she looked at me broke my heart slightly. Wistful.

I laughed. 'Yes,' I said softly. 'He's a very good man. Honorable. He's a bit shy, but it's endearing, I think. He just lives so much in his head. There's something of the old world in him.'

'Oh, absolutely,' she said. 'He seems like a real . . . gentleman. It's almost weird. But I love weird. Not to mention tall and smoking hot. Spill it, Lil. Tell me more about him!'

We turned on Cornelia Street, heading up to West Fourth. She towered over me in her boots.

'Well, he was divorced, just last year. I think that made him turn more inward. It was pretty painful for him.'

'What was his wife like?'

'A socialite type. She never came in the store, and he didn't talk about her much. Blond, a bit prim maybe. I think their families were close. I never understood the connection, but I guess that's why it didn't last.'

'Sounds awful,' she said. 'Um. Not that I'm typecasting. Does he come from a lot of money or something? I'm always amazed by these urbane, Manhattan types. It's still so foreign to me.'

'I think so. His mother, yes. His father, less so.'

'Oh, God. I'm going to feel like a weirdo at this ball, aren't I? Not that I'm not used to it.'

'You'll be wonderful,' I said. 'You'll be the most beautiful girl there.'

'You're sweet,' she said. 'I don't mind, though. Seriously. It'll be a blast. And I'm excited about this dress! I've really wanted a new project. And now I'm thinking of the ice blue. I mean, I'd been thinking of using black fabric, you know, maybe with touches of pink, but that's what I always do. I like your idea, doing something softer.'

A leaf skittered across the sidewalk in front of us. I imagined picking it up and dropping it, having an ice blue silk gown appear before us. The look on her face as she turned toward the mirror, transformed. I bent down and snatched up the leaf, crumpled it in my hand.

'Ethereal,' I said. 'It will suit you, with your pale skin and those blue eyes.'

'Yeah. And I just want to go all-out princess if I'm doing the blue. I was thinking a corset top, silk ribbons lacing up the back. For the lower half, maybe a petticoat, like in a darker blue, with a couple of layers of silk on top.'

'What about some tulle?' I asked. 'On top of the silk? Maybe we could find some beads or sequins to thread through it.'

I could see it perfectly. With Cinderella I had imagined the gown and it had appeared in my hands.

'Oh, I like that,' she said.

We walked down the stairs, into the West Fourth Street subway. An A train was pulling in just as we moved onto the platform.

I sat down and grasped a bar as the train lurched forward.

'You okay?' she asked, slipping into the seat next to me.

'Subways make me nervous. I usually just walk everywhere.'

'I'm way too lazy for that,' she said. We were pressed together, our legs touching. 'Plus, I like the people-watching. It's my favorite thing about this city.'

'How long have you been in New York?' I tried to remember if I had read it in her journal, which had gone back at least a few years.

'Five years,' she said. 'I can't believe it's been that long. I wanted to come here so badly when I was in high school. I lived right in the middle of cow country, nothing but farmland whichever way you turn and a big university stuck in the center of it. When I'd come to New York, just to visit, it seemed like everything was larger than life. I always felt like a completely different person.'

The train wheezed and shimmied down the tunnel; the lights flickered on and off and back on again.

'Like, when I was here,' she continued, 'I was who I was supposed to be. Everything seemed possible here. It still does. Sometimes I'm walking down the street now, not seeing anything, so caught up in my life, and then I remember what it was like when I first came here, how massive everything seemed. And I just get swept up all over again.'

I laughed. 'I feel like I've been around for centuries. I can barely even remember being a kid, being young.' But even as I said the words, I knew I was lying. Of course I could remember – the images were as clear as if I'd been skimming across the surface of the fairy lake only moments before, the air like water all around me. The memories flooded through me: how the world looked from high, high in the air, how the trees all blurred as I darted down, laughing, to the grass. These were the memories that were crystal clear to me. Not the haze of years that had passed since I'd fallen to earth, the random images that floated up to me as if from an abyss. Not the present, the here and now, that always felt so distant and strange. Though not now, I realized, not this moment right now. It felt good to talk to Veronica. I was surprised by it, how wonderful the world seemed with Veronica next to me, ready to hurl herself into it.

'Lil, you act like you've got one foot in the grave,' she said. 'You may be on the mature side, but you're still hot. I bet guys check you out all the time, don't they?'

'Veronica!' I said. 'Don't make fun of an old lady.'

'I'm not,' she said. 'And you're not that old, either. Look at Sophia Loren. Vanessa Redgrave. I saw her on Broadway, and she was stunning. Better-looking than half my friends. Oh, and you should have seen my grandmother. A ring on every finger until the day she died. Even on her deathbed, she refused to take them off.'

I looked into the window across from us and focused in on my own reflection. The lines etched in my face, the white hair. It was ridiculous to imagine that I was anything but what I was now.

'Being young is overrated, anyway,' she said.

I laughed. 'Only a very young person could say that. When you're young, you have no way to understand how painful it is, watching the world drop away. Your own body turn in on itself.'

'I'm not afraid of dying,' she said, standing up. 'That final adventure, right?'

'That, my child, is because you're young,' I said.

She poked me. 'When I'm old, I'm coming to find you. We'll duke it out with our canes.'

We got off the train and walked up Eighth Avenue, to Thirty-eighth Street. Fabric and notions stores lined the streets. The windows were full of dresses, mannequins swathed in bright, gauzy materials. We stopped in front of a window and peered in. Tiny gold beads streamed down a vivid red silk lined in shiny gold. A lime green swirled through with orange, like sherbet.

'Oh, these are like saris,' she said. 'I was almost thinking of heading out to Jackson Heights and getting one.'

'Miss Lillian!' The voice, coming from the other side of the street, cut through me.

I turned around, my heart sinking.

'Who's that?' Veronica asked. 'You know that guy?'

'My landlord.' I wanted to disappear.

Leo approached us, cutting across the street. 'I was just at the post office,' he said, 'when I saw you.' He looked over at Veronica. 'I'm Leo. Pleased to meet you.'

'Veronica,' she said, holding out her hand.

He took her hand and smiled. I was surprised to see how charming he looked, standing there in jeans and a suit jacket, his hands in his pockets. His dark hair curling around his face. 'So what are you ladies up to today?'

'Not much,' I said.

'Shopping,' Veronica said. 'I'm making a dress. Lil here is helping me.'

'What's the occasion?'

'A gala event at the Pierre. She's setting me up with a *prince*.' She pursed her lips, and he laughed.

'I suppose you do need a dress, then.' His laugh was open, flirtatious. 'Well, I won't keep you, ladies.' He turned to me. 'Have you had a chance to go over the papers?'

'Not yet,' I said. And then, quickly, 'I will call you.'

'Do,' he said. 'It's urgent. You know where to find me.'

'Yes,' I said.

He looked at me one beat longer, then nodded, bowed slightly. 'It was a pleasure,' he said. 'And lovely to meet you, Veronica.'

She watched him go, then followed me into the shop. 'He's so cute,' she said. 'What's your secret, lady? How do you know all these guys?'

I felt sick. I put out my hand and started running it over cottons, wools, silks, and satins. There were rolls of fabric piled on either side of us and lining the walls.

'I don't know,' I said. 'Just lucky, I suppose.'

'I'll say. Where is your apartment, anyway?'

'Thirty-sixth Street.' I told her the address. 'Why?'

'So I can partake of your leftovers, of course!' She picked up a sparkly red fabric lined with silver beading and held the end up to her face. 'How does it look?'

Her eyes were bright and an intense blue next to the fabric. Her burnt orange hair looked strange next to the deep red and silver, sort of wonderful.

'It's stunning,' I said. I picked up a light aqua fabric hanging beside me. 'Look at this one.'

'Nice,' she said, reaching out and rubbing her fingers over it. 'So what was that about, anyway?'

'What?'

'With your landlord.'

'Oh, nothing,' I said. 'A repair. Something about the pipes.'

She nodded, distracted by a stretchy mustard-colored fabric covered over in blue butterflies. 'I feel truly traumatized by this fabric, Lil.'

'What about this one?' I asked, pointing to an olive green cotton with purple starbursts.

'You know there are entire stores in this neighborhood devoted to spandex? I'm sure you do, but I do think it's a fact worth repeating.'

'There's one called Stretch World, down the street.'

'Hey, do you think I should make the dress from spandex? I'm sure there's a lovely variety of colors. What do you think?'

I was about to respond when I saw it. An ice blue silk, like liquid silver. I walked toward it, ran my hands over it.

'Look at this,' I said.

She dropped the yellow thing and rushed over. 'Oh,' she said. 'That is stunning, isn't it?' She rubbed it with her fingers. 'And so soft. I could bathe in this!'

I rolled off a bit, held it up to her face. Her skin glowed next to it.

'I think it's perfect,' I said.

I was so close to tears I could barely speak. I couldn't have conjured anything better.

'Me, too. This is what I've been picturing since we talked.'

'And I have the perfect thing to go with it. Just a little extra touch. I'll bring it for you.' I thought of the scarf I had bought, that I'd kept folded in tissue in my dresser drawer. 'It'll make your outfit complete.'

'I feel like I'm getting married,' she said, laughing. 'I should have a line of girls in hideous pink taffeta walk out before me. I'm sure this is the closest I'll ever come, anyway.'

'We'll see about that.'

We found the other materials – the tulle, a very fine silver net, and dark blue organza, for the petticoat. The owner cut the fabric for her and wrapped it in a bag.

We left the store and entered a notions shop down the street. It was my favorite one: like someone's old attic, a beautiful mess with aged wood on the ceilings and towering dressers like card catalogs with lines of drawers filled with beads, buttons, zippers, sequins, hooks, needles, ribbons, and appliqués. Everything crammed up together. Rows and rows of thread and needles. While Veronica picked out thread and plastic boning strips for the corset, silver eyelets for the ribbon to lace through, all the materials to put the dress together, I opened drawer after drawer and ran my fingers through the piles inside. Gorgeous square silver buttons that felt like coins in my hand and clanked together. Tiny pink buttons you could see through, like delicate rosebuds. Heavy cloisonné beads that sounded like marbles rolling around inside.

Veronica was laughing with the man behind the counter. Showing him the fabrics and describing to him, in detail, the embroidery she planned for the front of the corset, thin blue ribbing in vertical strips. I could see he was thoroughly charmed.

Inside a drawer on the bottom row of the dresser was a small, faded box that would once have held jewelry. I pulled it out, heard a rattling inside, like melting icicles. I opened it and looked down on a collection of tiny vintage crystals. They caught the light and sparkled up at me. It could almost have been a gathering of fairies, right there.

'Veronica,' I called. 'Look.'

She came over, squealed with delight when she saw them. 'Imagine those scattered across the tulle, like a spray of water.'

'Yes. Exactly. Can you do something so elaborate in less than a week?' I asked.

'If I work like a madwoman,' she said, laughing, ebullient. 'But I *am* mad, and I *am* a woman. And I get obsessive with a project I'm really into. I want this dress to be like something you've never seen before. Like I'm from outer space, or the bottom of the ocean.'

I had a vision then, of Cinderella at her spinning wheel. But the girl before me didn't look a thing like Cinderella had, with her moon hair and pale eyes. Veronica was all color, life.

'Plus I want George to faint dead away when he sees me,' she said.

I scooped a few crystals into my palm, let them scatter back into the drawer. I breathed out, using all the magic I had left, all the magic surrounding me even then, my sister so close to me that I could almost hear her tinkling laughter. The crystals filled and sparked. *She was made for him.*

'Use these,' I said. 'And everything will be perfect.'

CHAPTER THIRTEEN

'Why don't you want to go? You have to go. Look how beautiful you are. Look at the carriage and the horses waiting for you.'

She lay in the grass, her hair messed and tangled, her dress stained and sticking to her skin, her feet bare. The shoes and diamonds sparkled in the grass, the weeds shot up all around.

I knelt on the grass and moved toward her. I touched her shoulder, her arm, to soothe her. I pushed up behind her and wrapped my arm around her waist.

The whole night smelled of jasmine and honeysuckle.

I knew I should be filling her up. I dug in to find my fairy powers, my magic, the strength and spirit that would infuse her and make her feel beautiful, make her ready for this night.

But I was empty. It seemed as if it was she who was entering me and not the other way around. My hand rested on her stomach, and I clenched my fist, clutching the silk, trying to stem the flow of pain from her into me. She leaned back, pushing her shoulders into my chest. Her neck was in my face, my hand under her cheek and tangled in her hair.

'I miss my mother so much,' she whispered. I could feel my palms growing damp with her sweat and tears. I was dizzy with it. Her grief seemed to hang over us, sink through skin and bone.

'I know you do,' I said. 'I know you miss her.'

'She was my best friend,' she said. 'She used to let me help her paint. We used to swim every day in the river. Every night she would spend an hour brushing my hair. I loved her smell, and the jewelry on her dresser that she let me try on. We used to dance around the room and laugh so hard I thought I would be sick from it.'

'Yes,' I said. 'Such happy memories. It is good to not forget. But you can't live in them. You can't forget the present.'

The words felt like splinters I was pulling out of skin. They sounded hollow and strange, even to me. I did not know what to say to her, even as I felt the stale words pushing through me. All I could see was the vision of her mother floating on the water. The curve of her lips just below mine.

'I have no present,' she said, her voice barely audible, and I understood.

We were two ciphers lying in the grass, ruined, the horses and the carriages shimmering in front of us, mirages flickering in and out, threatening at any moment to return to twigs and pumpkins, the earth. It seemed, right then, that the whole world was that way, empty, populated by ghosts. That there was nothing real at all. *Go back*, I told myself. *Go back to the fairy lake, your friends, your world.*

But I couldn't move. The silk and tears under my palm. Her starlit hair. The darkening night and the musky scent of the jasmine cloaking us, like a veil. I couldn't even imagine moving. I clutched her, buried my face into her neck.

'Don't cry,' I said. 'Please.'

'I just want to disappear,' she said.

Even as she said it, I could feel her slipping from my grasp, and I held on to her.

'Help me, Godmother,' she said. 'Help me go back to her.'

I could see her mother's body by the edge of the water, her stepmother's face hovering above hers in the dark room, the cooks and maids and stable hands abusing her. I could see her bent over the stone floor with a bucket by her side, covered in ash under the chimney. I could see her on the floor of the stable, clutching herself. I could see the blade against her skin, the moon shining against the river, the drops of blood hitting the water's surface.

I wanted all her pain, her dreams and thoughts and memories. Her skin and hair. The straw pressing into her. She was unspeakably beautiful. All of it was. This pain and desire and emptiness and grief, this terrible longing moving from her to me and back again. The world I knew – the fairy lake, my sister, my friends, our days spent flying through reeds and across treetops – seemed blank, dull. I wanted this. Her life moving through me. I wanted to love a human so much that I could feel pain like hers when they were gone.

I sat up suddenly. There was a buzzing against my ear, but when I turned, there was only empty space. I looked around. The carriage and horses were barely there now, just flickers against the darkening sky. Only the tip of the sun was visible from behind the mountains, a hot orange line searing over them. It seemed as if the whole world had stopped, and yet if I pricked my ears and listened very closely to the night air, I could hear the violins and flutes, the pop of wine being opened, the click of heels on the marble dance floor.

Soon it would be too late for her to go, and I would have failed everyone. This was my job. Who I was.

I tried to pull myself from her thoughts, wrench myself from the pain that was filling me. It was coming into me so quickly I could barely breathe.

'Cinderella,' I said, trying to make my voice firm. And then again: 'Cinderella!'

'What is it, Godmother?'

Her voice clutched at me, pulled me down like an anchor. I had to use all my strength to gain control of myself, what I was saying.

I spoke as calmly and deliberately as I could. 'The ball has started. I can't take you back to her, but I can take you to him. He is your future.'

She twisted around to stare up at me. 'I have no future.'

I reached into myself, and there was nothing there. I had no power now, I realized. No way to help her.

'You are so kind, Godmother,' she said, pushing herself up from the grass on her elbows. 'No one has ever been this kind to me.'

'I'm sorry,' I whispered.

'You can do anything. These shoes,' she said, reaching over and holding one up, watching it glow in the pale light, 'you just imagined them, didn't you?'

She was so calm now.

'They are tricks,' I whispered. 'That's all we can do in your world.'

'I imagine things all the time,' she said. 'But I can't do anything. I can't make one thing change. I have lived in this house for five years, you know. I haven't left it. Not even once.'

'I am here now,' I said, and I could feel the desperation hacking at my chest, 'to change things for you. To change your entire life. Don't you understand that? Everything will change.'

'It's too late for me,' she said. The night seemed to have gone black, all at once, and in the starlight she looked like a ghost. If I blinked, she might disappear, along with the horses and carriage.

'No,' I said. 'It's not. Upstairs, in your room, you were so happy! When you were transformed. Let's go back. I can do it all over again. A new dress, new everything.'

She looked at me, confused. 'I wasn't happy,' she said.

'You were,' I said. 'You dreamed of him. I came and made you beautiful, for him.'

I reached out for her, but it was as if she'd turned to ash. She slipped out of my reach and stared at me.

'I never dreamed of him,' she said.

I felt like I was floating. Like nothing was real. I crouched on my knees and leaned toward her. 'But I was in your head,' I whispered. 'I felt what you felt, saw what you saw. You were in a field. He was walking toward you.'

'No,' she said, her voice low. Shaking her head and moving back on the grass. She looked afraid now. I wanted to scream. Grab her by her shoulders and shake her until she admitted that what I said was true.

'Don't you remember? It was a big field. It stretched out in every direction. He was walking toward you. The prince. Reaching out to you.'

'No,' she said, firmer now. She straightened her back and looked right at me. 'I don't think about the prince. I never think about the prince.'

'I was there.'

'Sometimes I dream of my father,' she said before I could continue. 'A field we used to play in, he and I, when I was a child. When my mother was having an episode, he would take me there. I don't care about the palace. Any of that.'

'What do you mean?' I asked. I couldn't understand anything suddenly. 'You were made for him. To go to the ball and fall in love. You should be dancing with him right now. I thought—'

I stopped. Remembered the dream then. The man in the field, the longing that seared through her whole being.

'Godmother,' she said, 'if you are here to help me, then help me go back to them. My mother and father. Our house by the lake.'

'But—'

'I want to swim in the lake with my mother. I want to dance with her in the garden. I want the three of us to walk together in that field.'

'But I can't—'

'No, Godmother. You can do anything. Anything you want. I would give anything to be like you.'

I just stared at her, speechless.

'Please help me.'

She had not been happy, I realized. I had imagined it. Her eyes lighting up in the mirror as she watched herself. Her twirling around and kicking up the glass slippers, turning her ankles to see. Her skipping down the great hall, excitement crackling and streaming through her. Had I imagined all of it?

'You aren't real,' I said, and I felt tears on my cheeks as I spoke. 'I can't tell what is real.'

She gave me a strange smile. I could barely see her face in

the dark. 'I didn't know that fairies cried,' she said. Her voice was kind now, soft.

'I am supposed to send you,' I said. 'It's my role. What I was sent for. I have to send you. I have to.'

'Oh, Godmother,' she said, leaning toward me. Reaching out her arm and stroking my hair. 'You are so beautiful. I have never seen anyone so beautiful as you.'

'I'm not even human,' I said.

'Your hair is so red. I've never seen hair as red as yours, or eyes as green.'

'Stop,' I said. I grabbed her wrist. My thumb rubbed against the scar, which seared into me. 'Stop! They're not real. Don't you see? None of it is real! I'm not even human!'

'You're hurting me,' she said, and I dropped her wrist suddenly, saw the marks where my nails had cut into her, into the wound.

'I am not even human!'

The slippers were broken, I realized then. Shattered into bits. Long shards of glass spread out around her, next to us. I couldn't remember her having broken them. She looked right into me, her face inches away. I flinched. Her eyes were so hollow and dead. How had I not noticed before?

The day before the ball was a Friday, and I went to work at the normal time, knowing full well that it could be my last day. That it would be my last day. The alternative was unthinkable.

I walked up and down the aisles of the store, feeling the spines of the books under my palm. I opened the case behind the register one last time and took out the book. I stared again at my favorite pictures, the leaves running down the sides of the page, the words scribbled in French. Left there, just for me. *All my old loves will be returned to me.*

Yes.

George came down just before noon.

'Are you excited?' I asked him.

'Yeah,' he said. 'I'm excited. Not to put on a tux, and not to see my ex-wife, but Veronica seems great.'

'You think so?' I asked. I could barely contain my excitement. 'I think you two are perfect for each other. I think this will change everything.'

George laughed, then reached over and put his hand on mine. 'Thank you, Lil. You may be getting a little ahead of yourself, but I appreciate it, that you care so much.'

I watched his face. There was a sadness to him, something in his eyes that made me breathe in. It had always been there. It had been in Theodore's face, too, I realized. Even then I had responded to that.

'You're welcome,' I said. 'And I want to thank you as well, for everything you've done for me.'

He gave me a strange look. 'What do you mean?'

'Just letting me work here. Giving me a place. I didn't always have a place, you know.'

'What's up, Lil?' he asked. 'You're acting like you won't see me again.'

A bit of cool air swept through the room as a young couple came in the front door.

'No. I just want to thank you. I never have.'

For a moment the way he looked at me took me off guard. As if I were young, as if he could see into me.

'Well, it has been my pleasure, madam,' he said. 'You're

a mystery, you know that? Someday you should tell me your story.'

'Yes, I should,' I said, looking down.

And I thought, for a second, what if I told him? What if I told him and Veronica both? Just sat down and said, *This is who I am. This is who I was, this is what I did, and this is how I'm setting things right.* What if I told him I was leaving?

I would have given anything to have my powers again, right then, and be able to hear George's thoughts, feel what he felt. Humans had seemed so simple to me once, when I had not understood anything at all.

'I hope . . .' I didn't know how to say it. 'I hope this works out for you.' The way it was supposed to work out for Cinderella and the prince. I didn't know how to tell him what I had seen in him. What I wanted to see: him and Veronica, together, erasing all the longing and sadness from each other. He would laugh if I told him that.

'Thanks, Lil. Well, I'd better get going. I've got to pick up my tux, then head up to Chelsea to meet a client.'

'Oh,' I said, reaching out to him. 'Will you be back today?'

He looked at me in surprise, and I caught myself. 'I don't think so,' he said. 'But I'll see you Monday morning. Maybe we can have an early breakfast across the street. I'll tell you all about *the ball.*' He emphasized the last two words and smiled.

He does not believe he can be happy, I thought.

'That would be wonderful,' I said.

'I'll see you Monday.'

I watched him leave, his dark hair falling past his collar, his long body pushing out the door.

It hadn't occurred to me before then that I might miss the

human world when I left. How much I would miss George. But then I thought of everything I would be returning to.

I spent the rest of the day putting things in order, the way I always did. Restoring order to the shelves, helping people pick out just the right book, wrapping their purchase in a brown paper bag. I tried to get through all the boxes George had piled in back.

When I left work, I thought about going to the diner to eat but then decided to do something more special. I had so little time left. I considered going down to the water, but it was too soon, much too soon for that.

And suddenly New York seemed wide open, wonderful, enchanted. I wanted to go somewhere new. A place I'd never been. My mind ran through all the possibilities – the far-flung beaches, the zoo, the botanical gardens, the planetarium where constellations lit up all at once in the dark. And then I thought of what George had told me, about the fairy paintings at the Frick.

I didn't mind the long walk. I made my way over to Fifth Avenue, filled with excitement. The cars slid down the avenue like fish, their headlights glowing, and every building had an illuminated wrought-iron entryway with a doorman standing in it, ready to usher people in or out. There were posh people everywhere, with their small dogs, their town cars pulling up to the curbs, their perfumed skin and puffing hair. I walked past, invisible, my hands stuffed in my pockets. I glanced into the lobbies, saw marble floors and chandeliers sparkling, hanging down.

I thought of the palace and its silver stairs. How they had felt under my human form, the glass slippers clacking against metal.

An hour later I turned on Seventieth, and the street

was darker now, lined with town houses fronted by swooping banisters, greenery bursting out of the windows and doorways. There were whole worlds in each one, I thought, imagining what I might have been able to see once on a street like this. Of course, the world was so crowded now. The thoughts and dreams swirling here would likely move into a fairy and eat her alive. Wouldn't they? I laughed. I thought of Cinderella's stepmother and her dream: the banquet tables laid with food, the chests overflowing with jewels.

Men and women walked by holding hands, stepping out of cars, walking up into the palaces lining the streets. I thought of Veronica and George, how perfect and alive they were, the way her eyes would glitter when she looked at him, her lashes batting up and down like wings, and how flushed he would become under her gaze. I thought of her ice blue dress with the crystals shining off it, wrapping around her body and clashing with her hair.

I could see all of it.

The Frick came up on my right, surrounded by a regal dark fence. I took a breath and stepped through the main door, past the security guards and around the side, to the front desk.

Inside, it was a riot of color, all around. I was surprised that it was an old house, a mansion someone had lived in once. I could *feel* the presence of lives in the walls and air, even before I read about them.

I bought a ticket, then walked slowly through, one grand room after another, past the ornate furniture that was on the verge of crumbling, the fireplaces, the paintings that took up whole walls. Everything rubbed up against everything else. As I walked from room to room, I heard whispers, laughter. At one point I saw men and women standing around the couches with drinks in their hands, and stopped in my tracks. They were gone a moment later, the whole place turning so quiet I could hear my breath, my beating heart. The faint movements of the pacing guards.

I entered a great hallway, a long rectangle of a room lined in paintings. Every kind of painting, it seemed. Whole worlds clashed and collided with each other there. Stormy scenes, dark trees bent against blackening, melancholy skies. Portraits, faces staring out, spoke of other, ghostlier worlds. I thought of everyone, all the places and people I had known, the dreams I had taken up into myself and could still feel rustling there, deep down.

I stopped and stared into one of the paintings: a lit-up, butter-colored harbor with long boats teeming against the shoreline, where men and women wandered and worked and waited. The sky glowed and turned to dark, then to a bright dewy blue, almost translucent. Sugary. The water was green and brown and blue, constantly changing, almost alive. I could see the sun and the buildings reflected in it, growing and spreading across the surface, feel the cool sprays of it flicking onto my hands and face. *The sky*, I thought, *is going to break open.* I stepped closer, stared into one of the boats, the people working there and the sails dangling and folding down, like sheets hung out to dry, and then the faces, the people bent over, moving. I could hear them talking, shouting orders. I could hear the sounds of their feet stomping across the hull, the planks of wood, the water slapping against it, and the tug and groan as the boat stopped and swayed in the harbor.

'Ma'am?'

I recognized something. A familiar line of the jaw, arch of the forehead. A clock, I saw then, rising up across the water. Chiming one, two, three . . .

'Excuse me, ma'am?' A hand touched my arm. 'Ma'am, are you okay? I need you to step back behind this line.'

I looked down, disoriented. Green carpet, a yellow line.

I moved then, but I could feel the tears bubbling up in me, pressing against my eyelids. I looked back at the painting but it was all still now, quiet. A lovely scene lit from within, as if a heart were glowing from inside of it. The figures on the boat were motionless, drawn in black paint. The clock tower had disappeared.

A stairwell led to a cluster of rooms downstairs. A painting caught my eye immediately as I walked in. I stepped closer. The colors seemed to shimmer off the canvas, greens and blues and golds. I focused in. A fairy scene. Three fairies next to a lake, dancing on the grass beside it. Behind them, a scattering of lights.

I could reach into the painting and feel water, grass, light. I could feel the wind breaking against my face as I flew through it. The water skimmed against feathers as I dove in, exchanging the air for the fairy lake, pressing into the water, my wings spread out like sails as I went deeper and deeper into the other world. The elders sat at their thrones; the gnarled trees swayed back and forth in the water.

I checked the date of the painting: 1831. I leaned in but could not make out the fairies' faces. They could have been my own kind but also could have been any other fairy tribe. Had they shown themselves, too?

I didn't want to step away. The colors were rich, like juice or candy. My body, with its aches and fatigue, felt different, as if I were one gesture from flight. Back in the other world, flying had been as natural as breathing. I barely had to tilt my wings, think of air, before I was gliding through it. In the water I could dip my head and propel forward like a great fish, the water skimming through each feather, massaging them.

A guard stood at the edge of the room, watching me. I nodded to him, then saw the painting to the left of the one I'd been looking at.

It was a forest scene. A beautiful girl with pale blond hair lay in the grass, her body spread out and angled strangely. The grass was covered in blood. Over her hovered the small body of a fairy, the unmistakable sheen of wings. It was evening, and the moon was above, shining through the trees.

In the background you could see the coach, a horse barely visible against the black night. The trees dropped over the scene, their leaves pale green in the moonlight.

I couldn't breathe. I looked up at the guard, but he didn't seem to know what was happening. He was just standing there as if everything were normal.

The fairy was tiny, her wings a blur of movement, but still bright white. You could just make out the red of her hair, like a tiny flickering flame.

I looked at the plaque next to the painting.

1834, ANONYMOUS.

'What is this?' I said, turning to the guard.

He looked up at me, confused. 'Ma'am?'

'Do you know anything about this painting?' I asked.

'No,' he said. 'I'm sorry.'

I turned back to the canvas. Her pale skin, her peaceful face.

The blood, sickly and dark in the moonlight. I could have been right there. As if not one minute had gone by.

I studied the painting, tried to memorize every detail. There was something strange about the trees, I saw after a minute, and I looked more closely. Up in the right-hand corner, in the array of heart-shaped leaves dappled with moonlight, leaves that shifted from pale to dark green, there was a smattering of lights. *Fairies.*

'You were there,' I whispered. 'You were there, watching.'

The room was silent.

'Are you here now?'

In the corner of my eye: the curve of a wing, the blurred light above me. I turned, and there was nothing.

I did not know how to feel. What to think.

My head spun. Someone had recorded that ancient scene. And if it *had* happened, if it had become a part of history, hadn't it been destined to happen? What if everything had turned out the way it had been destined to all along? What if it had happened exactly as it was supposed to? Maybe they were never destined to be together, Cinderella and the prince. Maybe it was him and me, all along.

I felt dizzy. After a few more minutes, I went upstairs, moving back through the rooms, passing angels and mirrors and overstuffed couches and chairs and the guards staring out at me, until I heard the sound of water and entered a columned marble room with a long fountain in the center. The water tumbled down from it into a shallow pool below.

Above, the glass ceiling arced and glowed, filtering a strange light into the room and onto the water. Around the fountain, green plants jutted, and the leaves spread like long fans in the air. White flowers drooped from the stems. It was a courtyard, right in the middle of the building, with lights hanging from the ceiling around it.

On the other side from where I was standing, there was a statue, a tall bronze statue of a creature with flaring, jagged wings.

I dropped then, next to the water.

My face stared back at me, and I bent down into it. Relief poured through me.

I thought of Cinderella, what the modern world had made of her. The flat cartoons, the children's books, the films that surrounded her with birds and mice and all the creatures of the forest. That showed her with a pouf of hair and a dress like a cape. Her hand raised to her mouth, her eyes as big as saucers.

I hadn't realized until then how many times I had doubted myself.

Chapter fourteen

She was pulling me in. I'd heard of fairies who couldn't find their way once a human heart grabbed hold of them like this. The pain was moving from her to me so fast – the memories, her sickness – that soon there would be nothing left of me. My powers were already almost gone. *Concentrate*, I thought. I pulled myself up, lifted myself off the ground, stood over her.

'Cinderella,' I said, making the words that I would speak as fierce as I could, willing all my strength into them. 'You have to go to the ball. You cannot turn your back on your own destiny. I was sent here by the fairies, to get you there. Whatever you feel now, he will erase it.'

She just stared back at me with those hollow eyes.

'Cinderella,' I repeated. 'Are you listening to me?'

Her memories were so sharp in my mind. I squeezed my eyes shut, trying to will them away, but they flared up at me like suns. I saw all that her stepmother and stepsisters had done to her. What the servants had done to her. The beatings she had received, the ways her body had been abused. I was angry, suddenly, at my world. Swooping down to save her and give her a new life when we should have seen what the old one was doing to her. She was obviously damaged, those eyes, the bruises on her skin, her dark heart. And her thoughts. I could hear them. Little twitterings between the locks of her moonlight hair: 'I am not fit for a prince.' 'I am nothing.' 'A little cinder girl.'

'Please,' she said. 'I do not want to go.'

I stared at her. She had everything. We had given her the greatest gift a human girl could have, and she was willing to toss it away.

The anger came up on me in a flash. 'This is your fate,' I said. I wanted to spit the words at her, turn them into knives and arrows. 'What we have fated for you. Do you think you can ignore that? We all have to do what we are fated to do. Every one of us.'

Again I could feel the ball and what was happening there. It pulled me so strongly. I could feel Cinderella's memories roiling around inside me, but they were no longer wiping out everything else.

And I could feel him. Waiting for me. Taste his lips as he stalked across the marble floor, his eyes sweeping in every direction.

'No, Godmother,' she said, shrinking back from me. 'I can't go. Please do not be angry with me.'

I bent down, leaned into her. The tone of my voice changed, shifted. 'You would defy fate?' Even on the ground, with tears running down her cheeks, she looked like a princess. I could *feel* him. I knew what would happen the moment he saw her. 'A little cinder girl like you?'

She did not move. She didn't even seem to have heard me at

first, but then she looked up, straight into me, and for a moment I thought I saw something ferocious in her staring back. Could she hate me? Me, who had been sent to help her?

I tried to dip into it, what she was feeling, but something was stopping me, something in her. Why couldn't I change her? Why couldn't I enter her thoughts, fill her with excitement and desire?

The horses and carriage glimmered faintly, barely visible in the darkness, and the thoughts seemed to rush up on me: *Because I am the one who desires him.* And then, *Because I could go in her place.*

Even as my mind reeled against it, told me that this was something *I could not have*, I felt a soaring from deep within my body. I wanted this. This night.

She was right: She did not deserve it.

And someone needed to go to the ball, make the prince fall in love. It was supposed to be her, but I could go in her place. They might never know it was not her. Later I could fix everything.

I took a deep breath. 'Fine, Cinderella,' I said. 'You will not go, then.'

I would need to dress as she had. I would need everything back again, the way it was.

'Please, Godmother,' she said. 'If you came here to help me, take me back to them. My mother and father.'

I looked up at the moon. Now that I knew what I was going to do, I had to hurry. 'I have to leave you,' I said. 'We have only until midnight. But I will come back.'

'Please,' she said, standing up and reaching for me. 'Don't go. Please help me. I need you!'

'No,' I said. I pushed her away. 'I will be back soon. Wait here.'

I turned, concentrated. Focused all my energy. I reached down and picked up a leaf. I rubbed it between my thumbs, felt it start to come apart, threw it to the ground.

A pair of glass slippers appeared. Glittered like two chunks of ice from the grass.

I walked to a tree, pried away a bit of bark with my fingers. I crumbled it in my hands and dropped it over me, imagining, as it fell, my hair sweeping past my shoulders. I gathered up a pile of leaves and blew them over my body. A dress appeared on my form, like a river shifting in the light.

'What are you doing?' she said behind me.

'I will not be long,' I said as I slid my feet into the slippers, one by one. 'I will be back soon.'

'Why are you dressed like that?' she said. 'Stay and help me, please! I can't go back there. I need you!'

I looked at her. She was desperate now, trembling. Her memories tumbled over me, and I swatted them off. I had offered her the perfect life, and she had refused it. How could we ever have thought she could be with the prince?

And then something in me softened. It was not her fault. None of it was.

'Wait here, my child,' I said. 'I will return soon. I promise. I will help you then.' I reached out and pulled her to me, held her close. 'Shh,' I said, stroking her hair. 'Just wait a little while longer, and I will help you.'

'Hurry,' she said. 'Please.'

I let go of her, then turned and stepped into the coach, which seemed to flicker to life as I entered it. The horses stamped their feet, and the driver looked back at me, his face translucent, the night fully visible behind him.

I felt amazing, powerful. In this world I could have everything. I could devour it. Him. I could go to the ball and make them forget everything else. I could have the powers the fairy world gave me but also be one of them. I could wield this power and still feel the love and pain and desire move through me. The rot and despair.

I leaned toward the window, reaching for the door, and then the horses snapped into action, the driver yelled into the night air, and we were off. The coach bounced and rumbled along the narrow road. I looked back at her, lying in the grass now, under the moon, her dress already flickering as the magic began to wear away, and at the same time I could feel him, waiting.

And for that moment I felt as if everything was exactly as it should be.

Veronica lived right off Tompkins Square Park, on Seventh Street between Avenues A and B. The early evening was crisp, and it was the first time it felt as though summer was actually ending. The whole city seemed to be coming to life again after the months of heat and haze.

I cut through the park to get to her. I slipped along the paths that were usually open to the world but now felt like part of some secret, enchanted place. I loved everything. I ran my fingers along the benches and railings and the bark of the trees. I pulled off pieces of bark, bits of leaf and twig, and gathered them in my palms. A few people lay sleeping on the benches – homeless men with bags piled beneath them – but even they seemed enchanted, like princes who had fallen under a spell. I imagined myself perched on a tree branch, watching Veronica, and had to stifle my laugh.

I stepped up to her building. *This is it,* I thought. Every moment, every horrible day I'd spent on this earth, had led me here. My pain was forgotten. Trying to fly, trying to find them all before now – I had just been impatient. All the signs had been there. And they had all led me to this moment, right now.

Bit by bit I dropped the bark and leaves and twigs to the ground, imagining, as they fell, a dress and a pair of shoes and a pair of crystal earrings rising in their places.

I rang her bell. She buzzed me in. As I walked down the hallway, I could barely breathe.

She stood waiting for me, and as soon as I saw her, I knew it had worked. All the magic I had summoned up for her. 'Your hair,' I said, smiling. It was so blond it was almost white. It was stunning next to her pale skin, her bright blue eyes.

'Yes!' she said. She gleamed with excitement, tilted her head left and then right. 'What do you think?'

'You look beautiful. You look . . . classic. I had no idea you could look so . . .'

'Glamorous?' she asked.

'Very glamorous,' I said. 'And it's so long suddenly . . .' Her hair swung down to her shoulders, curling up at the ends. Perfect moon hair.

'Isn't it great? They're extensions. Kim did them for me. I didn't think I'd have time with finishing the dress and all, but we just stayed up the whole night and did it. I thought about having hair down to my lower back but went for the Veronica Lake look instead. I mean, it seems fitting.'

'It does,' I said. 'It is.'

'Are you okay?' she asked. 'You look like you've seen a ghost.'

'I think I have,' I said. 'You just . . . look so much like someone I used to know.'

'Veronica Lake, maybe? Marlene Dietrich?' She posed, batted her lashes.

'Maybe,' I said.

'So come inside,' she said. 'Make yourself at home. I know it's a mess. I meant to clean, though. Which I think counts for something. But yeah, there's clutter. I don't have medical insurance, but I've got two hundred pairs of shoes and fifty corsets.'

I stepped in. Her one-room apartment was like a jewelry box flung open: a crazy-quilt-covered bed practically lay on top of a sagging purple velvet couch; a dressmaker's mannequin with a sheet thrown over it stood next to it; clothes and lingerie and swatches of fabric were draped across the furniture and chairs and sewing table; gauzy red curtains hung in front of the windows. There seemed to be enough for two or three apartments crammed into one room. An old-fashioned vanity was sandwiched between the bed and the kitchen counter, and I walked over, fascinated by the elaborate hand mirror, the pots of gloss and blush and glitter and jewelry that lay on top.

'So how did it go? Where's the dress?' I asked. 'I'm dying to see it.'

'You know what we need first, Lil?' she asked. 'Some sangria and some ambience.' She lit a stick of incense that was poking out of a can on the coffee table, then went over to the refrigerator. 'Go ahead, make yourself at home.'

I waded through the clutter on the floor to the couch. A black lace bra was draped over the arm, and I pushed it off and sat down.

She opened the small refrigerator and took out wine and seltzer and fruit. She reached down and pulled a bottle of liquor from a shelf below.

'So you really think this is the guy for me?' she asked, looking over at me.

'Yes,' I said. 'I do.'

'How do you know?'

'I can see it.'

'I wish I could. I would have saved myself a lot of heartache, that's for sure.'

I looked around. Herbs and dried flowers hung in the doorways. *To attract fairies*, I thought, smiling. A deck of tarot cards lay on her windowsill.

A few minutes later, she handed me my drink. I sat forward and took a long sip, surprised by its sweetness.

'Okay,' she said, rubbing her hands together. 'Ready?'

'Yes.'

'I spent hours of my life on this thing, Lil.'

'Show me!'

She moved to the mannequin, lifted the sheet, and flung it off.

I closed my eyes, pictured it. Willed it into being. And then I opened them.

The dress was a confection of ice blues and crystals, layers of silk and tulle, a petticoat underneath that made the skirt fluff out on either side. The tulle, strung through with crystals, hung over the silk like a watery net, just as I had envisioned. Underneath, the blue shimmered, seemed to change color.

I reached over, ran my palm along the fabric.

'Look at the back,' she said, turning the mannequin so

that I could see the line of tiny silver eyelets laced through with silk ribbon. 'This silk is so soft. Cutting it was like cutting butter.'

'It feels like butter,' I said. I imagined it, my legs moving against it as I walked, the silk like water against me. 'It's beautiful. It's . . . it's just stunning. I couldn't have imagined anything better.'

She reached over and hugged me spontaneously. 'Thank you for everything.'

'You're welcome,' I said. 'I envy you, the night you're going to have.'

'I just wish you were coming, too.'

'Now, don't be silly. You need to get ready, my child. The clock is ticking.'

She sighed. 'It always is.'

She sat down at the vanity. Her long back facing me, curving in at the waist. Her hair dropping past her shoulders. I could see her face in the mirror, watching herself. Even in her T-shirt and black jeans, she was luminous.

She uncapped a small tube and held a wand up to her eye, drawing a thick black line along the curve of her lid. She did the same on the other side, pulling the line so that it swept up and out at the corner. 'So I was wondering,' she said, looking at me in the mirror, 'about the story you told us in the salon.'

'Story?'

She seemed nervous suddenly, shy. 'The boy you loved. I don't mean to be nosy. I don't know how much you like talking about it. I'm just . . . Did you fall in love again, after that?'

'No,' I said. And then, more quietly, 'No. That was it for me.' The words hung in the air in front of me. I felt like I needed to explain them away, but I didn't know how. How could I explain all of it?

She dipped her finger into a pot of glitter, stroked it across her eyelids. To my surprise I realized she was close to tears. That she didn't want me to see.

She took a breath. 'Why? What was it about him? Or you?'

'I don't know,' I said. My mind beat up against her questions. I had asked myself so many times over the years, but I could never fully understand why I'd reacted the way I had. 'I guess . . . In a way I fell in love with the entire world when I met him. You know how one person can become so massive? I hadn't paid much attention to the world before that.'

She picked up a small brush and dipped it into some eye shadow spread out like artist's paint in front of her. I could see that her hands were shaking. 'How do you mean?'

I wanted so badly to tell her. Could I tell her? My wings curled at the edges, ready to spread out. Couldn't I just say, 'I was a fairy'? Tell her that I had fallen in love with a human who didn't belong to me, who'd been made for someone else? That tragedy was intertwined with our story? That I'd done a terrible thing? But how could I explain why I had done it? That I was only now setting it right all these centuries later?

And she looked just like Cinderella. Not Maybeth at all. I had to acknowledge that now.

She turned in her chair and folded her legs up under her. Her makeup was half done. Her eyes black-lined and glittering, like huge jewels. She waited for me to go on.

'I lived in my own world,' I said haltingly, 'where everything was perfect. Perfect. In that world nothing bad could ever happen. Everything was beautiful. More than beautiful. It was a place without desire of any kind.' I paused. 'I had never felt human before that. I hadn't had any interest in human things, except from a distance. I hadn't understood them.'

'Go on,' she said, nodding.

'So when I saw him for the first time, I fell in love with everything at once. I loved how it felt to long for someone, to think about him and feel myself in his thoughts, to toss and turn because I couldn't stop thinking about how the back of his neck felt under my palm. When I knew what it was like to desire something, I felt alive for the first time. Human. The way I had been before – so reserved, cold, spoiled – didn't feel right any-more. And when I couldn't have him . . . Before that, I did not know what it meant to lose anything. Where I came from, my world, no one ever lost anything at all.'

I stopped, exhausted suddenly. There was so much beating in me, so much that I couldn't express.

'I understand,' she said simply.

'I know you do.'

'You do?'

She was crying then. Just a girl, I thought. That's all she was.

'Why don't you tell me?' I said, my voice as gentle as I could make it.

'I don't . . . I don't know how to talk about it. When I think about it, I feel like I'm going to die. I stopped talking about it. I know I should be healing, getting over it.'

'No,' I said. 'You are so young.'

'My . . . He just . . . It all happened in one second, you know? Everything was normal, and then he was gone.'

'It's okay,' I said, standing up, going to her. 'Shh. You don't have to talk about it if it's too hard.'

I sat on the bench next to her.

'I dream about him, Lil. I work so hard to forget him, and then I go to sleep and . . . I just miss him.'

'I'm sorry,' I said.

She lifted her head, looked at me. 'I'm terrified. I don't think I can ever love anyone else. I'm always lonely, but I can't . . .'

'I know,' I said, stroking her hair.

'I never talk about it,' she said, 'how much it hurts me, all the time. It's empty without him. I'm empty. I'm afraid it will always be like this.'

'It won't,' I said. 'It just takes time. You are so young, Veronica.'

She sat up, wiping her face. 'I want to be better,' she said. 'I was so into this night, making this dress. I felt truly happy, you know? But I feel guilty, feeling happy when he isn't here.'

'I know.'

I could have been back in the other world. Her moon hair, her shimmering face, her wide, wet-jewel eyes. *I'm sorry*, I wanted to say. *I'm sorry that I left you.*

'Did it ever get easier for you, Lil?' she asked.

I stared at her. What could I say to her? It had never been easier for me. But she wasn't like me. She still had her world, her self.

'Yes,' I said. 'It gets easier. But I made a mistake in this life, Veronica. I gave up on the world. I gave up on everything. You can't do that.'

'What if I never get over it?' she whispered.

In the distance I could hear a church bell chiming the hour.

I stared into her, willing every bit of power I had into her, everything I had left from the other world. What I should have done for her, for Cinderella. 'You will get over it,' I said fiercely. 'It is hard. It is the hardest thing in your world. But you must keep doing it, keep living. You have to. Do you understand?'

'Everyone thinks I'm such a flake,' she said. 'Always dating all these guys, these guys who are all wrong, but it's because, because I can't——'

'I know,' I said. 'It feels impossible, I know. It is the hardest thing, letting go of someone. But you have to do it.'

'I feel like there are black holes all around me. The moment I feel okay, I step into one. I can always step into one.'

Her eyes were so hollow, the way Cinderella's had been. I felt as if she were right on the edge of something and that I would need to use every bit of strength to pull her back.

'I know,' I said. 'When I was young, centuries ago, I envied humans for that. For being able to feel that. For being capable of such love and such grief. There is something wonderful in all of it. Do you know that? What you have. The world you have. There's so much love behind everything, so much beauty. You cannot give up on it. Do you understand?'

'Yes.'

I concentrated, put everything I had into her. I would not make the same mistake again. 'This is what the world is,' I said. 'Exactly this. This is what it means to be human.'

We were quiet for a few moments.

'I didn't mean to dump all this on you, Lil,' she said finally. 'You're being so amazing and——'

'It's why I'm here,' I said.

She nodded, smiled at me through her tears. 'I must be a mess.'

'You're fine,' I said, smoothing back her hair. And she was.

Her hair glittered in front of me. Her skin as soft as silk. I looked at her and thought of pearls, the insides of shells. 'You'll be fine.'

'Thank you,' she said.

'Now, get up,' I said. 'And let's put this on you.' I stood. Carefully, as if the dress were made of glass, I unlaced it and lifted it from the mannequin.

She stood, shaky. Wiping her eyes. She pulled off her jeans, took off her T-shirt. Her body was pale and glowing. She was wearing shimmering silk stockings and a strapless bra.

Already she looked like she'd been fashioned from foam and sea.

She stepped into the dress. I helped her move it into place, then tightened the lace in back, tying it into a bow. I adjusted the dress in front and smoothed her hair where it was tousled, next to her face.

'How does it look?' she whispered. 'Is it okay?'

'Yes,' I said. 'It's beautiful.'

She would be okay, I thought. She would be more than okay: She would be happy.

We stepped out of her apartment, out of her building, into the street. We headed up Avenue B. The air was thick with the scent of a light rain, which was just beginning to fall. A cab was approaching, the roof sign lit to show that it was available.

'I'll get this for you,' I said. I lifted my arm. The cab stopped at our side. I smiled and pulled the door open for her.

She looked at me. 'Thank you,' she said, and reached over, for the second time that night, and hugged me. 'Thank you for everything. I'll come by first thing in the morning to tell you all about it.'

'You're welcome,' I said. I could feel tears pricking at my eyes. A relief so strong it was almost unbearable. Finally. It was right. She was okay now. She would be okay. I wondered if I should tell her that by morning I would be on my way home, to the other world.

I chose not to say anything. She was okay now. She would be fine.

She bent down and slid into the cab, careful to keep her hair in place, the silk of her dress smooth and straight.

'Have a wonderful time,' I said. 'Just let yourself feel everything. All of it.'

'I will,' she said. 'Thank you, Lil. Thank you for being such a good friend to me.'

And in that moment it was all perfect: The smoky early autumn air, the glitter on her face, her moonlit hair hanging to her shoulders. The pale blue dress with its ribbons and smattering of crystals. Her pale slippers disappearing behind the door.

I watched the cab rush up the street, its taillights fading out.

I closed my eyes. I couldn't hear or smell the ball, but I was almost there. I could have been there. The silver stairs. The towers. The moat and the candles. The scent of gardenia. The air, smoky from all the torches. The rain and the heat. The love and grief and beauty. The whole world, all the kingdom, everything ground down and stopped until there was only this.

My part had ended. This is where it ended. Where it should have ended. When I would have left her.

I remained alone on Avenue B, and despite the miracle that had just occurred, the street was the same as always. Groups of young people wandering along the sidewalk, the curving shapes of pipes from inside the hookah bar on the corner. A Vespa sputtering past. An old Cadillac. A Volvo. Another cab.

I reached into my purse and felt something soft in my hand. I looked down. I was holding her scarf, the one I had found for her. I couldn't believe I had forgotten to give it to her. I started to call her name, but she was gone, the taxi out of view.

It felt like an omen. My body seemed to shift, turn in on itself. I couldn't breathe suddenly. I had left her once before when I should have protected her.

I lifted my arm.

'The Pierre Hotel,' I said as the taxi came to a stop beside me.

CHAPTER FIFTEEN

I was breathless with excitement as the carriage moved through the night. I could feel him – dancing with girl after girl, his eyes pinned to the door at the top of the staircase, waiting for me to appear in front of him. His heart in his mouth. I knew he had not stopped thinking of me after the day I appeared in his chamber. His mind was full of me, my red hair and green eyes, my pale human skin. Like autumn leaves and milk. Of course, if Cinderella walked through the palace doors, she would make him forget me and that day in his chamber, the most important day of my life. I had to face that now: how that day had meant more to me than any day I'd spent in the fairy world. I would give up all of it for him – coasting along the fairy lake, gliding in the air above it. I would give it up for another day like that one, with him.

I loved the feel of the ground rushing under me, the rumble of the carriage, the sensation of silk on skin, the glass encasing my feet. I heard the ball as we rushed toward it, saw the great heaps of food spread out on the golden banquet tables, the thousand candles lit up and floating in the moat, stuck in the stone walls and along the banisters of the great staircases, the hundred silver steps outside leading to the palace's front gate. The line of golden carriages out front. The ladies and lords inside, everyone drunk with music and wine and promise. Cinderella's stepmother and stepsisters in lace and pearls and emeralds, waiting to be plucked from the crowd. And he in the center of it, staring up at the door, the top of the staircase.

Waiting for me.

The carriage rushed ahead.

And then there they were: the silver steps. Blinding me. So sharp and shining, perfect. And over them, at the top of the stairs, the great clock, its hands encrusted with jewels.

I stepped out of the carriage. The glass slipper clicked against the silver, and then I was rushing up the steps, as fast as I could, so fast I couldn't see anything, could only feel the movement from deep in my body, the need to get there, to be with him again. *This*, I thought. *This now. This is what it means to be human.* I couldn't hear, could barely see. It had all just come down to this. Him waiting, me running, the hands of the clock moving forward.

I rolled down the window, stuck my hand out, and moved my face into the breeze. We made a left on Fourteenth Street, then turned up First Avenue.

The cabdriver seemed to linger at every red light, slow down just before every yellow. He was talking loudly on his cell phone in a language I couldn't recognize. I wanted to scream.

'Please,' I said, tapping the thick divider. 'I'm in a hurry!'

He gestured to the red light and shrugged, then spoke into his cell phone more loudly than he had before.

I would not miss New York City cabs in the other world, I thought, sitting back and closing my eyes. Clenching both my hands into fists.

Veronica would be fine. She was not like Cinderella, who had been broken long before that night. Hadn't she been?

I forced myself to breathe, even as the taxi lurched into traffic.

What were the fairies doing right now, I wondered. Floating on the water? Landing on tree branches and swinging down? Taking naps in flower blossoms? Or were they right there in the taxi flitting around my neck and ears?

'Help me,' I whispered. 'Please. Make sure she is safe.'

The night was getting colder. The taxi moved forward. Thirty-fourth Street became Fortieth, then Forty-sixth. I rolled up the window and watched the street signs pass by, feeling myself getting lighter and lighter. My wings were tingling. I could almost hear the clomping of hooves. *I am coming*, I thought. *Just wait a little bit longer.*

'Pierre Hotel,' he said.

And there they were. Carriages, the forest, the castle. There were the coachmen and the guards standing around, ready to escort every lord and lady through the palace doors and into the ball inside.

I raced up the silver steps, into the palace. The torches flaring on either side of me. One of the palace guards stepped forward to escort me into the room.

And there he was. The prince, stepping out of the crowd of lords and ladies, just as I knew he would. The guard moved back to his station.

'It's you,' he said. His beautiful mouth. He lifted his hand to me.

'Yes,' I said. 'I never forgot you, Theodore.'

'Come inside,' he said, and he smiled at me, looked right into me, the way he had once, when I was hovering at the edge of a room, with no place at all in this world.

I took his hand and let him lead me inside, to where the dancers slid across the marble floor, which shone under us.

Everyone turned to watch us.

He took my hand in his. His other palm pressed against my waist. It seemed to move right through me, straight to the center of my body. I lifted my face to his.

'I was so afraid you wouldn't come,' he said. The music, light and quick, dropped over us. 'I haven't been able to stop thinking about you. You're all I think about.'

We began to dance. He pushed me out into the crowd and then pulled me back again, his hand on mine and his face in front of my face and his lips so close to mine. I could taste his breath, smell his scent, and I could see myself reflected as he twirled me about, his hand around my waist, pushing me out and bringing me back to him. Like dying and coming back to life.

He stared at me as if I could disappear any second, and he did not take his eyes off me. The music forced him away and back again, away and back again. His hand clutched mine so tightly it was beginning to hurt.

A line of ladies stood watching us. Having left the floor, standing with glasses of wine or punch in their hands. I could hear them whispering, 'Who is she? Where did she come from?' I could feel the heartbreak of the girls who'd spent weeks dreaming of this night and already realized he was for me.

Cinderella's sisters stood miserably by the stairway, unable to stop watching us.

I could hear their thoughts: *Why won't he dance with us?* But they knew why. No one had ever seen anyone like me. I was not of their world, despite the blood beating through me, my human form, my pale skin, and the sweat forming on my brow.

My body moved easily with the music. I stared back at him, into his sugar-water eyes. I felt he could see things in me that no one else could. This desire. Fairies were not supposed to want for anything. But I did. It was a secret, a gift, for him.

The music ended. He pulled me to him, my palm against his chest, and I could feel his heart beating. I had never felt a human heart before. 'Come outside with me,' he whispered, his voice ragged. My whole body flared into something else. I loved this new feeling. I felt the silk on my skin, his heart under my palm, his face next to my face.

I could smell the rain. At one end of the ballroom, a set of elaborate doors led to a long balcony that looked out over the palace gardens. Strings of gardenias had been wrapped around the railing. The scent was so strong, made stronger by the rain just beginning to fall, that it filled the ballroom.

He led me to the balcony, moving through the crowd of his subjects, who all stepped back and bowed or curtsied as he went past.

It was exquisite, ecstatic.

Outside, the rain was light. I felt wild, in love with the feelings moving through me, with his eyes that saw me, that pinned me to the spot. I pulled him to me. He slipped my gown from my shoulders. I could taste him now, like figs plucked straight from the tree.

As the clock began to chime, I pressed into him, as hard as I could, nearly suffocating him.

He didn't seem to notice, or to hear the flapping wings. He could not feel the air turn cold with it. I looked up and saw their faces, their bodies in flight, bearing down on me.

The clock chimed three times, four.

The doorman nodded and let me inside.

As I passed through the lobby of the Pierre and headed toward the ballroom, I saw men and women in the most wondrous clothes. Handsome men in bow ties and tuxes, ladies in slinky elegant dresses. They were standing about the hotel lobby, taking off jackets and scarves, blocking my way.

I pushed through. Into the next room, up the stairs.

I made my way down the hall, my heart pounding. Glancing to my right, I caught sight of a dowdy old lady rushing forward, and I almost laughed out loud. That might have been me once, I thought, but not now. I was here to help her, to make sure that the human girl met the prince and lived happily ever after. I was not of this world. My hair fell down to my shoulders like fire. I could hear the sounds of the orchestra, the tapping of feet along the marble floor. The swish of my dress as I ran down the hallway to the main ballroom.

This is who I am. I was doing exactly what I was supposed to do.

I reached the door. Inside, a roar of laughter and talking.

'Excuse me, ma'am?'

'Yes,' I said, turning, noting the suited man's surprised look.

'Can I help you, ma'am?'

He was shocked by my beauty, I thought, lowering my eyes and looking back up at him.

'Thank you, sir,' I said. 'I am fine.' I turned away, searched for her in the throng of people. I could not help it if my beauty made him mad.

And then I spotted her. She was impossible to miss, with her long body and starlight hair and the shimmering blue of her gown, against all the shorter, less beautiful women in tight black. I could hear her laughing, her head bent back, as it always was. George standing next to her with a glass of wine in his hand, making her laugh.

She was alive. She was safe. She was happy. The glow on her face! I had never seen her so happy as that, with the lights from the chandeliers glittering down on her skin, her face turned to him, and her mouth spread into a smile. She wasn't the least bit self-conscious, I realized. Together they were the most beautiful couple there. And so young. I had forgotten how young she was. She had always longed to be anywhere but where she was, and now she was here, and it was all different, everything was changed, and he would love her until she turned to ash.

What was he saying?

I leaned in, tried to hear, but whatever it was she was laughing at, she stopped. A moment later he put down the glass and led her to the floor. I watched her wrap her long arms around his neck, him slip his palms across her back.

I could feel his palms across mine.

I heard their wings against my ear, like insects on a summer night. A whirring all around me.

'I have to go,' I said, pulling away from him.

'I don't understand,' he said, his voice soft, so soft it felt as if it were coming from inside me. 'Let me help you.'

'No,' I said, my voice breaking. 'It's midnight.'

I could feel it all coming apart, feel him slipping away from me, everything cracking open, how fragile he was, how fragile she was, how everything was so fleeting, only seconds, wanting so much to be near him and knowing I could never be closer to him than this, that this is what it meant to be human, not being able to stop time, always grasping, but for that one moment, despite the pain moving through me, my broken heart, it was all so beautiful, and I was in love with all of it. *All of it.*

The clock chimed ten times, eleven times, twelve.

'I have to—' I looked into his stricken face, but I could already feel it receding from me. Their faces coming into relief. The elders. Behind me. All around me. I had to go now. There was nothing I could say to him. I pushed back into the ballroom, pulling up, fixing my dress, past the gilded old ladies, the portly men with sashes around their waists.

'At least tell me how to find you,' he called after me, and I could hear the grief in his voice, feel it in my heart at the same moment as I turned and ran through the great hall, down the grand silver stairs to where the carriages waited, my hair unraveling, my shoe falling from my foot. I ran forward, almost able to see the outline of my carriage waiting out front.

Why had they come?

And then a more horrifying thought: Did they know I had left her?

What would they do to me?

'Go!' I cried to the coachman as I threw myself inside. 'Go!!'

And he cracked the whip, and the horses, just glimmers now, raced into the night, back to her. Behind me I could hear the beating of wings.

The night air was colder now than it had been before, and I shivered in the thin dress. The ride seemed to stretch out, take twice as long as it had before.

Finally we approached the clearing. Everything was suddenly quiet. As if the whole world had gone to sleep.

The moon lit the field. I leaned forward, and there she was. Like magic. Lying where I'd left her, still in the gown, the shoes in pieces beside her. Her moon hair falling to the grass around her.

The carriage pulled to a stop, the horses reared up in front of us. I kicked off the remaining glass slipper and stepped into the grass, which was wet against my bare feet as I tiptoed over to her. I did not want to wake her. She looked so peaceful there, so beautiful with the moon pouring down over her.

'I've come back,' I whispered. 'Just like I promised.'

CHAPTER SIXTEEN

woke to the sound of pounding, someone banging on my door. The sound seeped in, insistent, interrupting. I just pressed my head into my pillow, tried to claw my way back into my dream.

The wings, the water.

'Lil!' I heard.

I sat up, disoriented. A thirst dug deep into my throat and chest. I tried to remember the night before, but it was all a blur. The air blew in cool through the open window, the unmistakable scents of autumn and exhaust mixing together. *Water*, I thought.

'Lil, wake up! It's me, V!'

I tried to blink away my dizziness as I swung my legs and lifted myself from the mattress, my old bones creaking with each shift and start. I bent my wings in and wrapped a cardigan around me, holding it closed.

'Just a minute!' I called out.

I remembered the ball, his arm around my waist.

I stumbled from my bed to the living room, grabbing onto the doorframe to balance myself. I opened the door, and she stood in front of me, her now-platinum hair sweeping down to her shoulders. I searched her face for news.

'Hey,' she said.

'Good morning,' I said. 'Come in.'

'Oh, wow,' she said, whistling under her breath, walking past me and into the room. 'What happened in here?'

I looked around, saw the place with her eyes. The drifts of mail, the mound of newspapers by the door. The bags of garbage, overflowing in the kitchen. Books everywhere, opened and on their sides.

I felt a tinge of embarrassment but pushed it away. None of that mattered now.

'Here,' I said, 'let me clear a spot for you on the couch.' I rushed over, moved a pile of books to the floor. *Cottingley Fairies* was spread open next to the stack, and I shut it quickly. 'Do you want some tea?'

'No, no,' she said. She moved to the couch, looking slowly over the place, taking it in. A look of slight horror on her face that she was trying to conceal. She looked at me. 'Thank you again, Lil, for being so amazing yesterday. I really . . . It meant a lot to me.' She was holding something. A package she was shifting back and forth, from hand to hand.

'You're welcome,' I said.

She sat down on the couch and I sat across from her, on the chair. She seemed distracted, strange. She placed the package down on a pile of papers and then pulled it back quickly, onto her lap. She seemed unsure of how to do anything.

'So how was it?' I asked, unable to wait any longer. 'What happened?'

'Oh,' she said, looking up at me. 'It was gorgeous. Beautiful food and music, and that place! You were right. I loved it. I felt like I was in a Garbo movie or something. And George is such a nice guy, Lil. A really cool guy. I like him a lot.'

'A cool guy?'

She smiled, seeming to relax a bit. She looked down shyly and then back up at me. 'I think he's amazing.' She was glowing, I realized, and it was all I could do to keep myself from jumping up and shouting with joy.

'You do? Oh, that's wonderful. I knew it. I knew it.'

'He was such a gentleman. Awkward and sweet. We talked about all kinds of things, too. Literature and film and art, where we've been, our families and where we come from. His background is so cool. Did you know that his grandfather invented the seamless stocking?'

'No,' I said, smiling. 'I didn't.' She looked so much like her, like Cinderella. Her moonlit hair, her luminous skin.

'He just made me feel so . . . alive. Like I have things to say. He was interested in my work, Lil. He's even coming by the salon tomorrow to see some of my hair pieces and wigs. I talked to him about some of my sewing stuff and he was actually interested. Guys are never interested. Oh, and he loved the dress!'

'He did?' I clapped my hands, delighted.

'Oh yeah. He kept telling me how impressed he was, how beautiful it was. I told him it was your idea.'

I waved my hand. 'Don't be silly.'

'And he really loves you, Lil. It was so sweet. He told me he thinks you're the best person he knows.'

'He did?'

'Yes. He said he wishes he could tell you how much you

mean to him. How you're always looking over him, looking out for him. He would die if he knew I was telling you this.'

'That's . . . I don't know what to say.' Just then I thought I saw a flash out of the corner of my eye. A sparkle. It was almost time.

'I thought you'd want to know that he feels that way.'

'Thank you,' I said, tearing up. 'Yes. So . . . you'll be seeing him again?'

'Yeah, tomorrow. He's coming to the store and then I think he's taking me to dinner. He couldn't believe I'd never been to Peter Luger, so we might go there if he can get us in. I don't really care where we go. I'm just excited to see him again.'

'So you think he might . . . do you think you might fall in love with him?'

She laughed. 'I feel like such a dork, Lil. But. I mean you never know. But . . . yeah.' She smiled. Another perfect moment. *Soon*, I thought.

Tears fell down my face. I could not stop them.

Her face shifted. 'Lil,' she said. 'I really need to talk to you about something else.' She ran her fingers along the coffee table, flicked off a thick layer of dust. 'I ran into Leo downstairs.'

'Leo?' For a moment I wasn't sure who she was talking about. 'Your landlord? Leo?'

'Oh. What about him?'

'I just ran into him downstairs, so we said hi. He told me he's been trying to talk to you forever. He said you never called him. You didn't tell me this place is getting sold. Why didn't you tell me? You do have a place to go, right?'

'Oh, Veronica,' I said, wiping my cheeks. 'It's okay. It doesn't matter now.'

'What do you mean it doesn't matter? You have to leave. He's been trying to tell you, he said. I'm worried about you, Lil. It's like you're not paying attention. You seem so . . . I don't know. I mean, this place . . .' She gestured to the room, to the piles of papers and books and unopened mail.

'Veronica. It's okay now. I've set things right.' My heart went to her. She cared so much, but she had no idea what was actually happening. Of course she was worried. If I was ever going to tell her, it had to be now. This moment. Put her mind at ease. Explain to her why she didn't have to worry, and why I was going away. I took a breath, and then I spoke. 'I want you to know something. I have so little time now. I want you to know what I am, why I was sent to you.'

Veronica stared at me with her huge eyes, bright blue in the morning light. She seemed different without her makeup, her face bare and young-looking. 'What?' she asked. 'Tell me.'

'I've never . . . I've never told anyone this, any of this.' I pushed out the words as if they were rocks pressing against my tongue, my cheeks. 'Something happened, a long time ago. An accident.'

I had to hurry. My wings felt like they were cutting into me, slicing through my skin and bone, straight to my heart. It was all coming to an end, and everything was in me at once: loss, joy, regret, relief, guilt, everything I could have done, should have done. What I had had once, and lost. All the years of being alone. The knowledge that in this world things died and didn't come back.

Veronica pushed herself off the couch, came and sat at my side, still clutching the package. 'I know what this is about,' she said carefully.

'You do?' I was hopeful suddenly, that she had known all along.

'It's your sister, isn't it? I remind you of her. I understand.'

I stared at her, uncomprehending.

She set the package down next to her and put her hand on my arm, then reached up and kissed my cheek. A shudder went through me. My wings tensed.

'Leo gave me all this stuff to give to you,' she whispered, nodding to the package. I looked at it for the first time, confused. A regular yellow mailing envelope. 'He said he found it going through his grandfather's things. I hope it's okay that I looked at it.'

'What are you talking about?'

She reached in to hug me, her arm snaking around my shoulder. I flinched and pulled away. Veronica held on to me.

'Lil, let me be your friend. You can talk to me about what happened, you know. I knew that something had happened to you and now I want you to know that you can talk to me about it, about anything.'

I could feel her hand pressing against my wings. Surely she had felt them by now – the soft piles of feathers, the thin bones. I waited, ignoring the pain that shot through me, slicing right into me. It was all almost over.

'You have to talk about things,' she said. 'You know? Everyone has to talk about things.'

I was starting to feel claustrophobic. Her hand pressing against bone. Her breath against my skin. I flinched away from her. Why wouldn't she just listen to me? We had so little time!

'Listen, Veronica,' I said quickly, the words tumbling out. 'I have to tell you this. What I am. Why none of this matters anymore. I am . . .' I paused. To my horror, I sounded reedy, weak. My voice seemed like it came from another body. I wondered, for a split second, if I was breaking something. If by speaking it I would change things somehow. But she had to know this! We were out of time and she had to know who I was and who I'd been, why everything she was saying was a mistake. Why it would all be okay now. I started again. 'I am,' I said, 'the fairy godmother. I was a fairy, in the other world.' The words seemed to fall from my mouth all wrong, breaking on the wood floor like bits of china. 'I came here to set things right, because of what I did.' It poured out of me, just like that.

She just stared at me with those wide blue eyes. A look of shock on her face I tried to ignore. In the sunlight, with her blond hair hanging down, her makeup-less face, she and Cinderella could have been twins.

I had to make her understand. 'I was supposed to get Cinderella to the ball. I was her fairy godmother, the one who sent her to the ball. That's what I was supposed to do, but I failed.'

'No, Lil,' she said interrupting me. Talking slowly, gently. 'I know what happened. Your sister. That's what this is about.'

'No! Listen to me!' She was supposed to be my friend. Why was she looking at me like that? I wanted to scream with frustration. 'She never made it to the ball. See? I was supposed to get her there, that's all I was supposed to do, and I failed. I was banished. I fell to earth. They banished me, don't you see? From my own world!'

'It wasn't your fault, Lil,' she said. She picked up the package then, and opened it, let the contents fall out onto the coffee table. Old photos, yellowed newspaper articles, bits of paper.

'It was my fault. I was supposed to protect her. That's why I came here, why I can't fly anymore. Why I had to set things right.' It all seemed to tumble out of me. The words, my tears, nothing sounding right. I had no control, over anything. I was dizzy. The light in the room seeming to sparkle, moving in and out. They were coming. I was almost there. 'Listen to me!'

'You couldn't have saved her, Lil. You were just a girl yourself. You were at a beautiful dance, you were young. You could not have known what would happen to her that night.'

'No!' I said. My wings were like snakes on my back, struggling to free themselves. 'Are you hearing me? I was a *fairy*. And protecting her, looking over her, that was my *purpose*, what I was supposed to do. And I didn't do it because I was in love with the prince myself, because I was selfish and left her alone. That's why they banished me. I was a fairy, like the fairies in your book. I was Cinderella's fairy godmother, long ago.'

I could hear wings, the beating of wings.

She took my hand. More gentle than I'd ever seen her. 'You are an amazing person, Lil. I know you loved her. But what that man did . . . you could not have known.' She picked up a few of the newspaper clippings from the table. 'I think you'll want to go through this stuff. There are some beautiful photos, Lil. Some of you and her, of that night. I just . . . I want to help you.'

She didn't understand at all. She was supposed to be my friend, my one friend, and I could not make her understand me.

'It must have been terrible to lose her,' she said, her eyes filling with tears. 'I can't imagine. What that man did to her, and then my god what she did to herself . . .'

'But I . . .'

She kept talking, her voice soft, relentless. 'I know you are the one who found her by the water, bleeding. I read about all of it, Lil. It was in the papers, the next day, all of them, and Leo's grandfather kept the clippings. See? It must have been . . . unbelievable. I am so sorry for what happened to you.'

I glanced down at the table, the pictures of two young women, the newspaper article lying face up, the words 'Society Girl Takes Own Life After Violent Attack' blinking up at me. My head was spinning, the room hot and closing in. 'No, Veronica!' I said. 'You're wrong! I'm telling you *what I am*. You felt my wings. You see these feathers. I am going to have to leave soon, and I want you to understand. You did everything you needed to. You and George, the ball. It's perfect. *You* helped *me*. There is nothing to worry about anymore. It's fixed, all of it. That was all so long ago and now it's been fixed!'

'I don't . . .'

'I will show you, then,' I said, as I stood up. Turned and lifted my shirt. I could hear the flapping of my wings, and a euphoria moved through me. She would understand perfectly now. My wings unfurled, feather by feather. I felt like I didn't have any boundaries, no skin, nothing. 'Do you see?' I asked.

I could feel my wings tapping the walls, hear the crash of a picture frame falling to the ground.

To my shock, she just looked terrified. She was reaching down to the table, searching through the materials. 'Wait, Lil,' she said, pulling a photograph out of the pile. 'Look.' She strode forward, holding the picture up to my face. 'Lil!' she said. 'Look.'

The whole room filled with feathers. They drifted down, like snow. Why couldn't she see them? They were falling right on her, gathering on her shoulders, in her hair.

She thrust the photograph in my face. It was black and white.

Two girls at a dance. Dancing together, smiling at the camera. People standing around them in suits and gowns, holding drinks. One in a dark dress and one in a long, pale silk gown. Both beautiful, radiant. The shoes, the slippers, as clear as glass. Behind them was the water. A clock rising up.

'Lil, none of it was your fault. I know everything. You couldn't have saved her. It wasn't your fault. You were a girl. There was no way you could have known what would happen.'

Something crept up on me then. A feeling, a memory.

'Lil, it is okay to miss her. I know that everything you said to me was true, but you have to miss people. You have to remember them!'

I took the photograph from her and stared down into it. My face and hers. One framed by hair like moonlight, the other like autumn leaves. We had both been so beautiful. Young. The whole world spread before us.

I turned it over.

'*1952, October 17.*'

My head hurt. I pressed my palms to my head. My wings cut into my back, like someone was stabbing me.

'Let me help you,' Veronica said.

'*Winter Garden Palace.*'

I was supposed to have protected her, but I had left her there. By herself. I shouldn't have left her alone. She was so beautiful, young. Much younger than me. But I had left her outside, someplace we weren't supposed to be. We didn't have invitations. Only one of us could go in, on the arm of that man. She was supposed to wait for me. And she did. She stayed there. I had left her alone just to be with someone I would never see again, someone who had first been hers. Should have been hers. And look what they had done to her.

The room was filled with feathers. My wings flapped back and forth.

What occurs in the world of faerie will become manifest in the world of men.

'Cinderella,' I said, jumping down from the carriage and making my way over to her. I could still feel the press of his fingers on my skin. 'It's time to go.'

I stood over her. She was asleep. So calm, peaceful. She never really got to rest, did she? I felt a wave of love for her as I bent down and put my face next to hers. My cheek touched her cheek. She did not move.

'Get up,' I said, more loudly now. Her face was cold under mine. 'Get up, my child. We need to go.'

I stood. The moon shifted. It was only then that I saw that the grass was covered in blood. The moon was just bright enough to illuminate it. And her wrists. The glass.

I realized then: Her dress was ruined, the slippers in shards. Her wrists cut open.

'No,' I whispered. The glass slippers were in pieces around her. 'What have you done?' I dropped down beside her, barely able to breathe. 'I'm here! I came back. Wake up!'

I was supposed to take care of her. She was supposed to live happily ever after. I put my hands on her shoulders, shook her as hard as I could. 'I only left for a while,' I whispered. 'It was barely any time at all.'

She did not move.

'Cinderella!' I cried, pushing her so that she was lying on

her back, putting my palms on her face to revive her. 'Wake up!'

A terrible pit of grief opened inside me. Tears blurred my vision. I could feel glass in my knees but let it cut into me.

'Wake up, child! I am here now!'

She couldn't have been gone for more than moments. Just moments.

'What have you done to yourself?'

Desperate, I gathered up leaves and dirt, then opened my palm, let the mixture slide down her arms and chest. 'Come back,' I said, tears running down my face. I rubbed it into her skin, focusing every feeling and desire inside me onto her. 'I'm sorry I left you, but I'm here now. I won't ever leave you again.' Her body was cold, unmoving. 'Please,' I whispered, dipping my face down her neck to her shoulders. 'You can't die. Not like this.'

She was supposed to have borne many children. Lived until she was a hundred, surrounded by her heirs. He was supposed to have loved her until then, stayed mad for her even as her skin dropped off her bones and her hair turned to ash. She had been made for him.

'Forgive me,' I said, lying next to her, pulling her to me. Everything inside me, shattered.

We were supposed to have protected her. I was supposed to have protected her. How could she be so fragile? She, who had been made for him and who was destined to be queen.

It was then that I heard them bearing down, the flapping of wings and the voices of the elders, condemning me.

And then I was no longer holding her, and I could not make my way back to her. The world had no boundaries suddenly. I was falling, screaming, clutching at the air. I crashed into something. My eyes opened onto grass, dirt.

I looked up and everything was changed. It was not my world. And it was not their world, not as I had seen it before.

I stood on the ground, rooted to the spot. My limbs white and bulging. I wobbled as I tried moving. I was heavy. Enormous.

'Help me!' I cried, and the sound of my voice startled me.

There was only quiet. I could not detect anything beyond the muttering of wind in the black trees, the dull swish of the moving grass.

'Cinderella!!' I screamed. The sound rattled through me, and I coughed the way humans do, my body clenched together.

I had heard stories about banished fairies, stories that made me lie awake with my eyes wide open.

'Maybeth!' I called. 'Gladys! Lucibell!' I pressed my palms against my throat and tried to force the sound out, to ignore the sensation rushing through my throat and over my lips. 'Where are you?'

But I knew they were gone now, too. That they weren't coming back.

A rustling sound distracted me, made me turn my head. A small boy stood staring, his hands hanging at his sides.

'Bird,' he said then, pointing.

'What?'

He smiled, made a flapping motion. 'Wings.'

As he said it, I felt a strange sensation in my back, like knives cutting into me. I could feel something moving, a slight breeze rush past my cheeks.

'No,' I whispered. 'No.'

I turned my head and something soft rubbed against my cheek. I tilted my head farther.

A feather. Bright white.

Finally I saw her, Maybeth, a flicker on the edge of the room. And beside her, Gladys. Lucibell. A trio of lights.

Veronica couldn't see my wings. How could I have thought that a human could understand? I was a *fairy*. I had made humans go mad, just by showing my face. Of course Veronica couldn't see. She was just a girl, after all. A regular human girl.

'I need to say good-bye,' I said, suddenly calm. 'I don't come from your world, Veronica.'

Come back, they said. *Come to the water.*

'I was a fairy godmother,' I said. 'I came here to help you. You are a beautiful, beautiful girl, and you will be happy. Everything is okay now. Go, my child.'

I stretched out my arms and moved them up and down, letting the feathers caress them. So soft, as soft as fur.

All I could hear was the flapping of wings, the whispers of my fairy sisters finally come back to me. I could almost taste the water sprinkling onto my face and hands as it would when I got home again. I would glide through the air with the other fairies, looking for the glittering blue lake where our two worlds – air and water – met. Laughing, we'd slip into the water and let everything go soft, quiet.

'Lil!' I heard, but it was so faint, barely a whisper. I turned around and saw Veronica through the haze of the feathers.

'I have to go now,' I said, trying not to hit her with my wings. 'I have to go home.'

I smiled and turned to the door. I could barely breathe. I had known they would come back. All this time, even despite everything, I had known that they would someday return for me. Maybeth was my sister, Gladys and Lucibell had been my very best friends, and I knew they would forgive me. I knew they would find a way.

Come to the water, I heard, louder now, and I pushed out of the building, into the street. All the pain lifted from me as I walked toward the voice. Toward her.

My muscles warmed and stretched out as I headed south. My wings flared behind me, but no one seemed to notice. They really couldn't see. I laughed out loud, ecstatic. Already I was changing, shifting, becoming invisible to them. Leaving their world behind.

It was a beautiful world. It always had been. Full of so much pain and beauty and grief and love, people you cared for so much that losing them could shatter everything. It was all so beautiful. Veronica and George, the rows of books, the whole crazy, pressed-in city. But it was, finally, their world. Not mine.

I put one foot in front of the other and just went and went, not caring if I walked into people, smashing into them with my shoulders and elbows. All I could think of was the pure lake water from the other world, how you could look down and see palaces and coral, crazy multicolored fish passing underneath. The hush as you passed into it, opening your eyes onto a sky blue, slow-moving universe.

Come, they all said, their wings tickling my face. I laughed with joy.

My sister. The lake. The sensation of flying through the air, of having skin that was smooth and beautiful and pale. Wings spreading out on either side of me.

I walked along the river, the water straining against my

senses. I followed the sound of wings to the pier, my pier, with the small clock tower at the end of it. The clock glowed from the other side, mirroring and magnifying the one I stood below. The sky was bright blue. I came right up on the water.

'Where are you?' I whispered, looking in, and tears of relief ran down my face.

I saw them. Maybeth and Gladys and Lucibell. There they were. Staring up at me from under the surface of the water, laughing, in human form so I could see them, their wings spread out behind them. I laughed, too. I was so happy. I looked around at the bored commuters, all oblivious to this miracle taking place just under their noses. No one could see them but me.

I pressed against the rail, climbed up onto it.

All the years, centuries of walking the earth, weighed down by what I'd done, what I'd lost, the pain in my heart and gut, these useless wings that now, even now, were flaring up behind me, and for once it was okay. I could shuck off my shirt, let them expand out on either side of me, a huge white heart, me at the center, always alone and burdened and never for a moment being able to forget what I'd done, and now it was over, they had returned to me, they were taking me back, calling me home. And only then, right then, the moment I thought it, the fairies disappeared and Cinderella was there, her face rippling in the water beneath the pier, as beautiful as the first time I saw her.

She was looking up at me, smiling. 'I forgive you,' she said. 'I am okay now. Everything is okay.'

'I'm sorry,' I said, but I knew she could not hear me over the sound of the air, the sound of the water. 'I missed you so much.'

'Come back to me,' she said, reaching out for me, the tips of her fingers surfacing from the water.

I heard a woman scream from the pier, voices shouting, but there was no time to turn and tell them it was okay, that this was all I had wanted, that everything was okay now and I was only going home.

I leaned forward, smiling down into the water, and let my wings unfurl slowly behind me. And then I took a deep breath, and went to her.

ACKNOWLEDGMENTS

I had a ton of help while writing this book, from all sorts of people who read and gave me feedback and encouraged me and let me benefit from their brilliance. I am grateful to all of you, especially Jennifer Belle, Lindsey Moore, Elaine Markson, Gary Johnson, Heather Proulx, Catherine Cobain, Ron Bernstein, Eric Schnall, Jeanine Cummins, Massie Jones, Joi Brozek, David Bar Katz, Robert V. Wolf, Anton Strout, Mary McMyne, Angela Amstutz, Dinah Prince Daly, Kelvin Palaciosa, Rebeca Dain, John Lawton, Scott Jones, Jeremy Tescher, Shax Riegler, River Jordan, Valerie Cates, Orly Trieber, Chelsea Ray, Barb Burris, Heather McConnell, Brenna Sniderman, Alina Vogel, Jason Chopoorian, Kathy Patrick, Maryann Curione, Philip Mead, Christine Duplessis, Anthony Madrid, and Warren Ellis.

And thank you to those who inspired bits of this book: Julius Lang and the Center for Court Innovation for making me love the garment district, Lana Guerra for being the coolest hairdresser ever, Kevin Heafy for having a gym at the Chelsea Hotel, Steve Turnbull for collecting bookly ephemera, Tommy Colomara for introducing me to the ferry boats at Pier A, and Kevin Davis for telling me about modern-day balls. And thank you, again, to Eric, who made me go to the Frick, to Joi, who had truffle martinis with me at the Pierre, and to Massie, who actually designed Veronica's dress during one long phone call.

And of course I thank my family: Jean Turgeon, Catherine Turgeon, Alfred Turgeon, John Krinbill, and Mary Margaret Krinbill, who, with failing eyesight, read an early draft of *Godmother* through a magnifying machine.

I mean really.